ABOVE THE LAW

What Reviewers Say About
Carsen Taite's Work

It Should be a Crime

"Law professor Morgan Bradley and her student Parker Casey are potential love interests, but throw in a high-profile murder trial, and you've got an entertaining book that can be read in one sitting. Taite also practices criminal law and she weaves her insider knowledge of the criminal justice system into the love story seamlessly and with excellent timing. I find romances lacking when the characters change completely upon falling in love, but this was not the case here. I look forward to reading more from Taite."—*Curve Magazine*

"This [*It Should be a Crime*] is just Taite's second novel…but it's as if she has bookshelves full of bestsellers under her belt."—*Gay List Daily*

"Taite, a criminal defense attorney herself, has given her readers a behind the scenes look at what goes on during the days before a trial. Her descriptions of lawyer/client talks, investigations, police procedures, etc. are fascinating. Taite keeps the action moving, her characters clear, and never allows her story to get bogged down in paperwork. *It Should be a Crime* has a fast-moving plot and some extraordinarily hot sex."—*Just About Write*

Do Not Disturb

"Taite's tale of sexual tension is entertaining in itself, but a number of secondary characters…add substantial color to romantic inevitability"—Richard Labonte, *Book Marks*

Beyond Innocence

"Taite keeps you guessing with delicious delay until the very last minute…Taite's time in the courtroom lends *Beyond Innocence* a terrific verisimilitude someone not in the profession couldn't impart. And damned if she doesn't make practicing law interesting."—*Out in Print*

"As you would expect, sparks and legal writs fly. What I liked about this book were the shades of grey (no, not the smutty Shades of Grey)—both in the relationship as well as the cases."—*C-spot Reviews*

Battle Axe

"This second book is satisfying, substantial, and slick. Plus, it has heart and love coupled with Luca's array of weapons and a badass verbal repertoire… I cannot imagine anyone not having a great time riding shotgun through all of Luca's escapades. I recommend hopping on Luca's band wagon and having a blast."—*Rainbow Book Reviews*

"Taite breathes life into her characters with elemental finesse… A great read, told in the vein of a good old detective-type novel filled with criminal elements, thugs, and mobsters that will entertain and amuse."—*Lambda Literary*

Rush

"A simply beautiful interplay of police procedural magic, murder, FBI presence, misguided protective cover-ups, and a superheated love affair…a Gold Star from me and major encouragement for all readers to dive right in and consume this story with gusto!" —*Rainbow Book Reviews*

Switchblade

"I enjoyed the book and it was a fun read—mystery, action, humor, and a bit of romance. Who could ask for more? If you've read and enjoyed Taite's legal novels, you'll like this. If you've read and enjoyed the two other books in this series, this one will definitely satisfy your Luca fix and I highly recommend picking it up. Highly recommended."—*C-spot Reviews*

"Dallas's intrepid female bounty hunter, Luca Bennett, is back in another adventure. Fantastic! Between her many friends and lovers, her interesting family, her fly by the seat of her pants lifestyle, and a whole host of detractors there is rarely a dull moment."—*Rainbow Book Reviews*

Courtship

"The political drama is just top-notch. The emotional and sexual tensions are intertwined with great timing and flair. I truly adored this book from beginning to end. Fantabulous!"—*Rainbow Book Reviews*

"Taite keeps the stakes high as two beautiful and brilliant women fueled by professional ambitions face daunting emotional choices… As backroom politics, secrets, betrayals, and threats race to be resolved without political damage to the president, the cat-and-mouse relationship game between Addison and Julia has the reader rooting for them. Taite prolongs the fever-pitch tension to the final pages. This pleasant read with intelligent heroines, snappy dialogue, and political suspense will satisfy Taite's devoted fans and new readers alike."—*Publisher's Weekly*

Lay Down the Law

"Recognized for the pithy realism of her characters and settings drawn from a Texas legal milieu, Taite pays homage to the prime-time soap opera Dallas in pairing a cartel-busting U.S. attorney, Peyton Davis, with a charity-minded oil heiress, Lily Gantry."
—*Publishers Weekly*

"Suspenseful, intriguingly tense, and with a great developing love story, this book is delightfully solid on all fronts. This gets my A-1 recommendation!"—*Rainbow Book Reviews*

Reasonable Doubt

"I was drawn into the mystery plot line and quickly became enthralled with the book. It was suspenseful without being too intense but there were some great twists to keep me guessing. It's a very good book. I cannot wait to read the next in line that Ms. Taite has to offer."
—*Prism Book Alliance*

Visit us at www.boldstrokesbooks.com

By the Author

Truelesbianlove.com

It Should Be a Crime

Do Not Disturb

Nothing but the Truth

The Best Defense

Beyond Innocence

Rush

Courtship

Reasonable Doubt

The Luca Bennett Mystery Series

Slingshot

Battle Axe

Switchblade

Lone Star Law Series

Lay Down the Law

Above the Law

ABOVE THE LAW

by
Carsen Taite

2016

ABOVE THE LAW

ISBN 13: 978-1-62639-558-9

THIS TRADE PAPERBACK ORIGINAL IS PUBLISHED BY
BOLD STROKES BOOKS, INC.
P.O. BOX 249
VALLEY FALLS, NY 12185

FIRST EDITION: JUNE 2016

CREDITS
EDITOR: CINDY CRESAP
PRODUCTION DESIGN: SUSAN RAMUNDO
COVER DESIGN BY SHERI (GRAPHICARTIST2020@HOTMAIL.COM)

Acknowledgments

A series is a big commitment, both for the author and the reader. I've developed a keen appreciation for the fact that while I need to leave enough threads hanging at the end of each book so I can weave the next story out of the same cloth, I understand that means my readers are left hanging as well. Thanks to all you patient souls who read the first book, *Lay Down the Law*, in the Lone Star Law series. Your emails and social media posts supporting my work fueled the inspiration for this volume. Rest assured, there's another installment in the works.

Thanks to all the usual suspects who helped me bring this book to life. Rad for giving my stories a place to thrive. Sandy Lowe for patiently tending to every detail along the way. Cindy Cresap, my editor, who makes me laugh even while she's schoolin' me about crazy hyphen rules. Sheri, thanks for another amazing cover. A huge shout out to the entire Bold Strokes team, from PR to proofreading—thanks for everything you do!

Ashley Bartlett and VK Powell—the best first readers in the world! Thanks for always being willing to work with me up until the clock strikes midnight on deadline day.

Thanks to fellow author Kim Baldwin for her insights into network news and thanks to outstanding indie film director, Robert Camina, for taking the time to answer all my questions about documentary filmmaking.

Lainey, thanks for all the sacrifices you make, big and small, to allow me to pursue my dreams. I love you more every day.

To all my readers—thanks for making this journey so worthwhile. I cherish all the emails, notes, and words of encouragement. This story is for you.

Dedication

To Lainey, above all.

CHAPTER ONE

Signing out. Text you when it's done. Yours, D.
Dale looked at the words she'd typed into her phone and closed her eyes. She'd sent the same words to Maria every time she'd gone into a potentially dangerous situation. The simple act of typing the text had been her lucky charm, her talisman. Until it wasn't.

A year had passed, and she couldn't shake the desire to type the text even though she knew no one would read it. Maria was gone— three words that never failed to dash a bucket of cold water on any lingering notions of sentiment, chilling her inside and out.

She pressed her thumb against the backspace button, slowly and methodically erasing every trace of her good-bye, but her eyes stayed closed and, against the backdrop of self-imposed darkness, she replayed the worst moments of the worst day of her life.

She'd powered her phone back up the minute the plane touched down. The sunrise flight from El Paso had only lasted an hour and a half, but the agent she'd met with there had promised she'd have the reports of Zeta Cartel activity in her e-mail inbox by the time she returned to Dallas. Before she could open her email account, her phone started blowing up with messages, voice and text. Her boss, Hector Diego, had called three times, and she had calls from several unfamiliar numbers, as well as a series of texts from the office with vague requests for a callback. She thumbed through them all and seized on the one call from a friend, ATF Agent Mary Lovelace. She touched the number and waited for Mary to pick up the line. She didn't wait long.

"Dale, where are you?"

"At Love Field. Just landed. What's up?" She pushed aside a rising sense of panic fueled by the unfamiliar anxious undercurrent in Mary's voice. She'd met Mary during one of her tours in the Middle East where they both served in the Marine Corps. Sure and steady was their calling card, and Maria often joked that when they were on the job, folks would only be able to register one beating pulse between them.

"I'm ten minutes away," Mary said, her voice tight with urgency. "I'm coming to get you."

The offer of a ride was welcome since she'd been planning to catch a cab to the office, but she couldn't help but feel something was off. "What's the deal? Hector's blowing up my phone, and he knows I was on a flight. Seriously, it's like you guys can't make it without me sometimes."

Mary's response was clipped and to the point. "Stay put. I'll explain when I get there." The line went dead before Dale could say another word, and her stomach roiled with unease. She hadn't checked a bag, so she paced outside, watching for the sight of Mary's Jeep and checking her watch as each of the promised ten minutes ticked slowly by before a loud honk shook her into awareness.

Mary pulled up next to her and leaned over to unlock the door. Dale barely had time to slide into her seat before Mary floored the accelerator, barely missing the Dallas cop on a Segway who shook his fist in their wake. When she looked back at Mary, her gaze was firmly fixed on the road ahead. "Where's the fire?"

"We'll be there in a minute."

Dale shifted in her seat. Mary's vague response fanned the flames of her anxiety, and as she watched familiar landmarks flash by, her apprehension became more acute. She asked again, and this time she didn't try to hide the urgency in her voice. "Where are we going?" When Mary hesitated, she pressed the point. "It looks like we're headed to my neighborhood. Are you going to tell me what's going on or am I going to have to jump out at the next stoplight and figure it out for myself?"

Mary turned the Jeep down the main street that led into the Oaklawn neighborhood Dale and Maria called home. She pulled over a block from their street and turned in her seat. "Dale, I'd give anything in the world if I didn't have to tell you this, but I need you to prepare yourself."

"Tell me what?" Dale scoured Mary's face for a clue, but she got nothing. Her stomach started churning, and she could feel a trickle of sweat along the back of her neck. "For Christ's sake, Lovelace, quit stringing me along."

"It's Maria. There was a shooting. It happened less than an hour ago when she was leaving the house."

Dale saw Mary place a hand on her thigh, but she barely registered the touch. Her heart thumped wildly, and her skin felt tight and suffocating. She fought for breath. "Where is she?"

Mary opened her mouth to answer, but her expression telegraphed the message before the words could leave her lips.

Dale's gut clenched. She pushed her door open, jumped out of the Jeep, and started running. She could hear Mary's voice calling out to her as the cement sidewalk blurred under her feet, but her entire focus was on the loud pounding of her boots against the pavement, guiding her home.

She pulled up short at the yellow ribbon of tape. Her yard, her house, a crime scene. Unbelievable.

"Ma'am, I'm going to have to ask you to step back."

Her head took a slow motion turn toward the voice, and she registered the uniform, the badge. A local cop she didn't know, but whose face she would never forget. Before she could growl her anger that it was he, not her, who was a trespasser, a hand touched her arm and she whirled to face her boss. She had only one question. "Where is she?"

Diego shook his head, and his eyes cast shadows of regret. "I'm sorry, Dale. She's gone."

Dale closed her eyes, praying when she opened them, time would have turned back to yesterday when she'd lingered in bed and *tried to tempt Maria to do the same. She'd teased and cajoled, but Maria insisted she'd be late for a hearing. "When you get home," she'd said. "We'll spend an entire weekend in bed. I promise."*

Dale, reeling from the memory, opened her eyes, but nothing changed. Her lawn was crawling with law enforcement personnel. Measuring, photographing, bagging, and tagging—all the things she would be doing if this weren't her house, her wife, her life. She might not be able to join in, but she had to know more. "What happened?"

Diego started talking, and she closed her eyes again to block out everything except his words. She cringed as he relayed the details provided by a neighbor who'd seen everything unfold.

Maria had walked out the front door. The neighbor waved from his own front yard. Maria called out a greeting and was bending down to retrieve the newspaper when a black SUV roared up to the curb. The neighbor had been startled at first, but the sound of rapid-fire gunshots spurred him into action. He ran back into his house and dialed 911 while straining to get a better view from his living room window. Before he was done with the call, the SUV drove off, leaving Maria sprawled on the lawn. With the phone still in his hand, he'd run across the street, screaming for help, but it was too late. Maria's body was riddled with gunshots. She was still and lifeless, lying in a river of blood.

Dale listened to the account, allowing the horrific images to penetrate her consciousness, but filing away her pain for later. Right now, paralysis was her friend, but she needed one more thing to make sure what they were telling her was real and not some tragic nightmare. "I need to see her."

Diego stared at her with a frown of reluctance, but finally nodded and grasped her arm. She stumbled, feeling faint, floating above her body—she wondered vaguely if she would ever feel normal again. A second later, she saw a different hand on her arm and she turned to see Mary standing beside her.

"I'll take her."

"I'll go with you."

"We're fine."

"I'm here if you need me."

Dale saw their mouths move, but their words drifted through the air like they were discussing someone else, something else. Anything besides her. It didn't matter—all the talk was just a delay of the inevitable. Without waiting for an escort, she stepped over the crime scene tape and walked slowly across her lawn toward a cluster of people kneeling on the ground. As she drew closer, she saw Mary out of the corner of her eye, waving everyone away until it was just her and the torn and bloody body of the woman she loved. She dropped to her knees, clutched her chest, and keened her sorrow, not caring who heard.

Dale shoved her phone into her pocket and slid her arms into the bulletproof vest, flinching as she adjusted the Velcro straps tight around her chest and shoulders. She hated the bulk and the vulnerability the vest symbolized, not to mention her left shoulder was still sore from the gunshot wound she'd gotten while checking out a lead at one of Cyrus Gantry's warehouses. If she didn't need to set an example for the rest of her team, the vest would have stayed in the back of her truck.

She waved at Mary, her second in command. "Do we have eyes in the building yet?"

Mary held up a finger, spoke a few words into her phone, and nodded. "Heat sensors picking up one body inside. Sniper from the house roof confirms, but he doesn't have a clear shot. Beams are in the way."

They'd received a tip from an unknown source early in the morning that Sergio Vargas would be doing a major deal at the barn on this property today. Dale wasn't big on anonymous tips with no opportunity to evaluate the source, but the prospect of bringing in the fugitive chief of the Zeta Cartel was worth taking a risk on shaky information. If Sergio Vargas was in that barn, chances were he wasn't just doing a one-time deal. He'd probably been hiding out here. The entire homestead was unoccupied, and this farm had been on the market for months. With no one to interrupt his dealings, this was the perfect setup for a drug lord on the run, and the fact that his co-captain and brother, Arturo Vargas, had been arrested just last week, probably made the solitude even more appealing. The owner had given the task force the run of the place to clear out any outlaws. Sergio Vargas's oasis was about to become the doorway to his prison cell.

Dale glanced back at Mary and the rest of the group. Everyone was amped and ready to charge, no matter what danger lurked on the other side. She'd carefully chosen the team with her today, purposefully not including a few of the task force members she'd been working with over the past year. The events of the last week signaled someone was leaking valuable information, and until she figured out who it was, she was on high alert.

"We'll go in from both sides with flashbangs. The object is to take Vargas alive. Do you understand?" She waited until each of the dozen agents nodded before saying anything else. "Everything by the book. If he resists, take him down, but no unnecessary force. And don't get hurt yourselves. I can't spare you, and I don't have time for the paperwork." She flashed a grin as she delivered the last words and led the way to the barn door, certain everyone on her team would follow.

When they were all in place, she shouted, "Federal agents. Come out with your hands in the air. You have five seconds to respond or we're coming in." She held up her hand and started ticking off the count on her fingers. When she reached five, she closed her hand in a fist and pointed to the door. Two agents were ready with a battering ram, but stood down when Mary tugged on the door and it opened.

Dale tossed a flashbang into the room, bracing for the loud noise and the acrid smell of smoke. Hoping the suspect's visibility was impaired, she crouched down and stepped into the room, sticking close to the wall while she tried to get a read on anything moving inside. The rest of her team followed with the exception of Mary, who was assigned to secure the door in case Vargas somehow made it past them. Even if he did escape, he wouldn't get very far. The sniper on the roof of the house next door was poised and ready to take the shot.

Through the haze, Dale detected a chair in the center of the room. Someone was seated in the chair, and as the smoke cleared, Dale saw that his hands were in his lap, held close together, and his head was covered. What the hell? She raised her gun and stealth-walked the short distance until she was standing directly behind him. Out of the corner of her eye, she saw one of the other agents approaching from the left, and she shook her head. With the gun still pointed at the guy's head, she sidestepped around to the front of the chair and issued a command. "Put your hands in the air. Right now!"

The guy shoved both hands skyward immediately. She was close enough to see everything clearly now. His hands were tightly bound together with twine and his head was covered with a burlap sack, most likely a castoff, found in the barn. His legs were bound to the chair with heavy rope, tied tight. If this was Sergio Vargas, someone had beaten them to him. Before she found out if they'd captured their intended prey, she shouted to the rest of her group. "Report."

Responding shouts of clear came from the front door, the stables, and the loft. Dale waited until everyone had reported in before waving Mary over. "Go ahead and unmask him."

She kept her gun trained on what she imagined was the spot right between his eyes, as Mary carefully lifted the sack from his head and, as every inch was revealed, Dale scrambled to make sense of what she was seeing. Finally, she could no longer deny the truth.

"Who the hell is this?" Mary said as she laid the bag on the ground. "Dale, what is it? You look white as a sheet."

Dale stepped closer, as if reality would change upon closer inspection. No, not a chance. The man they'd captured wasn't the highly sought Sergio Vargas, but someone she and others had been looking for. Someone she wasn't altogether sure would be welcome now that he'd been found. The sense of familiarity was like a punch in the gut. She leaned down and removed the gag from his mouth. "Not sure what to make of the fact we found you here. You care to explain?"

The man's voice cracked, but his tone was adamant. "I want a lawyer and I'm not talking to you without one."

Dale shook her head. "Of course you do." She motioned to Lieutenant Raphael Martinez, a Texas Ranger assigned to their task force. "Take him to division headquarters. I'll call AUSA Cruz and we'll figure out the charges. I have to make a stop on the way in. I'll meet you there." She walked out of the barn and back to her truck, but before she could open the door, she felt a tap on her shoulder and turned to face Mary.

"What was that all about? You know that guy?"

Dale sighed. "Let's just say he's a person of interest in the Cyrus Gantry case." Mary nodded, and Dale made a split second decision to tell her the rest. "Oh, and he's AUSA Peyton Davis's brother, Neil."

CHAPTER TWO

L indsey leaned toward Senator Levenger and posed the final question of the interview. "Are you prepared, right now, to tell the viewers of *Spotlight America* whether or not you plan to resign?"

The senior senator from Ohio cleared his throat and shot a furtive look at his attorney who was sitting across the room. As the seconds of silence ticked by, Levenger's face reddened, but Lindsey simply waited for the answer. Clearly, he'd believed the show booker's promise that she would stick to an agreed outline of acceptable questions. Lindsey had made no such promise, and she struck a pose of nonchalance as he stuttered his response. Something about duty, family, and remaining loyal to his constituents. She nodded as he spoke, but steadfastly refused to throw him a lifeline, instead preferring to let him hang himself with his own scattered attempt at an explanation.

An hour later, while she was carving into a steak at Del Frisco's Grille, she got the call. She stared at the display on her cell phone and took a deep breath before answering. "Ryan here."

"Ms. Ryan, I have Mr. Prince on the line."

"Of course you do." With a sigh, she pushed her plate aside. "Put him through."

"Lindsey, what the hell were you thinking?"

"Uh, I don't know, Larry. Maybe I was thinking a senator who can't keep his hands to himself might have a constituency that wants to know if he plans to try to weather the shitstorm he sailed into. Even you can't deny it was a fair question."

"Fair? Who ever said we were supposed to be fair? Besides, we promised his attorney we wouldn't ask the resignation question in order to get the exclusive, but I guess you think it was fair to pop him with it anyway, right there on live TV?"

"Sorry. I may have forgotten about that promise." She hadn't, and Larry didn't believe for a moment she had, but she didn't give a shit. Good journalism wasn't about agreeing to what the story should be in advance, no matter what the network and their sponsors believed.

"Funny, I would've thought what happened after your interview with General Tyson would make you especially careful, for a while at least."

Lindsey chewed a bite of steak instead of responding. General Randall Tyson had gotten everything he deserved as a result of the fallout from her interview. He'd openly ridiculed the president who'd appointed him as the commander of US Forces in Afghanistan, and then acted appalled when she refused his demands to edit his insults out of her broadcast. Several of the network's key sponsors had been outraged at what they viewed as her lack of patriotism. To placate the network bigwigs, including Larry, she'd acted appropriately chastised, but when faced with Senator Levenger's actions, her investigative instincts pushed her to ask the tough questions. "I only asked the senator what everyone else wants to, and you know it."

"Whatever. I've got a new project for you on location in Dallas."

Lindsey's appetite plummeted at the abrupt change in subject. "We had an agreement. No more traveling for a while."

"I may have forgotten that promise."

Larry delivered the words in a singsong voice, and Lindsey wanted to punch him in the throat. "Don't be an ass. We had a deal."

"We do have a deal, but this is a puff piece. You'll barely have to work. Infomercial about the DEA. Interview some real folks, put together a story about how they're restructuring to meet the changing times. They have some big event coming up." She heard the sound of shuffling papers before he continued. "It's the tenth National Take-Back Initiative. People bring their drugs in, like those gun turn-in programs. Cover that and make it into something."

"Sounds candy ass. Can't you have someone else do it?"

"Susan promised someone with credibility would do the story. Naturally, I thought of you."

Lindsey scoured his words for the hidden mine. Susan was the executive producer for *Spotlight America* and a network muckety-muck. A person at her level usually collected favors instead of handing them out. "Who did Susan make this promise to?"

"I don't know and I don't want to know. Neither do you. The important thing is you still owe me for the fallout from General Tyson and the stunt you pulled today. You realize how difficult it is to get these politicians to come on the show after they've imploded all over the Internet?"

Lindsey took a deep breath and silently counted to five before answering in an even tone. "Don't get me started, Larry."

"Look, I know coming back was an adjustment, but you're not in a combat zone anymore. Relax and enjoy some well-deserved rest."

"In Texas?"

"You'll be down there a couple of weeks, tops. Cush trip. Hell, you'll probably spend most of it in a four-star hotel going through the dailies."

Maybe Larry had a point. Dallas wasn't New York, but it wasn't Afghanistan either. Puff pieces weren't her thing, but adjusting to life back in first-world civilization had been harder than she'd expected. She could use a little down time. "I want to pick my own crew."

A few beats of silence passed, and finally Larry said, "Uh, okay. I mean sure, camera, sound—you pick."

"Producer?"

"I think we've already got someone lined up for the spot. She already did some of the prep work, and she's ready to leave whenever you're up to speed."

Lindsey was certain she wasn't imagining the nervous edge in Larry's voice. "Larry, who is it?"

"Damn, I've got another call coming in. I'll have Beth call you with the details."

He hung up before she could get another word in, and she stared at her phone wishing she could pull back her consent. He was up to something, and she wished she knew what it was. In the meantime, she could line up the rest of her crew. She scrolled through her phone contacts until she found the number for Alice Jordan, one of the industry's top cameramen, and she punched in her number. Alice answered on the first ring.

"Jordan."

"Hey, it's Lindsey. Put on your boots and hat and fly with me to Dallas."

"Hey, girl. They got you on that piece? What did they have to offer to get you to agree?"

"You know about it already?"

"Sure. Elaina's been making a big deal about it. She's been working us to death on another project so she can finish up in time to head down there."

Lindsey was only mildly shocked at the sound of her ex's name. She and Elaina Beall had broken up a couple of years ago, and they'd somehow managed to avoid the awkwardness of working together since. So, Elaina was the producer who'd already been picked for the project. No wonder Larry hadn't wanted to mention her name. He probably thought she'd come unhinged at the thought of working with Elaina for the first time since their very public power couple breakup. She wasn't looking forward to it, and frankly, she was surprised Elaina had agreed to take the job. Elaina had spent their entire relationship bemoaning Lindsey's singular focus. Work always came first—a mantra Elaina had resented from day one.

Maybe she'd changed, and maybe working together on a human interest piece devoid of controversy was the perfect way to mend fences.

CHAPTER THREE

Dale drove her truck up the long, rocky drive to the Circle Six ranch, rehearsing how to break the news to Peyton Davis that her brother had turned up under more than a little suspicious circumstances. When she reached the main house, she saw Peyton standing on the porch with a scowl on her face. She climbed out of the truck and called out as she walked toward the house. "Sorry to just drop by. Is this a bad time?"

Peyton shook her head. "It's fine. I heard you driving up, but I was hoping it was Lily. She was supposed to be home a couple of hours ago."

Dale heard a slight edge of panic in Peyton's normally calm voice, and she couldn't help but flash back to the memory of Maria's death she'd relived earlier that day. "Where is she?"

"She left just before lunch to go out to Valencia Acres. She and Sophia haven't had a chance to visit in person since last week."

"I guess they have a lot to talk about," Dale said. Lily, Peyton's girlfriend, had met her birth mother, Sophia Valencia, who she'd been told her entire life was dead, for the first time the week before. Unfortunately, their meeting had been marred when she'd learned that Sophia's brothers, her uncles, were the notorious Sergio and Arturo Vargas, co-heads of the Zeta Cartel and at the very top of the most wanted list being hunted by Peyton's federal task force.

Dale was well aware that the fact that Sergio was still on the run had Peyton worried about Lily's safety. She didn't blame her. Sergio and his brother were responsible for dozens of gruesome murders and, although she'd never been able to prove it, she suspected they were at least tangentially responsible for Maria's death.

As for Lily, she wouldn't be safe until both of her uncles were in custody. She'd personally debriefed Lily after a shootout at Sophia's ranch that culminated in Arturo's arrest. Before he was taken into custody, Arturo had taunted Sophia about the circumstances that led her to spend most of her life having no contact with her daughter. When Lily was only days old, Sergio and Arturo had taken Lily from her mother and handed her over to Cyrus Gantry, Lily's natural father. In return for the privilege, Cyrus had spent his life beholden to the criminal element, while lying to his only child about her parentage, insisting she had been adopted after her mother died in childbirth, a lie that once found out, would drive Lily to distrust his every word. Cyrus's troubles were compounded by the fact that Peyton, the woman Lily loved, was investigating him for money laundering.

Despite her own sense of foreboding, Dale searched for something encouraging to say. While she was thinking, Peyton's mother, Helen Davis, appeared in the doorway, her expression drawn with worry.

"Is she home?" Helen asked.

Peyton shook her head. "No, but I hear someone else coming up the drive. If it's not her, I'm going to head out."

"Maybe they just lost track of time," Dale offered. She flicked a glance at Helen, and Peyton introduced them. "Mom, this is Dale Nelson, the lead agent on the task force."

Helen shook Dale's hand. "Nice to meet you, Dale. Any chance you could help Peyton here keep a cool head? She's been pacing the porch for the last hour."

Peyton shook her head. "I should've gone with her."

The sound of the car engine was closer, and Dale raised a hand to shield against the sunlight, but she could only make out that the vehicle was big. While the three of them stood still, watching and hoping for the best, Dale listened as Helen offered words of advice to her daughter.

"The girl needed to be with her mother without you looking over her shoulder. There'll be plenty of time for you to get to know Sophia." Helen put her hand on Peyton's arm. "Lily's a tough one. She had to get that from someone, and it sure wasn't Cyrus. I bet Sophia can handle any trouble that comes along. You can't protect her from everything."

Dale nodded at the wisdom of Helen's words, but she sincerely hoped Peyton would never have to learn that last truth the hard way.

A second later, an SUV burst out of a cloud of dust and pulled to a stop right in front of the porch. Dale watched Peyton vault over the railing, run down the walk, and yank Lily's door open. She couldn't hear their exchange, but she imagined their words were laced with comfort and affection. She was happy for them, but couldn't help but feel a trace of pain as she witnessed the relief of their reunion.

Peyton looped her arm through Lily's as they walked toward the house and Lily called out a greeting. "Hello, Agent Nelson. Good to see you again. Mrs. Davis, I'm sorry I'm late, but there was a wreck on the highway and traffic was crawling. My phone was in the backseat, and I didn't want to risk a wreck trying to get it. I didn't mean to worry you."

Before Dale could say anything, Helen pulled Lily into a fierce hug and said, "Don't you Mrs. Davis me, young lady. I'm just glad you're home. Now, I imagine these gals have a bit of business to discuss, so come inside and have some iced-tea with me."

"Wait," Dale said.

"What's up?" Peyton asked.

"Maybe all three of you should hear this."

"Out with it," Peyton said.

"We got a tip on Sergio Vargas earlier today, and we conducted a raid at a farm over in Denton this morning."

"Let me guess," Peyton said. "He got away."

"He wasn't there. At least not when we arrived. But he'd been there and left us a present." Dale shifted in place, unsure how her news would be received. "Your brother Neil was in the barn, tied up and left behind."

"What the hell?"

"I'm not sure what to make of it, but the minute we found him, he clammed up, asking for a lawyer. I thought maybe he might talk to you. I can give you a ride in."

Dale watched Peyton struggle to process the news that her brother, who'd disappeared after she'd caught him manipulating the family business, had turned up under even more nefarious circumstances. Peyton's expression quickly changed from disbelief to anger.

"You should go," Lily said, placing an arm around Peyton's waist. "He might talk to you, and answers are what you need. Family's complicated."

Lily's words and touch seemed to have a calming effect on Peyton who agreed to accompany Dale to the DEA office where Neil was being detained. As they drove into town, Dale couldn't help but wonder what Peyton would have done if Lily weren't around and, as she once again relived the pain of her own loss, she hoped she would never have to find out.

Dale waited until they were on the highway before attempting to engage Peyton in conversation. "I think he just got in over his head."

"Neil's always had big dreams, but he doesn't understand having to work to make them come true. He's the perfect pawn for a get-rich-quick scheme, but he's also culpable for his actions. He has no one else to blame for the mess he's made."

"Like Lily said, family's complicated."

"Understatement of the year. What about you? You have much family?"

Dale winced at the question. She realized Peyton was asking about extended family, brothers and sisters, mom and dad, but the question nagged at the sore spot she feared would never go away. Maria Escobar, her wife and the prosecutor who'd held Peyton's job before her, had been her family, her most precious treasure. Time had numbed the pain, but she didn't think she could ever think family without feeling the enormous void Maria's death had left in her life. She'd watched the way Peyton ran to Lily's side at the ranch—eager to see her, desperate to know she was safe, affectionate no matter who was watching. She'd had that once, and now it was gone.

"Sorry, that was insensitive."

Dale shook her head. "It was a fair question. I have an older brother and a younger sister. They both live near our parents in Austin. Law enforcement, through and through. Guess it only made sense I married a prosecutor."

"I hear she was as tough as they come."

Tough. Not a word she would have used to describe Maria, but it was true. Tough when it came to her job, but gentle in every way Dale needed when she came home after a day of watching ugliness try to take over the world. Maria had convinced her they could be safe in the home they'd built for themselves. That it would be the one place where viciousness of the world could not penetrate.

She'd been wrong. Their home had offered no protection when Maria walked out the front door into a haze of gunfire. The medical examiner told her Maria had died in seconds, but Dale knew when she was being pacified. No one knew what Maria had suffered, what she'd thought in those final seconds, how she'd felt. All Dale knew was her own feelings—anger, sadness, guilt, but most of all, loneliness. What Peyton had found in Lily, she'd had all that and more. When it was ripped from her, she'd known she'd never have it again. The job was all she had, and she'd vowed to spend every waking moment until her dying breath finding justice for Maria and for all the other innocent victims of the vicious Cartels.

"Are you okay?"

Dale looked over at Peyton whose eyes reflected concern. "Yeah, I'm good." Peyton's expression didn't change, but she nodded and didn't ask anything else. Good thing since she didn't plan to answer any more questions. Maria wasn't a topic for casual conversation. She'd grown to respect Peyton since she'd shown up to take over the task force, but they weren't at the point where they swapped sad stories. Just to make sure, she took the lead and changed the subject. "Let's talk about Neil. What are you going to say to him?"

"I wish I knew. Have you got enough to charge him with anything?"

"Not yet."

"Good. I think we need to make sure he knows he's free to leave and then go from there. I'm pretty sure I can rile him enough to get him to talk to me. He likes to brag, especially to me."

"You really want to let him go?"

"No, but making him think we do is probably the only way we can use anything he says. If he's not free to go, we're going to have to read him his rights, which pretty much kills any chance of him mistaking this conversation for a simple brother sister conversation."

Dale heard the rumble of anger in Peyton's voice. "You're really pissed at him."

"He had everything he could ever want and squandered it. I walked away from the ranch, the horse breeding, all of it, mostly because I knew I could be happy doing something else, but running the Circle Six was the only future he could see, and then he wasted the opportunity with his schemes. We're in real danger of losing the ranch if we don't honor some of the agreements he made, but if we do, we risk losing everything we wanted the ranch to be. I never should have left, and I never should have given away my birthright, especially to someone who wasn't worthy of it."

Dale reached over and placed a hand on Peyton's shoulder. She got it. The passion, the anger, the purpose. Being on the job came with all of those, and she couldn't help but feel she'd let her love for Maria distract her from the danger of their work. Part of her purpose was to protect, but the most precious person in her life had died on her watch because she'd been distracted by the desire to bring home a bigger prize. If she had things to do over, she would have… Hell, she'd been over it a thousand times, but she'd never come up with anything plausible except it should have been her on the lawn that day. Riddled with bullets, bleeding out, dying in the line of duty.

But she hadn't died, and every day she lived, she could either regret her choices or make them worth something. She'd never bring Maria back, but she could make sure the work they'd done together continued so others could be spared. She wouldn't let anything get in the way of running to ground every last drug dealer and anyone who helped them, which led her to bring up a subject she'd been dreading. "Peyton, I get the whole thing with your brother, and I know it was my idea that you come down and talk to him, but at some point we should talk about how you're going to handle Cyrus Gantry. If you're prosecuting his case, then folks are going to call the entire prosecution into question based on your relationship with his daughter."

Peyton didn't respond at first, but Dale waited out the silence, determined to get some answers. Maybe Peyton would think she'd overstepped, but she wasn't about to let the AUSA's love life muck up the investigation she'd dedicated her every waking moment to.

"You're right, and the Vargas connection is a problem too," Peyton said. "I've got to steer clear of the cases against all of them, and I will."

"Good. Who's taking your place?"

"Well, I'm not quitting the task force entirely. I'll work on some tangential cases, but I'm going to recommend that Bianca take the lead on the case against Cyrus and the Vargas brothers."

"She's a little green, don't you think?" Dale asked, unsure if replacing a conflicted prosecutor with an inexperienced one was the best solution.

"There's only one way she's going to learn. I get how important this is, and I promise, if I didn't think she was ready, I would be the first to say so. Trust me on this just like I'm trusting you to make sure this case remains the number one priority for the task force."

"You don't have to worry about me." Dale pulled into the parking lot of the Dallas division of the DEA where Neil was being held. "I don't plan on letting anything get in the way."

CHAPTER FOUR

L indsey pointed at the nondescript building to the right. "That's the address."

Jed Larabee, the sound engineer she'd chosen for the team, made a sharp turn into the parking lot, and Lindsey consulted her notes one last time before they arrived at the field office for the Dallas DEA. Larry hadn't provided much in the way of guidance for what the network wanted for the story, and she had only two bullet points as a guide: the DEA's drug Take-Back Initiative and the recent shakedown of synthetic drug suppliers. Yawn. Based on her research of crime stats in the area, this stuff was fluff and she'd said as much to Elaina on the flight from New York.

Elaina's response was pure company line: "People aren't just interested in hearing about violent crimes. They want to know about things that affect everyday situations. Prescription drugs and what their kids are buying at the local smoke shops may not be interesting to you, but they are important topics to our viewers."

Her question and Elaina's answer had been the sum total of conversation they'd shared on the trip down, and she'd been relieved to drop Elaina at the hotel with Alice while she and Jed did some reconnaissance for the filming they'd start in a couple of days.

"This building's beyond boring," Jed said. "I'll let Elaina know so she can start looking for some other landmark to film for the opening shots."

Lindsey nodded. He was right. The brick facade signaled office building rather than the home of a bunch of badass cops hunting down drug lords. Even if the subject matter for this piece was dry, they'd need something exciting for the ad clips if they wanted to get anyone to tune in. She made a note and then closed her notebook. "I have a feeling this entire assignment is going to be boring. Thanks for agreeing to come along."

"Thanks for picking me. I'll go along with dull every once in a while because you'll be more likely to grab me for the next juicy one, which I'm hoping is vintage Ryan. Cool?"

Lindsey smiled. "Cool." Her reputation for digging deep to get the meaty stories was legend, and it felt good to have most of her crew on board for more significant work. With the exception of Elaina. Once upon a time, Elaina had worried less about pacifying everyone and been more interested in real news. They never would have gotten together if that hadn't been the case, but nowadays, Elaina was a network lackey, hesitant to buck the system, which was likely why Larry had handpicked her for this assignment.

Well, she'd been handpicked too, and Larry and everyone else at the network should know by now what they were getting when they put her in charge of a project. She'd do this piece because she owed Larry one, but after that, she was going to find something substantial to wrap her brain around. She put her hand on the door handle. "Let's go get this over with."

A few minutes later, she and Jed were sitting in a conference room with Special Agent in Charge Hector Diego. The DEA had rolled out the red carpet, complete with an array of sandwiches, miniature desserts, and a large selection of soft drinks, and she was disappointed they'd eaten before they'd arrived. Lindsey had conducted dozens of police station interviews in her career, and she'd never been greeted by catered food. The happenstance raised her antennae, and she stayed on guard as she introduced Jed and discussed what they hoped to learn on this visit.

"Jed will need to check out the areas where we will be conducting interviews to determine what kind of equipment we need. For my purposes today, I just want to get a feel for the office and meet a few of the people I'll be interviewing so I can formulate a schedule. I anticipate we'll start filming interviews tomorrow or the next day if that works for you."

"Of course, of course. Whatever you need." Diego shoved a binder with an official DEA seal on the front, across his desk to her. "The network sent a list of topics you plan to cover while you are here, and we have no issues with providing you full access regarding the specified areas. You'll want to interview some of the local agencies that assist with the program as well. Here's some background information to help you focus your questions."

Lindsey bristled at his conclusory tone, but tried not to let her reaction show. Clearly, Diego was intent on directing her efforts and making sure she stayed within the agreed upon bounds. She'd expected as much, but now that she was here, close to where many other more significant investigations were being conducted, her promise to curtail her natural curiosity was stifling. If she didn't find something to pique her interest, how could she expect to keep viewers interested?

An idea popped into her head, and she shot a look at Jed, trusting he wouldn't rat her out for going off script. "Thanks, Agent Diego." She tapped her fingers on the binder. "I've reviewed a lot of the material already, but I'm sure this will be helpful as well. You know what else would be particularly helpful?"

He cocked his head. "What?"

"A liaison." Lindsey leaned forward in her chair and assumed her best *I'm just a silly woman and I could use help from a big, strong man like yourself* posture. "I know your entire agency is probably overburdened by all of the organized crime activity in the area, but if there was any way you could spare an agent who could, I don't know, kind of oversee this project and guide us through the interviews, I think we could have a much more polished final product. What do you think?" Batting her eyes would be too much, so she punctuated her question with what she hoped was a pleasant, yet hopeful, smile.

Diego shifted in his seat. "Well, I guess that's a good idea. I had one of our secretaries lined up to help with coordinating interviews, but an agent might be more help to you. In fact, I have an idea of someone we could use, and I think she's here right now. Hang on. I'll be right back."

Jed barely waited until Diego left the room before he burst into laughter. "Thanks for the bonus. I had no idea I was going to get a glimpse of Lindsey Ryan, distressed reporter in search of a savior. Pretty smooth."

She smacked him on the arm. "Shut up." She pointed at the ceiling and whispered. "Someone's probably listening. I just figured he'd assign us some rookie who might accidentally tell us something way more interesting than the stats we can read on DEA.gov."

"Good plan. I'll cross my fingers."

They didn't have to wait long. Within ten minutes, Diego was back. At first it appeared as though he was alone, but when he cleared the threshold, another figure filled the doorway. She was tall and rangy, dressed in skin-hugging Levi's, a tight black T-shirt, and black leather boots. The stranger tugged off her sunglasses, and Lindsey sucked in a breath at the sight of her stormy blue eyes. Fiercely dark, they telegraphed depth and danger.

"Ms. Ryan, Mr. Larabee, I'd like to introduce Special Agent Dale Nelson. She's been with the agency for a number of years and knows everyone here. Agent Nelson will be at your disposal during the term of your stay. I'm sure you'll let me know if you need anything else."

Without another word, he was gone, leaving them with Agent Dark and Handsome. Lindsey tried not to stare, instead launching into the first question that came to mind. "He just surprised you with this, didn't he? I mean, you must've just walked in seeing as how you still had your sunglasses on when…" Lindsey stopped talking, certain she was rambling and sure she was making a horrible first impression.

Dale looked between them before answering. "Yes."

Straightforward. Good. She could work with straightforward. "Do you have some time now to meet? We could go over our plan for the week. I'd like to get your input on a few of the interviews we have scheduled."

"Now's no good." Dale put her sunglasses back on. "I'm in the middle of something. I'll call you when I break free."

Lindsey only had a brief second to react before Dale started walking toward the door. In a flash, she was out of her seat. "Wait."

Dale turned, her mouth fixed in a thin line. Lindsey wished she'd take her glasses off again so she could tell if the expression in her eyes was curious or annoyed. She'd bet on the latter. Still, no matter how annoyed Dale might be, Lindsey couldn't help but want to prolong the connection, if only for a few minutes. She stuck out her hand and silently counted the seconds as Dale looked down and then finally grasped it. The grip was firm and strong. Exactly what she'd expected. She let the touch linger just a shade longer than she figured Dale was comfortable with and then reluctantly let go.

Dale nodded at her and then at Jed and strode out the door.

It wasn't until they were in the car, headed to the hotel, that Lindsey realized she hadn't given Dale her number and Dale hadn't asked.

❖

"What the hell was that all about?" Dale slammed Diego's door shut behind her and crossed her arms while she waited for him to respond. Peyton was waiting, but she didn't want to start talking to Neil until she straightened things out with her boss.

He didn't even look up. "Sit down, Nelson."

"No, thanks. I won't be here long. Can't, since you've got me doing double duty. Not sure why you think I have time to show a reporter around. I'm loaded up as it is. I was on my way to interview a suspect when I got here."

"Seriously, Dale. Take a seat."

She caught the tone, gentle but firm, and complied. "What's going on?"

"Word is the task force work is about to be put on hold for a while."

"What?" He had to be joking. They'd been working these leads for months, and they were just now seeing some progress. "You can't be serious."

"It's not coming from me. Word is Gellar is shifting his office's focus, and part of that is disbanding the team." He pushed some papers around on his desk, clearly uncomfortable to be having this conversation with her. "Look, I know these cases are personal to you, but—"

"These cases are personal to a lot of people, including the people Gellar is supposed to be representing. What's the deal? He made his case against his archenemy, Cyrus Gantry, and now he's done? Gantry's money laundering is nothing compared to the evil the Vargas brothers engage in every day. Our work is far from over."

"I hear you, but it's not my call. Maybe it's a blessing in disguise. Take a breather. You're already breaking protocol by working so soon after taking a bullet. Show this reporter and her crew around for a while and then we'll find you a good case to get involved in. They're focusing on the Take-Back Initiative, and we've already given them a list of people to interview, things to focus on. Just guide them through it, and when the event's over, you'll be off the hook."

The reporter. Lindsey Ryan. She'd known who she was the instant she saw her. Everyone knew who she was. She'd been embedded with several military units over the course of the invasion in Afghanistan and her appearances on *Spotlight America* were well known. To top it off, she made no secrets about her sexuality, which meant she was a poster girl for lesbians everywhere. "Did you pick me for this because she's a lesbian?"

He looked genuinely surprised at her question. "To tell you the truth, it was a split second decision and I'm giving you the gig because you should be on light duty anyway, and with the task force winding down, you're the perfect choice. I guess it doesn't hurt that your tours in Afghanistan give you a connection to Ms. Ryan. Be nice. This piece they're doing is important to the director. Very important."

Image control. She got it. In the past year, the agency had taken a hit both in the press and on Capitol Hill when it was discovered that certain agents were using hookers as confidential informants and taking favors in the process. Funding was always in jeopardy, but after Hooker-Gate, getting money from Congress had been next to impossible.

She'd do her part for the good of the division, but she wasn't going to cozy up to Lindsey Ryan and start swapping war stories. Reporting about war wasn't the same as actually fighting one. Ryan would tape her candy-ass fluff piece and jet back to New York, and she'd stay here and keep doing the real work that kept folks alive. In the meantime, she'd have to figure out how to keep the task force in operation without anyone knowing. The first step was convincing Diego she had drunk the Kool-Aid.

She stood up. "Okay, I'm in. I'll deal with Neil Davis and then I'll call Ryan and get her crew what they need to get started."

"Thanks, Dale. I owe you one."

Damn right you do. Dale walked straight from Diego's office to the room where Peyton's brother had been since they'd brought him in early in the day. Peyton was waiting outside the door. "He still in there?" Dale asked.

"Yes. I was waiting on you to go in, but I'd about decided you'd ducked out the back door."

"My disappearance is the least of your worries." Dale glanced around, but several other agents were wandering the halls, and she'd rather have the talk about the fate of the task force with Peyton in private. "When we're done here, we need to talk."

Peyton raised her eyebrows, but to her credit didn't ask any questions. "Deal." She motioned to the door. "You ready to start with him?"

A few minutes later, Peyton was seated across the table from her brother and engaged in a silent standoff. Dale could see a definite family resemblance, but where Peyton sat tall and confident, Neil slumped in his chair, and his red eyes and sullen expression signaled defeat. It was hard to take the backseat on any interrogation, but she deferred to Peyton's position as Neil's sister and decided to trust her strategy. For now.

"Neil, Mom is worried sick about you."

"Mom never worried about me a day in her life. How could she? All she ever did was think about her precious Peyton. No matter what the rest of us did to keep the ranch going, you were waiting for the right moment to take it all away from us."

Dale watched Peyton closely, but she couldn't detect even a hint of defensiveness in response to his provocative remarks. She remembered Peyton had one other brother, Zach, and she wondered if he was as bitter toward his older sister as Neil.

"I don't want to take anything from you," Peyton said, her tone neutral, calm even. "In fact, you're free to leave here right now if that's what you want. I only want to talk to you and help you, if I can. Considering the circumstances, I thought you might consider an offer of help after what you've been through."

"You don't have a clue what I've been through." Neil growled the words.

"Why don't you tell me? I know the people you're working with are dangerous, deadly even. You should know that by now since I'm pretty sure you didn't tie yourself up and risk getting shot by federal agents who'd been tipped off to storm that barn. I can help you, if you let me. Don't let all the hard work you've done on the ranch go to waste."

"Of course you'd say that since you're the only one who benefits from all the improvements I've made. Does Zach realize he's never going to own a piece of Circle Six or will you wait to spring that on him until he's given his life to making your inheritance as valuable as possible?"

Dale shot a look at Peyton who couldn't quite hide the toll her brother's words were taking. While she respected Peyton's desire to handle the interview on her own, she wanted to move it along, especially in light of what Diego had told her about the task force. She pushed away from the wall and stepped between Peyton and her brother. "Like your sister said, you're free to leave, but you haven't. What that tells me is you've either got something to tell us or you're just plain scared to show your face on the outside. Why don't you lose your pride and start talking, otherwise we're going to kick you out of here and let you fend for yourself with your new friends."

"If I talk, I die."

"Wrong. If they think you talk, you die. You walk out of here right now, the Vargases will think you talked whether you did or not. If you tell us what you know, we'll protect you. If not, you're on your own. I don't care who your sister is."

Neil hung his head, and Dale could tell he was wavering. He'd been off the grid for days, doing who knows what. He'd gotten cash from Cyrus Gantry in exchange for his promise to let Gantry Oil drill on the Davis ranch, but he hadn't had any money on him when they'd picked him up. She wondered if he'd blown it already. Either way, he seemed desperate, and she planned to take full advantage. She rapped a knuckle on the table. "Tick, tock. We've got other people we can talk to, but you better hope none of them point a finger at you."

He looked up at her, and his expression was a mix of resignation and resentment. "Fine, I'll talk, but not here."

"Where then?"

He looked over at Peyton. "I want to go home."

Peyton hesitated only a minute. "We'll take you now."

CHAPTER FIVE

L indsey pushed the button to the eighth floor. She and Jed had just returned from the DEA office and were in the elevator on their way to Elaina's room for a planning session. Elaina had called when they were on the way back to the hotel and suggested the meeting, intimating they could use Lindsey's room, but Lindsey didn't offer. As the talent, she had the best accommodations, but the idea of having Elaina lounging in her suite made the decision easy. All she really wanted to do was find something to eat since she'd burned through lunch hours ago. The minute this meeting was over, she was going to have a serious date with room service.

She turned to Jed. "Let's get something straight before we go in there."

He grinned. "Yes, boss."

She smacked him on the arm. "Seriously. I need your help. Elaina's working some network agenda on this project, but I want to keep an open mind."

"I got it. Play along to get along, but be prepared to go rogue."

Lindsey reflected on her promise to Larry. Going rogue was what she was known for, but he was right; she did owe him a favor. If she did this assignment by the book, she'd be off the hook and free to tackle a new project. One of her own choosing. "No, we're not going rogue, but I do want to have some of my signature on this piece, no matter how vanilla it is, so be prepared to add in some angles if the opportunity arises. We'll have to be creative since I'm pretty sure Elaina was instructed to watch me like a hawk."

"And how are you feeling about that? Have you two worked together since…"

"Nope. This is the first time. Aren't you lucky?" Relationships in their industry took place in a fishbowl. When the relationship imploded the way theirs had, everyone got to witness the fallout. She'd seen worse debris from others, but all breakups were awkward for the people in the audience. "So far, things have been civil, and that's all I could hope for."

"I don't know how to say this," Jed said. "So, I'm just going to be blunt. There are better producers out there. Ones who are more in tune with your style."

"I know." Part of their personal clash had come when the romance wore off and Lindsey realized how differently she and Elaina approached their work. Elaina cared about ratings, viewership, and the bottom line—all the things that made the network love her. On the other hand, Lindsey cared about the story, and everything else was incidental. She'd go to any lengths to find the truth even when no one else, including viewers, wanted to know the real story. Her doggedness had never diminished the popularity of her work, but Elaina had assured her there would come a day when she would have to sacrifice her integrity in exchange for the opportunity to reach a broader audience. That assurance had been the death knell of their relationship. It hadn't taken Lindsey long to realize she was better off alone than with someone who would never understand her. She'd never let anything get in the way of her quest for the truth.

"She's perfect for this piece," she told Jed. "And that's all that matters for now."

She knocked on the door of Elaina's room and smiled when Alice answered the door. She and Alice had worked together on dozens of stories. There was no better cameraman in the business, and she was certain Alice had the same questions as Jed about why they'd been picked for an assignment that a trained monkey could do. She leaned in to give Alice a hug and whispered, "Thanks for doing this. I owe you one."

"Always glad to get a call from you," Alice whispered back. She stepped aside to let Lindsey enter the room.

Elaina's digs weren't quite as fancy as her own, but they ran a close second. Lindsey started to walk over to where Elaina was seated at a sizable desk, but she stopped abruptly when she spotted several trays of food sitting on the coffee table in the sitting area. "Oh my God, I'm starving." She grabbed half a sandwich and scarfed it in three bites. She reached for a napkin and when she looked back up, Elaina was standing beside her, wearing a sweet smile.

"I figured you'd be hungry," Elaina said. "I don't know how you manage to eat the way you do and keep looking this good."

Lindsey cleared her throat, hoping she wouldn't choke on a breadcrumb, but didn't ask for clarification about what "this" was. She wasn't interested in flirting with her ex or reminiscing about how she'd always worked through meals and then come home starving. Elaina might know all her little quirks, but those were all surface level, not the stuff that really mattered. She diverted. "Hey, Jed, you better get over here before I eat all this food. Consider this your only warning." She heaped a plate high with sandwiches, pasta salad, and fruit and took it to the desk where Elaina's stuff was spread out. "How about we make this a working dinner? What's first on the agenda?"

Elaina scrambled to shove the papers into a folder and then opened a fancy leather planner the size of a Volkswagen. "I've arranged with the local affiliate to provide us with a room for filming some of the non DEA interviews, but I'd like to do all the agency clips either at the DEA division office or in the field, same with the other local agencies. Jed, can you work with that?"

He gulped a bite of sandwich and nodded. "Sure. We took a good look around while we were at the DEA office. It's not ideal, but I can make it work. What kind of in the field filming do you have in mind?"

Elaina leaned back in her chair. "I don't know. Maybe Lindsey could tag along with one of the agents." She looked down at her planner. "Since our focus is the Take-Back Initiative, Lindsey, you could get them to show you where they plan to hold the main event along with some of the local outlets, stuff like that." She pointed at her computer. "The guy in charge, Agent Diego, sent over a bio for the liaison you asked for, Special Agent Dale Nelson. He's a decorated Marine who served in Afghanistan, and I think he could be the perfect hook for the story. Might be good to follow him around and work the human interest angle. From the war on terror to the war on drugs. Different battles, same skills. Something like that."

As Elaina droned on, Lindsey tried to hide a grin. Jed was kicking her under the table, and his own grin was infectious. Alice was the first to catch on. "What's so funny?"

"Nothing," Lindsey said as she delivered a return kick to Jed's shin. But Jed was not to be deterred.

"She's going to figure it out sooner or later," he said.

She sighed. He was right. She turned to Elaina. "Dale Nelson is a she, not a he."

It took a few seconds for Elaina to register her words, but when she did, her eyes narrowed. "Hmmm, that might change things. I'll have to think about it."

"Why?" Lindsey suspected she knew the answer, but she wondered if Elaina would be so crass as to admit her reasoning for rethinking Dale as the focus of the human interest angle. *Please let her not be that callous.*

"It's just different is all. Doesn't have the same broad-based appeal."

"Broad-based appeal? Care to explain what that's code for?" Damn. No matter how much she'd hoped Elaina would change, her hoping couldn't make it so. Lindsey's appetite vanished, and a clawing sense of claustrophobia drove her to stand and pace. "A woman serves her country overseas and comes home to do more of the same and that's less compelling than a man who does the same thing? Like death and destruction can only be appreciated if we placate the majority by showing them only a pure reflection of themselves?"

Elaina glanced at Jed and Alice, probably looking for moral support, but they both shook their heads as if to say "not my battle." When Elaina finally addressed her, she sidestepped the question. "It's not a matter of what you or I think. Our job is to reach the common denominator, and there's a method to getting there. Not everyone likes the idea of women in the military, and you might lose your opportunity to reach your audience and get the message across. You know that even though you like to pretend you don't."

Lindsey shook her head. Elaina wasn't going to give in. They could continue their standoff or she could grab what little advantage she could by turning Elaina's own words back around. "Didn't realize you were so focused on making this a substantive piece with a moral and everything, but I'm glad to hear it. I've got some great ideas for ways we can beef up this story. Trust me, Dale will be the perfect centerpiece for what you have in mind."

She was bluffing since all she knew about Dale was that she was gruff, handsome, and annoyed as hell that she'd been thrust into this assignment. One word from Elaina and Dale would likely jump at the chance to ditch this gig, but no way was Lindsey going to let that happen. Even with the little information she'd heard so far, she was certain Dale would be the key to making this story more interesting.

❖

"You two should eat something too. Come on. We've got plenty."

Dale looked up from watching Neil scarf his way through a plate of pot roast into the welcoming eyes of Helen Davis and wondered, not for the first time, how one woman had given birth to two such incredibly different children. Peyton was one of the most honorable people she'd ever met, and Neil was a selfish, entitled brat. She had no desire to break bread with him. She glanced at Peyton who nodded.

"Mom, I've got to talk to Dale. We'll be back in a few minutes." Peyton motioned for Dale to follow, and they walked out front and sat on the front porch. "She pushes food on people. It's her way."

"Sorry if I was rude, but I actually do need to talk to you about something and I couldn't do it in front of your brother."

"Sounds serious. Shoot."

Dale hesitated for a second before plunging to the heart of what she wanted to know. "Did you know Gellar is shutting down the task force?"

"What?"

"It's true."

"It can't be. He can't do that."

Years of experience talking to liars told her Peyton's reaction was genuine. The next question was what they were going to do about it. "Diego told me. He got the word from the director. I expect you'll hear about it firsthand when you meet with Gellar tomorrow. In fact, that's probably the real reason he wants to meet with you."

"We can't let this happen. Not now when we're just starting to make headway."

"You're preaching to the choir. Diego's got me lined up to work with some reporter who's doing a piece on the agency for *Spotlight America*. It's a PR thing about our drug Take-Back program. Supposed to make us look good after all the fallout from the hooker deal last year. Guess the director needs to go to Congress for more funding. Anyway, I can probably shake her to get some work done. Think you can sneak around if needed?"

"If I'm not out of a job entirely. They transferred me back here to head up this task force. If Gellar dissolves it, he may not see his way clear to keeping me on."

"You've got to stay on. Bianca's good, but she needs more experience, and she won't stand up to Gellar. If we're going to prosecute the Vargases, we need you."

"I hear you, but maybe it's for the best. My dad is getting sicker by the day, and there's the whole conflict with Lily's father."

Dale heard what she was saying, but she wasn't going to take no for an answer. "I get that it's a sacrifice. My wife died fighting these people. Your relationship with Lily, the fact that it's personal, just makes you more suited to the job. People fight the hardest when they're fighting for something they care about." She'd seen the concept in action every day that she'd served in active duty, and she believed it to her core.

The creak of the screen door interrupted Peyton's response. Helen stuck her head out. "I'm officially declaring your business on hold for now," she said. "Come on in and eat before everything gets cold."

Dale looked at Peyton who merely shrugged. What the hell, she was starving and it did smell wonderful. "Yes, ma'am." She started to walk through the door, but Helen placed a hand on her shoulder before she could get past.

"Dale, don't you worry about Peyton. She'll do the right thing. I can always count on her that way. Her daddy may be sick and her girl may be caught in the middle, but Peyton won't leave you hanging." Helen delivered the last words with a pointed look at Peyton, and Peyton offered what appeared to be a grudging smile. Dale made a mental note never to assume a conversation in the Davis household was private.

A few minutes later, they were seated around the table with Neil. Lily had excused herself to go make some phone calls, and Helen said something about checking her horses, but Dale suspected they both wanted to give them some privacy to ask Neil the hard questions. She and Peyton had agreed that Dale would do most of the talking.

"Like I said at the office, you're not being charged with anything. Frankly, I don't know if you've done anything illegal, but I have to say you sure are acting like someone who has something to hide."

Neil dropped his fork and let it clatter against his plate. "Maybe you're just overly suspicious."

Dale leaned back in her chair, purposely meeting his aggressive stance with calm tones. "Maybe. But I've got an eye for folks in trouble. They start hiding things, like the financial condition of this ranch and the fact they've made sketchy business deals, from loved ones. They miss important meetings and go on the run. And they get themselves tied up and left as bait for a bunch of federal agents."

"Sketchy business deals?" He stabbed his finger at Peyton. "She's talking about the father of your girlfriend. If you think Cyrus Gantry is bad news, then what are you doing dating his precious daughter and the heir to his fortune?"

The only sign he'd gotten under Peyton's skin was the hitch in her breath, but she quickly took control. "Spare me the lecture. If fathers and their children were exactly the same, you'd be more like Dad and be content to earn your money through hard work rather than gambling with the wealth of others. You sold rights you didn't have to Cyrus Gantry and took a nice little bonus off the top." Neil's expression told them both he hadn't expected her to find out about his side deal. "The question now is, why did you get paid in cash? Maybe all that money wasn't for the drilling rights. Have you been helping Cyrus launder money for the Vargas brothers? All I want is information, but if you don't pony up what you know, then I'll be after blood."

As Dale watched the exchange, she was more certain than ever that Peyton was the right person to bring the Vargases to justice. She'd never let personal conflict trump her desire for right over wrong, and that was exactly why she had to keep the task force alive. But if she was going to ask Peyton to make it work, she had to be willing to do the same which meant dodging Lindsey Ryan, and that wouldn't be easy.

She was familiar with Lindsey's work, respected it even. Lindsey asked tough questions and went to great lengths to bring realism to her stories. Unfortunately, the qualities she admired in Lindsey were the ones she would have to be most wary of because if Lindsey figured out she was working off the books, she wouldn't rest until she uncovered the details. And that was the problem with investigative reporters—when they sifted through other people's dirt, their goal was to sling mud. Nothing sold like a full-fledged messy scandal, and no one sold it better than an intelligent, attractive reporter like Lindsey Ryan.

She pictured Lindsey as she'd been when she met her at the office. She was as vibrant off screen as she was on, but what Dale noticed was her bearing. Stance confident, eyes sharp—Lindsey was unapologetic about asking questions, and she grilled her subjects for the details behind the answers. If she were going to pull off working double duty, she'd have to figure out how to keep Lindsey both close and distant at the same time. But for now, she turned her attention back to the exchange between Neil and Peyton.

"Cyrus Gantry isn't what you think he is," Neil said.

Peyton rested her hands on the table. "Enlighten me then."

"He's a good man who'd do anything to protect his family."

"You care to define 'anything'?"

Neil flicked a glance at Dale. "Do I need a lawyer?"

"Your sister's a lawyer," Dale replied. "If it were up to me, I'd have found something to charge you with already since I understand you skipped town with money that belonged to your family after you got mixed up with Cyrus. Your best bet is to start talking and tell us something we don't already know."

Neil took a breath and blurted, "The Vargases told Cyrus they would kill Lily if he didn't do as they asked."

Dale leaned in closer. "That's what we're talking about. Tell me more."

"I don't know how it started, but a few years ago, when oil prices were tanking, they approached Cyrus about a way he could make extra cash off the books by laundering money for their drug operation. He told them no fucking way, but they wouldn't take no for an answer. They sent him close-up photos of Lily in all kinds of places at different times of the day to show him they could get to her anytime they wanted. Finally, he gave in."

Dale would've had a hard time believing Neil's story, if Peyton hadn't told her about how the Vargas brothers had forced Lily's mother to give her up to be raised by Cyrus. And then, just last week, they'd tried to kill Sophia for telling Lily the truth. She wondered how much, if any, of the sordid backstory Neil knew. "Why didn't he reach out for protection? Seems like that would've made a helluva lot more sense than throwing in with drug dealers."

He shrugged. "I don't know. Most of his contact with the Vargases was through go-betweens. They were careful not to deal with Cyrus in public, where he could take any action against them. What was Cyrus supposed to report? All I know is sometimes a man has to take things into his own hands when he's threatened."

His pointed glance at Peyton spoke volumes, but Dale wasn't interested in helping them explore their family dynamics. "Okay, so tell me what you do know, starting with why he trusted you with this information and what you were doing to help Cyrus."

"I didn't have to do much. He wanted to lease the land out by the north pasture for drilling. He had his engineers do some preliminary testing, and he showed me a report that said there was a viable oil source. Peyton and Zach ran his team off before they got a chance to put a hole in the ground."

"That's it? That was your only involvement?" Neil ducked his head, and Dale knew there was more to his story. "This only works if you tell us everything. You hold out and I'll haul you back to my office."

"He'd already advanced me a big sum of money."

"Let me guess—you didn't have it anymore."

"I didn't have most of it."

"So, you owed him."

"Yes."

"And what did Cyrus have you do to work it off?"

"He wanted me to get him information about Peyton. What she was working on and if it involved him."

"So you spied on your sister?"

"No, I told him there was no way Peyton would confide in me and I had to stay gone a while, until the family cooled off about the investment with Cyrus. I offered to try to flush out the Vargases instead. And I found them, but they were waiting for me. Guess I'm lucky to be alive."

Dale drummed her fingers on the table as she contemplated whether Neil was telling the truth. Seemed pretty implausible that he'd turned from rancher to wannabe oil baron to drug informant in the space of a few months. Still, something about the way he delivered the details of his tale rang true. She turned to Peyton. "You have something he can write on?"

"Absolutely." Peyton walked over to a drawer and pulled out a pad of paper and a pen.

When she placed them in front of Neil, he asked, "What?"

"Start writing," Dale said. "I want every detail of every conversation you've had with anyone at Gantry Oil and the Vargas brothers on that paper before you leave this room." She stood and motioned for Peyton to follow. When they were out of hearing range, she asked, "You buy any of this?"

"I don't know what to buy anymore, but I do think it's possible Cyrus was acting out of fear. He may be a sorry ass example of a father, but he loves Lily in his own twisted way."

"Do you think Cyrus really believed Lily's uncles would harm her?"

"Hard to believe, I know, but they think Lily is a blight on the family. Ironic, right?"

Dale nodded, and the hard steel in Peyton's voice made her pause before saying, "We should probably talk to Lily's mother. Seems like she could shed a lot of light on the family dynamic beyond what she's already told you." She jerked her head toward the kitchen. "What do you want to do about your brother?"

"I don't know. You have any ideas?"

"I say let's cut him loose and see what he does. If he's a patsy, he'll steer clear of Cyrus and the Vargases, but if he's on the payroll, we'll know soon enough."

Less than an hour later, Dale left the ranch. She didn't envy the folks around the Davis dinner table that evening.

She drove back to the office and spent the rest of the day clearing her desk ahead of the busy next day. The first thing she'd do in the morning was meet with Lindsey Ryan and get her set up so she could work on her own, and then she planned to duck out and catch up with Peyton after her meeting with Gellar. If Gellar really was determined to dismantle the task force, they'd have to come up with a plan to keep their investigation going and keep their work secret.

When she finally looked up, the sky was pitch-dark and the clock on the wall read eight o'clock. She reached for the phone, but withdrew her hand before punching the familiar buttons to tell her dead wife she'd be home late. A year later, old habits still trumped the reality that she had no one to go home to anymore.

CHAPTER SIX

Lindsey shut off her alarm and stretched. She'd slept later than she'd planned, but hotel rooms with their freezing temperatures and blackout curtains did that to her. The bonus was she was well rested and ready for a packed day. She reached for the phone and ordered breakfast: eggs, pancakes, bacon, and coffee. Lots of coffee. She'd need a ton of fortification today since she planned to spend it with her reluctant liaison, Dale Nelson.

Dale. While she waited for breakfast to be delivered, she tugged on shorts and a hoodie and fished through her bag to find her laptop. Once it powered up, she typed in Dale's name. With no other identifiers, the search results were a mixed bag, and she scrolled through stories about a line of fancy yachts, a Canadian mass murderer, and a renowned meteorologist without any mention of Special Agent Nelson. She punched her way back to the search engine and added more words: DEA, Dallas, Marine, and several pages of stories appeared. All of them mentioning the enigmatic woman she'd met the day before, but the first one—the only one with a photo—seized her attention.

The photo was black-and-white, and Dale was in profile, standing in front of a ranch-style house. Several reporters with microphones clustered around her, and Lindsey could tell by the set of Dale's jaw, she was angry. The caption simply said: Crime Hits Home for DEA Agent. Lindsey's gut wrenched at the combination of the expression on Dale's face and the foreboding words. She scrolled through the article, skipping through phrases faster and faster, eager to know what happened yet dreading what she might learn.

AUSA Maria Escobar...apparently surprised by gunman... body riddled with dozens of blasts from automatic weapons... known for her ruthless prosecution of members of the Texas Mexican Mafia...survived by her wife, Special Agent Dale Nelson.

No small wonder Dale looked angry. There she was standing in front of the house she'd shared with her wife, mere hours after Maria had been assassinated on the front lawn, and reporters were vying for her attention. Lindsey wondered if she would've risked Dale's wrath to get a quote?

Maybe, once upon a time. When she'd first started out, Lindsey had believed nothing should stand between a reporter and the whole story, no matter how messy, no matter how ugly the truth was. Years later, her ideals had been tempered by the inhumanity she'd seen in the world. There was more than enough meanness, cruelty, and atrocity for her to document without having to stoke the flames of her subject's pain. She might always report the truth, but there was enough pain in the world without her creating more of it. The photo of Dale was striking, the caption provocative, but her heart ached for the way their intrusion had robbed Dale of important moments of quiet grief.

She glanced at the date of the release. Just over a year ago. Were the shades of Dale's past still casting shadows over her life now? Curiosity drove her to click open a few other stories, and she devoured each one. Dale served as a MP in Afghanistan and she had been awarded a Navy Cross for an act of heroism that appeared to be classified. She'd met Maria, who was serving as a JAG officer, during her time in the service, and they married soon after they both returned to the States. They'd both been working on a task force formed by the local US Attorney, Herschel Gellar. Their mission was to curb the tide of crime and violence perpetrated by the Zeta Cartel whose members were engaged in high dollar drug deals and a host of other violent crimes.

After scanning a dozen articles, Lindsey leaned back in her chair. So, now Special Agent Nelson was assigned to show her around town and educate her on the agency's drug Take-Back Initiative? Could there be any assignment more toothless than that?

She flashed back to her first look at Dale yesterday—jeans, boots, a tight black T-shirt, badge and gun on her belt, her unruly dark waves sticking out all over. She hadn't tried to hide her distaste at being assigned as a liaison to her crew. If the agency was set on redeeming their reputation with PR about public outreach, Dale wasn't buying the script. Something else was going on with Agent Nelson, and Lindsey was convinced whatever it was had to be the hook for this story.

A knock at the door jerked her out of her musings. She moved her laptop to make room for her huge breakfast, but when she swung open the door, instead of a room service waiter, Dale stood framed in the threshold, looking almost exactly the same as she had the day before. Lindsey stood stock-still for a second while she tried to process what was happening. Had they made an appointment and she'd forgotten about it? No, she was meticulous about details, and she hadn't even had a chance to give Dale her number before Dale ditched her at the DEA office.

"Are you going to invite me in?"

Lindsey snapped out of her reverie and looked down at her clothes. Dale caught her looking and said, "At least you aren't in your pajamas."

While Lindsey laughed off her embarrassment, she took a moment to reflect on Dale's tone. Not an ounce of flirtation had accompanied any of her words. Too bad. She looked as handsome today as she had the day before. If she wasn't considering Dale as the subject for her story, she might try to take advantage of the fact a bed was steps away, and it had been way too long since she had sex. She shoved away the thoughts before they went too far. "Come in, Agent. It's nice to see you, although I'm sure you can tell, I wasn't expecting company." Dale strode into the room, and Lindsey watched her eyes track the entire suite.

"Nice room. Big," Dale said. "You having to bunk with anyone else?"

"Uh, no, just me." Lindsey pointed at the large desk in the living area. "I'll be doing a lot of the work for the piece here, so I need the space." She didn't have a clue why she felt the need to justify the size of her suite, but she did. Before she could give it another thought, another knock sounded from the door. She glanced over at Dale, who was headed toward the desk where her laptop sat open, the results of her Google search on display. Thinking fast, she said, "Hey, do you mind getting the door? I'm going to change."

She didn't wait for a response, instead making a beeline for the desk. Dale cocked her head, but headed back to the door. Lindsey closed her laptop, grabbed a pair of pants, and called out over her shoulder, "You can sign for me. Thanks."

She practically dove into the bathroom. Once there she took a minute to catch her breath. *She probably thinks I'm insane.* One look in the mirror confirmed it. She hadn't bothered to brush her hair this morning, and it looked like small animals had burrowed a new home in her tangled waves. A closer look revealed a long sheet crease across her right cheek, evidence of a super sound night's sleep. She brushed her hair because that was the only one of the two problems she could solve and tugged on a pair of pants. If she were going to look like she'd just rolled out of bed, at least she wouldn't have bare legs.

When she emerged from the bathroom, Dale was sitting at the desk, eating a piece of bacon. She looked up and met Lindsey's eyes, but kept right on chewing as if daring Lindsey to say something.

"I asked for crisp," Lindsey said. "I hope it's crisp."

"You got what you paid for. Pretty expensive."

"Room service always is, but it's convenient. Maybe you can suggest some better places around here."

Dale finished off the slice of bacon and rubbed her hands on one of the cloth napkins. "You probably won't be here long enough. I can't imagine this story is going to take too much of your time. Are you ready to get started?"

Sensing she was being rushed, Lindsey grappled for control of the situation. "Actually, I was planning to spend the morning doing some background research." Suddenly, she was struck with a brilliant idea of how to spend some time with Dale and, hopefully, get her to open up about her work with the DEA. "But you can help with that. I've got a list of people I'll need to talk to and places where we might film. If you could take me around to see the locations, we can talk about the people while we drive. I just need a quick shower and I'll be good to go."

"What about the rest of your crew?"

It would be normal for her to have Jed or Alice along so they could assess the locations for lighting and sound, but Lindsey wanted this first outing to be just her and Dale. After what she'd read this morning, she wanted a chance to study Dale one-on-one and decide if her instincts about making her the center of this piece were spot-on. "They're working on some logistics this morning. Looks like you're stuck with me."

Dale frowned, but said, "Okay. I'll meet you downstairs in twenty minutes." She didn't wait for a response, and seconds later, was out the door. Lindsey grabbed one of the remaining pieces of bacon and contemplated her next move. She had twenty minutes to eat, shower, change, and explain to her crew that she was ditching them for the morning, but all she could think about was how fascinated she was with the enigmatic woman who'd just left her hotel room.

❖

Dale paced the lobby of the hotel. Fifteen of the twenty minutes had passed, and she was growing more and more agitated. It had started the minute Lindsey answered her hotel room door. She probably should have called first, but she'd wanted to make it clear from the get-go they were going to work on her timeline. After seeing Lindsey in short-shorts, looking like she'd just rolled out of bed, she'd been hard-pressed to hide the mysterious effect Lindsey had on her. She'd written the feeling off to the fact she'd been forced into this duty and her quick glance at the browser history on Lindsey's laptop revealed Lindsey had been reading up on her. She couldn't wait to get this little tour over with so she could get back to real work. As soon as Miss Lindsey Ryan got her ass down here, she planned to let her know she didn't have time to wait around.

To pass the last few minutes, she pulled out her phone and dialed Peyton's number. When she got her voice mail, she hung up and dialed Bianca who answered on the first ring. She didn't wait for niceties. "Hey, Cruz, what's going on over there?"

"Dale?" Bianca's voice dropped to a whisper. "I don't know. Gellar asked for all our files on Cyrus Gantry, and Peyton's been trying to get in to see him all morning, but she's been tight-lipped about what's going on. You have a clue?"

"I do, but we should talk in person." Dale mentally sorted through options of where the trusted members of the team could meet without raising suspicion. For the last couple of weeks, they'd been assembling at the Circle Six, but Neil Davis was back there now, and she was suspicious about his true allegiance. Still, she couldn't come up with a better option. "The usual place, this afternoon. We may need to work off the books for a while. What time can you make it?"

"I have a one o'clock docket, but it'll be fairly quick. I'll be there by four and I'll let the others know."

Dale spotted Lindsey walking toward her. "Gotta go." This version of Lindsey looked very different from the one she'd seen moments ago. Her tangled hair was brushed into smooth, shiny waves, and her jeans and blazer, while still sporty, were wrinkle free and not at all pajama-like. This Lindsey looked like the one she'd seen on TV, reporting from various hot spots around the world— the one who was here to do a story on the DEA and the one she'd have to avoid if she wanted to keep whatever they had planned for the task force secret. She chided herself for letting sleepy, rumpled, bare-legged Lindsey get under her skin.

"You didn't have to get off the phone on my account," Lindsey said with a smile.

"I didn't. You ready to get going?" She didn't wait for an answer before she started walking out of the lobby. Her truck was where she'd left it, right by the valet stand. She pulled the keys out of her pocket, unlocked the doors, and climbed into the driver's seat. The truck was pretty tall and didn't have rails, but Lindsey hopped inside easily. Dale mentally added a check in the plus column and drove out of the hotel parking lot.

"You must be in good with the valet if they let you use their premium space. You have to flash your badge for that kind of treatment?"

And just like that, Lindsey's tally went negative. "I always park close to the door and I always keep my keys. If you ever need a quick response, you'll be thankful I thought ahead."

"Duly noted."

Dale glanced over at Lindsey who was armed with a small messenger bag and what appeared to be a high-powered camera. "You plan to take pictures?"

"If I see something I want to capture. Why?"

"I guess I figured since your crew was filming you wouldn't need to take still shots as well. Especially not you."

"Especially not me, huh?"

She probably shouldn't have said that last part out loud. "Isn't one of the perks of being a big shot having other people do stuff for you?"

"You think I'm a big shot?"

Dale heard the flirtatious tone and did her best to ignore it. "I'm just repeating what I hear on TV."

"Don't believe everything you hear," Lindsey said. "I'll admit, I'll never win any awards for my photos, but I'm a pretty decent photographer, and seeing firsthand how best to frame a shot gives me valuable perspective when I'm reporting. Besides, there have been times when I didn't have a crew and I took photos to help me preserve images of things I saw. It helped me when I started to write the story."

Okay, so she was intelligent and pretty. Well, pretty wasn't the best word. Lindsey wasn't all put-together, package-pretty. She was a dangerous, barely-tamed kind of beautiful. In that way, Lindsey reminded her of Maria.

Dale shook her head. Would she always compare every woman she met to the one she'd lost? Probably. And why not? Maria had been her everything. They'd shared a lifetime of precious moments compressed into a short span of time together. They'd shared love of country, justice, and a willingness to sacrifice everything for the things they believed in, yet they had found time to nurture their love for each other as well. The hard work that often drove couples apart, brought them together until it demanded the ultimate sacrifice. Why did she ever bother comparing anyone else to Maria when she knew the result in advance?

"Did I bore you with my talk of photography?"

Dale snapped back into the present and took a deep breath. Her hands were clenching the steering wheel like it was a lifeline, and a trail of sweat trickled down the back of her neck. Praying Lindsey hadn't noticed her break with the present, she tried for levity. "Not as much as I'm about to bore you with the details of the Take-Back program." She pointed to Dallas City Hall. "There's where it's all going down. Right there on the front lawn. See, they even have banners up. Bring your old antibiotics and help save the world."

Dale turned down the next street and drove into a parking garage. The lot was pretty full and she had to park on the outskirts. "Damn, where's the cop-kissing valet when you need him?" she said. "Guess we'll have to walk a bit." She started to open her door, but noticed Lindsey hadn't made a move to take off her seat belt and she was staring straight ahead at the building. "You coming?"

Lindsey turned her head slowly and asked, "Mind if we sit here for a minute?"

Dale made a show of looking at her watch. "Sure. It's your time. You can use it however you like."

"Good. Let's talk. Tell me why this program is worthy of a news story."

Dale narrowed her eyes. "What are you getting at?"

"It's pretty clear you think it's silly. Why don't you tell me why you think so?"

Dale held up her hands in a gesture of surrender. "Hold on now. I never said that. I was just joking around."

"Okaaay."

Lindsey drew out the word, making it clear she wasn't buying it, but Dale wasn't about to confide her thoughts about the PR stunt her boss's bosses had dreamed up to deflect from the recent scandals that had plagued their department. Operation Discreet had gone down in flames when several congressmen on Ways and Means discovered agents had hired expensive prostitutes to work as confidential informants. DEA agents had provided top tier members of the Sinaloa Cartel with high dollar hookers, relying on the women to infiltrate the inner circle and report back. The plan had devolved when way more money was spent on "entertainment" than intelligence gathered. In addition, several of the women had been killed, their violently defiled bodies found by local police, and responsibility for their deaths disavowed by anyone in the agency. When a congressional staffer discovered what was going on, hearings were promptly scheduled, and heads rolled. The area director had been served up as a token to the torch-bearing legislators who'd threatened to withhold funding for any of the more worthy projects the agency had planned.

Months later, some of the heat had died down, but the rest of the agents were still paying the price for the harm done by the few. Hard-to-get resources, constant scrutiny, and other annoyances plagued the division, and someone had decided to make a big deal of the tenth Take-Back Initiative, complete with speeches and educating schoolchildren, as a way to distract the media.

She thought it was a colossal waste of time, but it wouldn't do her or any of the other agents any good to give Lindsey an angle to the story that would only distract from the agency's attempt to make a comeback. She measured her words. "It's a good program. Any time we can get drugs off the street, it's a good thing." She pointed at the building. "Now, would you like to take a look around?"

Lindsey read Dale's body language—the set jaw, the averted eyes, the folded arms. She knew she wasn't going to get any more information about how Dale really felt about this project. Not now anyway. That's okay. She could wait. She opened her door. "I would. Thanks. I know you probably have way more important things to do than tour me around town."

Dale shook her head. "Right now, this is the most important thing I could possibly be doing," she said and motioned for her to follow. There wasn't a detectable ounce of sarcasm in Dale's voice, but as Lindsey walked behind her into the building, she was certain Dale's words were laced with some double meaning.

An hour later, Lindsey emerged from the building. Dale had stepped out a few minutes before to take a call, leaving her to listen to the endless prattling of Harold Carter, the city employee who was in charge of the logistics of the event. In addition to walking her around the area outside where the stage would be erected, he'd given her a tour of city hall, including the alternate, but less desirable space they would use in the event of rain. While she pretended to listen to the boring recitation of detail, Lindsey's mind wandered to her companion for the day. Dale had patiently answered every question about the setup for the event and the logistics of collecting and disposing of all the drugs, but she could tell by the number of times Dale had glanced at her watch, she would rather be doing anything else. She couldn't blame her since she felt exactly the same way.

Damn Larry and Susan for sending her across the country to chase a silly story. She'd been in the business long enough to know how it would go down. In the few weeks before the story aired, the network would fill the airwaves with promo spots promising a tantalizing story about the DEA. They'd use her name to give viewers the expectation the story would be an expose. When the story finally aired, everyone would tune in, waiting and hoping for the twist that would never come. Ratings would be through the roof, making the sponsors and whoever else this story was designed to please happy—her own reputation for ruthless reporting be damned.

Truth was, her reputation was strong enough to survive, but that didn't mean she had to enjoy caving to the pressure. Maybe instead of trying to get Dale to play along, she'd see if Dale would give her a different story, one with more substance. She'd much rather be her ally than her adversary. She spotted Dale with her back to her, and headed her way, getting within a few feet before realizing Dale was still on the phone. She started to backtrack, but a few choice phrases piqued her curiosity and kept her in place. *We should talk in person. We may just need to work off the books on this one. I'll do whatever I have to.*

She didn't have a chance to process what she was hearing before Dale shoved her phone in her pocket and turned toward her. She didn't miss a beat. "You get everything you needed in there?"

Despite Dale's quick reaction, Lindsey thought she spied a hint of suspicion in Dale's eyes. She wasn't about to confess she'd been eavesdropping, but this might be the perfect moment to engage Dale about how this little project they'd both been assigned to was a colossal waste of time. "Can I be honest with you?"

Dale looked into her eyes and her mouth slid into a lazy smile. "Honesty is always welcome."

"I'm not even sure why I'm here. I mean next on my list is to ask you to introduce me to everyone who will be working the event, including the local cops. I get the impression all the people I meet are going to tell me what a great project this is and how it's a huge benefit to the local community and a valiant effort in the war on drugs." She paused and Dale raised her eyebrows and nodded for her to continue. "But you and I both know this project isn't going to make a real difference in anyone's life, and you're probably going to end up with buckets full of old antibiotics and expired ointment, but not much in the way of drugs that have any real street value."

She paused again, hoping Dale would riff off of her words and offer her own opinion about the negligible effect of the program, but Dale merely said, "If there's a question in there, I'm not sure what it was."

"I guess I'm wondering if you can think of something more worthy of an hour of prime time on a Friday night. I mean if you had the chance to reach twenty million viewers, what story would you tell?"

For a brief moment, Dale's eyes were bright and her expression was eager, but just as quickly, the mask of nonchalance returned.

She turned the key in the ignition. "I don't have any stories to tell. If you're not interested in this project, maybe you should fly back to New York and I can get back to the cases waiting on my desk."

The words were delivered in a flat tone without a trace of malice, but the message was clear: Dale wanted her to know she didn't care if she stayed or left. Lindsey's instincts told her there was more to it than that. She replayed the words she'd heard earlier: *We should talk in person. We may need to work off the books for a while.* What Dale really wanted was for her to report this silly story and get the hell out of her way for something way more interesting. The resistance only made her more curious about what Dale was up to and more determined to find out.

❖

Later that afternoon, Dale knocked on Peyton's office door. She'd rushed over to the federal building as soon as she ditched Lindsey back at her hotel, and as much as she dreaded hearing the upshot of Peyton's meeting with Gellar, she was relieved to escape Lindsey's probing questions.

"Come in."

She opened the door and stopped abruptly one step into the room. Peyton was behind her desk, and sprawled on the couch off to the side was her boss, United States Attorney Herschel Gellar. Dale could tell by Peyton's furrowed brow that her patience was wearing thin. "I'm sorry. I didn't realize you were in the middle of a meeting."

Gellar motioned for her to come on in. "Agent Nelson, glad you're here. Stick around. This involves you too."

She took a seat in one of the chairs facing Peyton's desk and waited for one of them to start talking.

"I've decided to make some changes around here," Gellar said. "Be more efficient. I'm not convinced this task force is a good use of resources. I'll be handling the Gantry investigation myself." He waved a hand at Peyton. "For obvious reasons, you'll be walled off from the case."

Peyton nodded, and Dale couldn't fault him for that part of his decision. Considering Peyton's relationship with Lily, it was the right call, but she couldn't help but ask, "What about the rest of the team?"

Gellar grunted. "Don't need a team anymore. We've got what we need. It's just a matter of catching that damn vagrant who's still on the loose. Any cop in a uniform can get that done." He stood and reached out a hand to Dale. "Agent Nelson, thanks for all your hard work, but I can take it from here. Besides, I'm sure you have much more important things to do than run down a fugitive."

Gellar left the room and Dale could only shake her head. Sure, she had much more important things to do, like keep a beautiful woman company while a ruthless drug lord was on the lam. She vowed again not to let Lindsey Ryan or her silly story get in the way of her real work, no matter what Herschel Gellar had to say about it.

CHAPTER SEVEN

Dale pulled up at Peyton's ranch and parked her truck to the left of the tiny sports car she recognized as Bianca's. How had she made it up the rocky drive in the low-riding car? After she stepped out of the truck, she stood still for a few minutes, soaking up the fresh country air.

She'd always lived in town, but lately she'd been considering getting a place farther out with some land and maybe a horse or two. The thought lasted the two minutes it usually did before her inner voice nagged about how hard it would be to keep up with a place like that all on her own. Since Maria's death, she'd shoved all her belongings in storage and moved into a small apartment near work. The two rooms were stifling, but better than looking out over the front lawn every day where her wife had been mowed down in the quiet neighborhood they'd chosen to spend the rest of their lives. The money from the sale of the house was in the bank, waiting for whenever she was ready to move on with her life. She figured it would be there a long time.

As if on cue, Peyton and Lily stepped out from the front of the main house. She'd had a ringside seat to their burgeoning romance, and while she was happy for them, she couldn't deny a tinge of envy as she witnessed their relationship unfold. Lily waved and she waved back, unable to resist her welcoming smile.

"Get in here, Dale," Lily called out. "Or you'll miss Fernanda's pie, and trust me, you don't want to miss this pie."

Dale couldn't help but return the smile. "Is it chocolate?"

"Yes."

"Meringue or cream?"

"Cream, of course."

Dale took the steps two at a time. "You said the magic word." She nodded to Peyton and said, "Everyone here?"

"All inside."

"Sorry I'm late. Had to shake a reporter. Lindsey Ryan's in town to do some human interest piece on the DEA, and Diego pawned her off on me."

"Lindsey Ryan?" Lily asked. "Wasn't she the reporter embedded with the troops in Afghanistan? I love her. What's she like?"

Dale paused before answering. Her opinion of Lindsey was still in flux, and her impressions of her percolated in the back of her mind. She settled on a vague, "She's okay." She saw Lily's eyebrows knit into a curious expression, but thankfully, Peyton saved her from further interrogation about her celebrity pest.

"Lily, we better get started."

Lily gave Peyton a peck on the cheek. "No problem. I'm meeting with one of the contractors at the house. You go do your business, and I'll go do mine."

She walked to the stable and Dale waited until she was out of earshot before saying, "You two moving in together?"

"As soon as the house is ready. It's been a while since it was lived in, so we're having some work done. Lily thinks it will be the perfect place for a wedding."

"A wedding, huh?"

"You have something you want to say?"

Peyton's challenge was clear, but Dale wasn't looking for a fight. "I won't deny it seems a bit quick, but it's none of my business. I wish you both the best."

Peyton's shoulders relaxed, but Dale could tell she still had something on her mind, and she asked her as much.

"I guess I just wondered if you ever think about dating again," Peyton said. "I mean I know how difficult our jobs are, but we all need someone to make it all worthwhile, someone to come home to."

Dale looked at the blue sky, the worn wood boards of the porch, the rocky gravel in the drive, everywhere but back at Peyton. She knew the answer and she'd known it since the moment she'd first met Maria. Maria had been her everything and, although a year had passed, the memories remained. Memories of their lives together. Memories of the future they'd planned. "I had that. Not sure you get to have it twice, and I'm not interested in figuring that out. No offense."

"None taken. I get it." Peyton's face flashed sympathy, but she dropped the subject and pointed inside. "You ready?"

She was ready for anything that would distract from the conversation they'd just had. It was the closest she'd come to discussing a future after Maria in a while, and it was as unpleasant as the first time her brother had brought up the subject a couple of months before. She'd told him the same thing she'd said to Peyton, but this time the words had been accompanied by a twinge of regret, like the knowledge she'd forever be alone weighed more heavily than ever.

The Davis kitchen was the makeshift war room, complete with a whiteboard and one remaining slice of pie. Dale helped herself and settled in at the table where Mary and Bianca were waiting. Peyton immediately took charge.

"This morning, Dale and I met with Herschel Gellar, and he told us the task force funds are being diverted to other areas. Effective immediately, the task force is disbanded and everyone is being reassigned. Dale's boss has confirmed it, and, Mary, I expect you'll be notified soon. Raphael and the others were reassigned yesterday, and I couldn't reach them to ask if they wanted to be here tonight. Bianca, you've already got a pretty big general caseload, so the only thing that will change for you is you might have a few more free hours in the day."

"And what about you?" Bianca asked.

"I've been assigned to the human trafficking unit," Peyton said. "I'll be working with the FBI primarily, but I'm not sure who yet."

"So what happens to the Vargas brothers investigation and…"

Mary Lovelace let the words trail off, but everyone in the room knew what she was really asking. They'd served a search warrant on

Cyrus Gantry, and agents were poring over the files they'd gathered from his offices. There was no question Peyton would have to be walled off from the investigation and possible prosecution, but did the disbanding of the task force mean the whole thing would be dropped?

"I'm not sure what's going to happen with the Vargases or Lily's father," Peyton said. "I recommended Bianca to take the lead, but Gellar says he's going to handle it himself."

"That should be interesting." Dale couldn't help but laugh. The US attorney might be the top prosecutor in the district, but rarely did he or she actually try cases. The role was primarily administrative, and that was certainly the case with Gellar. He loved to brag about the accomplishments of his division, but he was rarely directly responsible for any of them.

"I agree," said Peyton. "But here's the deal. The Vargases' game is too big to rely on Cyrus as their only source for laundering funds. Now that Cyrus is under the spotlight and Sergio is on the run, someone else is going to pop up as a major player, and when they do, I want to be ready to catch them in the act. Nothing we do as a team will be authorized by my office or any of your respective agencies, so I can't expect any of you to join me, but—"

"I'm in." Mary was the first to speak.

"Me too," said Bianca.

Dale caught Peyton's eye and smiled. "Pretty sure you know where I stand."

Peyton grinned. "I expected no less." Her expression became serious. "We need to develop a system for communicating with each other and cataloging the results of our investigation."

"Without getting caught," Bianca added. "How about everything goes through me? Since I'll have a general docket, it'll be easier for me to move around and communicate with all of you. I've got cases with DEA, ATF, and FBI on my docket right now."

"Who were those FBI agents who served the search warrant on Cyrus?"

"Jeffries and Cohen. Jeffries is a jerk, but Tanner Cohen is a good cop."

"Can you trust her?"

"Not sure, but she'll talk to me about what's going on, off the record. I can tell you she's not going to be happy that Gellar is taking over the prosecution on this. Means a lot more work for her."

Dale knew what she meant. It was hard enough putting together a case with a seasoned trial attorney at the US Attorney's office. Working with someone who had little to no litigation experience meant the case agents would be carrying most of the slack. If Gellar was a big enough pain in the ass through the process, Cohen might give them some inside info under the guise of commiserating. She filed away the idea for now. "Okay, so we coordinate through Bianca and we have our meetings here." She turned to Peyton. "What about your brother? Is he going to blab about a bunch of agents meeting here or do you have some cover in mind?"

"Matter of fact, I do." Peyton reached behind her and fished a deck of cards and a box of poker chips from a baker's rack. She fanned out the cards and started shuffling the desk like a Vegas crony. "Five card stud, anyone?"

While Peyton dealt the cards, Dale's mind started ticking off avenues of investigation she wanted to explore. She had no problem running her plans through Bianca. The question was how was she going to get everything done with Lindsey Ryan watching her every move?

❖

Lindsey walked into the restaurant and spotted Alice and Jed seated in a booth across the room. "Where's Elaina?"

"On the phone with Larry," Alice said. "It got kind of loud so she took it outside."

She was well acquainted with Elaina's temper and Larry's ability to push anyone's buttons. Secretly, she was happy to have a few minutes out of Elaina's watchful eye. She'd spent the balance of the day, after Dale dropped her back at the hotel, thinking about this project, and she wanted to run her ideas by Alice and Jed. She glanced over her shoulder, just to make sure Elaina wasn't in sight, but before she could get a word in, Alice beat her to it.

"Did you enjoy spending the day with tall, dark, and handsome?"

"Accurate assessment of her appearance—were you spying?"

"I might have been lurking around the lobby when you two were leaving this morning."

"Well, she might be a looker, but she could not be more annoyed at having to show us around. I have no idea why she got stuck with this assignment, but I can tell you she views it as a punishment."

"So, you're abandoning your plan to make her the centerpiece of this project?" Jed asked.

"Not a chance. She's got layers. Lots of layers. I've just got to peel them back, but carefully." She told them what she'd learned about Dale's wife.

"Wow," Alice said. "There's your angle. DEA agent makes ultimate sacrifice in the war on drugs."

Lindsey flinched at Alice's words and the way they echoed the headline she'd read that morning. Alice was right. Dale's wife's death was the perfect hook for the story; however, using it made her uncomfortable, but she couldn't put her finger on why. The facts were what they were. Maria Escobar's death had been a clear message to law enforcement: back off or die. That Maria's wife, Dale, remained steadfastly resolved to investigate drug crimes was a testament to her character and Maria's legacy. If the DEA wanted to beef up their image, they should be shouting this story from the rooftops. Maybe, by assigning Dale to her, they were letting her discover the story herself with the hope it would be more appealing than if they pitched it. Wouldn't surprise her if that were the case, but something about the whole thing made her wary. "I want to look into things a bit more before we settle on an angle. We have some interviews lined up for tomorrow with some other DEA agents and local police. Let's see how those pan out and then we can strategize about the angle."

"What angle?"

Elaina was standing to the right of their booth and Lindsey wondered how much of their conversation she'd heard. "Just tossing around ideas. I got a good lay of the land tour today and we're scheduled for interviews tomorrow. What did Larry want?"

"Nothing much. We went over a few details. So, you think we can wrap this up by the day of the event?"

Lindsey searched Elaina's face for a clue. The wrap it up comment indicated a budget concern, but she detected something more than money at play. She didn't want to rat Alice out, but she did want to know what Elaina and Larry had been arguing about, so she cast about for a way to ask. "Is Larry micromanaging as usual?"

"What? No, I mean, he's on us to get the story put to bed so it can air in the next couple of weeks, that's all."

"What's the hurry?"

"I don't know. Hey, are we doing our job or theirs? How about we focus on what you've got planned for the next few days and let the network worry about programming?"

"Sure." Lindsey offered the simple assurance, but she had no intention of letting her curiosity go unsated. Everything about this story, from the vanilla content, to the network's insistence that she be the anchor, signaled something was off, and she intended to get to the bottom of things.

CHAPTER EIGHT

The next morning, Dale pushed through the doors of Judge Niven's courtroom and slipped into a seat in the back row. Thankfully, she didn't see any other agents she knew. Bianca was at the front of the room, making a spirited argument for keeping the orange-jumpsuit wearing defendant seated at the other table in custody pending trial. Dale zoned out after a few minutes—this wasn't her case and she really didn't care what happened. She just wanted it to happen quickly since she didn't have much time before she was supposed to meet Lindsey and her crew for round two of busywork.

After the meeting at Peyton's last night, she'd done a little research on Lindsey, courtesy of LexisNexis. Lindsey owned a small apartment in Manhattan where her network was based, but it was currently sublet to someone else. She was single and had a substantial net worth, but without running a full credit report, Dale didn't have a clue where she kept her assets. She'd won several Emmys for her work, including one for her reporting while embedded with the US forces in Afghanistan. She'd spent more time as an embedded reporter than any other US journalist, her most recent stint with the Afghan Security Forces, reporting on the drawdown of US and NATO forces.

Dale had run into several reporters while she served, but they were there for the short term, not embedded like Lindsey, and their stories were nothing more than a glossy finish over the dirty truth of the war that claimed more lives than it saved. Like most living, breathing souls, she'd heard about Lindsey's expose on General Tyson, but she'd never watched any of Lindsey's war coverage, preferring not to relive any aspects of the experience she'd left behind. The only good thing that had come out of her three tours was meeting Maria, and she had many more pleasant memories of Maria right here at home.

When the bailiff called out "All rise," she was on her feet, unsure how much time had passed while she was lost in thought. When the judge ducked out the side door to his chambers, Bianca turned and motioned for her to wait. She watched while Bianca handed some papers to the defense attorney she'd just argued against, and then vigorously shook her head when he asked her to cut his client some slack. Bianca Cruz was a baby prosecutor, but she was catching on fast. Show strength, exude confidence, and grant mercy only sparingly were the keynotes to gaining respect.

When Bianca finally broke free, Dale joined her at the counsel table. "I have less than an hour before I have to meet the film crew. What do you have for me?"

Bianca dug around in her bag and pulled out a plain manila envelope about two inches thick. "I printed this out at home. It's a start—a list of the suspicious transactions Gantry made over the past year. The FBI financial guys put it together from the information they got from their C.I. I haven't had time to look for patterns. I also included a list of all known border crossings for anyone associated with the Vargases."

Dale took the folder and tucked it in her jacket. "I'll get through this today and call you tonight." Hopefully, she could carve out some time today to comb through the records. "Have you talked to Mary this morning?"

Bianca nodded. "Her boss has her back on the cases she had before she started working with us, a few of which are on my docket, which will give us cover if anyone catches us working together."

"Good. Any idea what Gellar's next move will be?"

"He's not sharing any info, but he does have the grand jury scheduled to meet later this week. I don't know if they have enough to hand down an indictment for Gantry, but they definitely have enough to indict Arturo."

Arturo Vargas had been moved from the hospital to a cell at Seagoville, and they'd been closely monitoring his phone calls and visitors for signs he was communicating with his fugitive brother, but so far it seemed he was keeping a low profile. "You think he'll go ahead and indict Arturo?"

"He might. Word is he thinks he can put pressure on Arturo to flip on Gantry."

Dale noted Bianca's skeptical expression. "You don't agree?"

"I don't think Arturo has anything to gain. By the time they finish stacking up the charges, he's looking at a life sentence. Even if Gellar filed a motion for a downward departure based on his cooperation, a judge isn't going to shave off enough to matter. Not for the head of a cartel. And that's the other thing—the little guys snitch, not the big ones. If Arturo talks, he's not necessarily going to implicate his brother, and I don't see that happening. Ever."

"Good points," Dale said. Bianca rose a few points on her respect meter. "You have any ideas about flushing out Sergio?"

Bianca looked around before whispering, "I do, but I don't want to talk about it here."

"At the ranch then?" Dale asked. They had another "poker game" scheduled for the next night.

Bianca shook her head. She scrawled a note on a piece of paper and folded it in half. As she handed it to Dale, her eyes appeared to lock on to something over Dale's shoulder, and she said, a touch too loudly, "Thanks, Agent. I appreciate you letting me know. Have a good day."

Before Dale could process what had happened, she saw Herschel Gellar enter the well of the courtroom. She slid the paper into her pocket. "No problem. The event is next Saturday and obviously, we'd like to have some folks from your office on hand to help out with the educational component. Thanks for spreading the word." She nodded to Gellar as she left the courtroom, and prayed Bianca was quick enough to handle his curiosity.

Moments later, she retrieved her truck from the parking garage down the street and drove to Lindsey's hotel on the other side of downtown. As she pulled into the parking lot, she reflected that whoever had put them up at this hotel didn't know their way around the city. The Anatole wasn't far from downtown, but there were other hotels that were more convenient to all the places they'd need to be over the next week. At least the spacious lot meant it was easy to find a space to park. She killed the engine and fished the note from Bianca out of her pocket. *7 p.m. J.R.'s. Just you.*

Dale drummed the seat cushion with her fingers. She'd expected a little more in the way of detail, but it looked like she'd have to wait until that evening to find out what Bianca had in mind. She tucked the note away and pulled another piece of paper from her glove box—the schedule she'd received from someone named Elaina on Lindsey's team. Today she was supposed to accompany the whole crew to interview a few local law enforcement officials. She'd already whined to Diego about it, but he hadn't budged. When she'd pointed out she was being wasted in the role of chauffeur, he'd insisted her presence was essential to ensure the program had a consistent message across all agencies. Her presence wouldn't guarantee that, but she didn't have a choice in the matter and she might as well accept it.

A sharp knock startled her out of her pondering. Her hand flew to her shoulder holster as she jerked her head to the window. Lindsey stood next to her truck, looking like a model in an expensive looking navy suit and perfect hair and makeup. Dale motioned for her to back up, and she opened the door and stepped out.

"Sorry if I scared you," Lindsey said, a teasing grin playing at the corners of her mouth. "I just happened to walk outside for a breath of fresh air when I saw you drive up."

"You didn't scare me," Dale lied. "I was just looking over the schedule. Pretty ambitious for a day's work."

"It's the story of my life. Too much to do and not enough time to get it all done. I've become the consummate overachiever."

"And you have the awards to prove it."

Lindsey smiled and cocked her head. "Aw, you noticed."

Heat rose up the back of Dale's neck, slow and tingly, and she brushed at her collar.

"Are you okay?" Lindsey asked.

Dale felt the flush through her entire head now, but the last thing she wanted to do was talk about it. "Uh, yeah, sure." She cast about for a change in subject, but before she could settle on something Lindsey asked, "Are you hungry?"

"Hungry?"

"Food, you know, sustenance. I'm starving. The others won't be ready for a little while. Do you mind if we grab something?"

Dale looked at the schedule in her hand. They did have a decent window before they were supposed to be at the first location. Besides, it was Lindsey's shoot. If they were late, what did she care? "Sure, why not?"

She jammed her keys in her pocket and followed Lindsey to a bistro inside the hotel. The hostess sat them at a booth in the back. Dale buried her face in the menu while she tried to process her body's strange reaction to Lindsey's flirty banter in the parking lot. "Twenty dollars for a salad! That's crazy."

"You don't strike me as a salad person."

"Good thing."

Lindsey swatted her with the menu. She'd caught a glimpse of this playful version of Dale yesterday and it was good to see it again. "Lunch is on me. Have whatever you want."

"I can buy my own lunch."

And just like that, crotchety Dale was back again. Lindsey set her menu on the table and leaned forward. "Look, I feel like we got off on the wrong foot and not just because you ate most of the bacon off my breakfast tray." She smiled and counted the beats until Dale returned the gesture. "So, I had you come a little early today because I wanted to see if we could start fresh. I figured we could share a meal, get to know each other. So have a steak, have a salad, whatever suits you. Next time you can pick the place and pay my way. Deal?"

She watched and waited for Dale's response, finally breathing a sigh of relief when she said, "Deal."

Dale ordered a burger and fries and Lindsey told the waitress to double the order.

"Now see, I would've pegged you for a salad girl," Dale said.

"Shows how much you know," Lindsey replied. "Five miles every morning means I can eat what I want, and I almost never want a salad."

"I approve."

"Are you used to women who only eat salads?" Lindsey winced internally at the unartful question. She hadn't asked Dale to lunch to dive into details about her deceased wife, but their playful banter seemed like a good time to broach more personal areas. However, now that she'd started down this road, she felt like a heel for acting like she knew less about Dale's personal life than she did.

"I'm not used to anything in particular."

Nice sidestep. Dale was going to be more difficult to crack than the average subject. "I have a tendency to accidentally date the salad-loving women. Doesn't bode well for the long-term." There, she'd tossed out the bait. Would Dale bite?

"I was married for seven years. We both worked our asses off, and when it was time to eat, we ate whatever we were hungry for at the time."

Lindsey listened carefully for any undercurrent in Dale's tone that signaled this avenue of conversation had hit a dead end. No, Dale sounded matter-of-fact, but she didn't detect any traces of anger or annoyance. "You *were* married."

"My wife, Maria, is dead. It's been a year."

Her voice was quiet and lifeless, and Lindsey wasn't sure where to go from here. She had a thousand questions, but they were all based on knowledge she'd now pretended she didn't already have. Where were you when your wife was shot down? What was the last thing you said to her and she to you? Have you been trying to find out who killed her? What progress have you made?

She couldn't ask any of these things. Not here, not now. In this moment, when Dale had displayed such vulnerability, the right thing to do was to be a person, not a reporter. The challenge was toeing the line between the two. She'd spent so much time digging for stories, she wasn't entirely sure she could compartmentalize her truth-seeking queries from well-intended curiosity. For now, she settled on a simple, "I'm sorry."

"You didn't do anything. It's just…"

Lindsey reached over and grasped Dale's hand. "You don't have to talk about it if you don't want to, but I'm here if you do."

Dale met her eyes, and Lindsey struggled to read the emotions reflected there, but before she could get a fix on them, Dale smiled and said, "Thanks, but I'd prefer if we talk about a lighter subject. Something along the lines of the great salad versus burger debate, if you don't mind."

"Fine by me."

Their food came quickly and they dove in. The rest of their conversation was light-hearted. Lindsey asked questions about Dallas in general. She'd flown through Dallas tons of times, but had never really spent any time in the city. Dale was describing her favorite burger joints when Lindsey got a text from Elaina that the crew was ready to go. She settled the check and they walked out of the restaurant.

Dale pulled the list of afternoon appointments out of her pocket and pointed at the attached map. "I see you already mapped out the locations for today."

"We're nothing if not efficient. Speaking of efficiency, Elaina managed to borrow a van from one of the local affiliates so we can all ride together."

"Oh, okay." Dale didn't know why, but the change in plans threw her a bit. She'd planned on driving. Maybe she'd expected more autonomy than being trapped in the van with the entire film crew would allow. She braced for meeting everyone else. "Where are they?"

Lindsey pointed at one of the circular drives on the side of the hotel. "Over there."

Dale stiffened as Lindsey grabbed her arm and started walking in the direction she'd indicated, but Lindsey didn't seem to notice. Forcing her stride into motion, Dale glanced down at Lindsey's hand, curled around her bicep. Smooth skin, manicured nails, no ring. Her Internet research hadn't revealed anything about a spouse or partner. Lindsey Ryan took care of herself, but not for someone waiting at home. More likely, she self-pampered for the camera and her career. What must it be like to have a job where someone younger and more beautiful was poised to take over the minute your ratings slipped?

She didn't have much time to contemplate the answer before they were next to a van from the local station Channel 8 news. The side door slid open, and she looked inside, recognizing the driver as the guy who'd accompanied Lindsey to the office earlier in the week. The other two passengers were women who could not have looked more different. One was dressed in jeans, a T-shirt, and Doc Martens. She was cute in a here's-my-younger-sister kind of way and she looked all of fifteen. The other woman looked like Lindsey did today, polished, professional, and dressed to the nines, but she didn't look like she would ever be comfortable in the outfit Lindsey had thrown on yesterday morning. She was classically beautiful, but in that too good to be true and completely untouchable kind of way. This chick probably slept in ironed sheets wearing expensive lingerie, and she definitely loved salads. Not at all her type.

The thought hit her like a stun gun—unexpected, hard, and painful. She couldn't remember the last time she'd thought about another woman being her type, but she knew it had to be before she'd met Maria. Peyton's words from earlier in the week echoed in her head and dug their claws into her heart. She hadn't thought about dating since she'd lost Maria, and a simple observation about whether another woman was attractive or not didn't mean her perspective had changed. Especially since she'd concluded she wasn't attracted to her at all.

"Climb in and I'll introduce you to everyone."

Dale turned at the sound of Lindsey's voice. She might not be attracted to the polished beauty in the van, but Lindsey...Lindsey was a different story. Today she was polished for the camera, but the image of Lindsey in her rumpled sweatshirt, hair pulled back in a jumbled mess, and no makeup yet looking absolutely stunning flashed in her mind. Her probing questions, her teasing tone, the way her eyes reflected kindness even when she was asking hard questions—all of these things rattled against the barriers she'd erected, and the realization caught her completely off guard.

The air around her grew thin, and she was crawling out of her skin. One thing was certain, no fucking way was she getting into a van with Lindsey Ryan. She muttered something about needing to drive her own vehicle and stalked back to her truck.

Lindsey watched, baffled, as Dale walked briskly away from the van. Just when she'd started to breach the barriers Dale had erected, she morphed from mildly reluctant tour guide to I can't be bothered to be near you. Dale had turned pale and distant just before she bolted, and Lindsey wanted desperately to know what had caused the change.

"What the hell was that about?"

Lindsey turned to Elaina. She was so absorbed in curiosity about Dale she'd almost forgotten about Elaina and the others. "New development. She's meeting us there." She shrugged and kept her face fixed in a nonchalant expression. "Work thing." She climbed into the van. "Let's go."

Elaina huffed, but told Jed to take them downtown. Lindsey consciously avoided the questioning looks from Jed and Alice. They'd seen the entire exchange and were probably wondering what in the hell had gotten into Dale. She wondered too and had no idea why she'd told the little white lie to cover for Dale's sudden attack of odd. In the moment, she'd sensed Dale was vulnerable and hadn't even tried to combat the powerful urge to protect her.

She'd have to get over that if she was going to do her job. And despite the network's assignment to keep this piece sweet and tidy, she was determined to find a meatier story, one worthy of her loyal viewers and her own integrity.

Dale was already in the lobby when they reached Dallas Police headquarters. Elaina ignored her and walked over to the officer on duty, but Lindsey hung back. When it became clear Dale wasn't going to approach, she told Alice and Jed she'd be right back and walked to where Dale was standing.

"You have an aversion to news vans?" she asked.

Dale's gaze remained fixed on some imaginary spot on the wall. "Not a big fan."

"I'm sensing you aren't a big fan of me either. I thought we were beginning to get along. Have I done something to make you mad?" Lindsey hated herself for asking the question, but as much as it might be construed as a sign of weakness, she really wanted to know the answer. She waited patiently while Dale's face cycled through a series of hard to interpret expressions before finally landing on a forced smile.

"It's not you."

"And you'd tell me if it was?"

"Did your job make you cynical or were you just born that way?"

Lindsey started to fire back a retort, but stopped to ponder Dale's response. It was a good question, and she wasn't sure of the answer. She'd been raised by a family full of conservatives, who blindly followed the loudest voice of their movement and discouraged any curiosity that questioned their beliefs. Maybe her intense desire to know all the facts, to find the truth, was a visceral reaction to the pressure not to. But she had no desire to bare her soul to anyone, let alone the subject of her next reveal. Luckily, Elaina chose that exact moment to interrupt.

"If you girls are done chatting, they're ready for us."

Lindsey saw Dale wince at the word "girls," and then raise her eyebrows when Elaina clutched her arm. She kept her eyes on Dale as she shrugged out of Elaina's grasp and said, in a dripping sweet tone, "We *girls* have been waiting on you, haven't we, Dale?"

The smile at the edge of Dale's lips was small and fleeting, but Lindsey saw it and was supremely satisfied she'd been able to make it appear. During the next couple of boring hours of setting up and interviewing the police chief about his organization's role in the drug Take-Back program, she reflected on that smile and vowed to go for an even bigger one next time.

CHAPTER NINE

Dale led Lindsey and the rest of the film crew into a conference room where Chief Turner and a few other local police officers were waiting. She'd worked with several DPD officers on cases in the past, handing them evidence on some of the minor cases the DEA had passed on because they weren't quite splashy enough to warrant federal dollars. Turner acknowledged her and introduced her to the others at the table. When he reached the one woman in the bunch, Dale beat him to the introduction. "Detective DeJesus, nice to see you again."

Andrea DeJesus half stood and shook her hand with a firm grasp. "Didn't know if you'd remember me."

"I always remember people who do my job for me." Andrea had brought the DEA in on a huge crystal meth bust the year before, and Dale remembered being impressed with the level of detail in the initial investigation. She'd even mentioned to Diego at the time that he should snatch Andrea up for their agency. Dale turned to the chief. "If all your vice detectives are as good as this one, you'll be putting us out of business." She started to say something else, but was interrupted by the distinct sound of a clearing throat behind her. She turned just as Lindsey leaned forward and whispered in her ear.

"Careful, you're making her blush."

Dale looked back and caught sight of a smile on Lindsey's face, but her eyes flashed a different emotion entirely. Annoyance?

Jealousy? Surely not. She decided she was reading too much into a fleeting facial expression and filed it away to examine later. Or not. For now, she'd focus on business. "Ms. Ryan, do you want to go over your questions for Chief Turner while your team sets up?"

Lindsey stepped back, out of her space. "Great idea, Agent Nelson. Chief, I'd rather ask you questions once we're on camera so we don't look rehearsed, but why don't you give me a little background about how your department got involved in this program?"

Dale walked to the other side of the room and did her best to tune them out. Her role for the next however long was babysitter, which was fine by her. She pulled out her phone and scrolled through her emails and texts. Peyton had sent a text confirming another poker game for the next night, and Bianca had sent a text to make sure she'd make the off the books meeting she'd scheduled for that evening. She texted them both back and started sifting through her growing email inbox. She was in the middle of reading through a report of the forensics from the raid on the barn when Lindsey's voice cut through her concentration.

"What assurances can you provide that the drugs you collect won't wind up in the hands of criminals? Isn't it true you've had trouble over the past year dealing with fallout after several of your senior detectives were caught selling contraband they'd collected from crime scenes?"

Holy shit. Dale pushed off the wall and started walking toward the conference room table where Chief Turner and his team sat like rotisserie chickens at the grocery story under the bright lights of Lindsey's interrogation. She tapped Elaina on the shoulder and whispered, "What the hell is she doing?"

Elaina raised one shoulder and put her finger on her lips. The dismissive gesture pissed Dale off and she strode over to stand directly behind the kid with the camera. She was out of Lindsey's view, but Chief Turner made eye contact and didn't bother to hide his annoyance at Lindsey's probing questions. No surprise there. This supposed puff piece had soured with the very first on-camera interview. Despite his obvious annoyance, Turner handled the question like a pro, telling Lindsey and her viewers the scandal that had rocked his department had been a wake-up call about the need for better protocols in handling the collection and storage of contraband evidence.

"Every mistake is an opportunity for us to become a better, more efficient force for justice in the community," Turner said. "While we would love to report we have no problems, I'm happy to report the issues we've had in the past make us stronger for the future."

Dale nodded. Well said. Thankfully, Lindsey didn't press the point and moved on to the specifics of the police department's involvement in the Take-Back day activities. A couple of the officers, including DeJesus, already participated in the department's DARE program in the local schools and would be offering several sessions at city hall on the official day. DeJesus explained what the sessions would entail, and Dale enjoyed watching the excitement on her face as she talked about working with kids.

Maria had enjoyed visiting schools and talking about the importance of law enforcement as a way to keep communities safe. She had been a perennial favorite at the local high schools and appeared every year on career day to tout the challenges and benefits of working with the US attorney's office. Her love for the job was at the top of the list of things Dale loved about her.

The rest of the interview was uneventful, and Lindsey ended the session on a high note by getting each of the officers to relate the event to something personal in their lives. Dale watched carefully for any signs that Lindsey might try to twist their words, but at this point in the process she seemed bored with the interview—a stark contrast to the way her eyes blazed with excitement when she was grilling the chief. *Need to be careful with that one—she feeds on drama.*

Dale followed the film crew out of the building, waiting until they were in the parking lot to say her piece, but instead of directing her comments to Lindsey, she spoke directly to the producer. "I was under the impression these interviews were about the DEA's program, not a witch hunt on the local police force."

"Sometimes our reporters ask questions to round out the story," Elaina said. "Don't worry. Everything will go through edits before it airs."

Elaina flicked a glance at Lindsey, and Lindsey frowned in response. Dale watched their unspoken exchange, certain she detected a push and pull between them that was at odds with the easy way Elaina had cuddled up to Lindsey when they'd arrived at police headquarters. Something was going on between these two, but she didn't have the time or patience to sort it out. She needed to make sure Lindsey's bulldog tendencies didn't stray over to the side investigation she had going with Peyton and the rest of the covert task force. No more lunches and no more sharing personal details about her own life. Strictly business with this one.

❖

Hours later, Dale walked into J.R.'s and spotted Bianca sitting in a corner booth. When she slid into her seat, she caught Bianca making a show of looking at her watch. "I know I'm late. Couldn't be helped."

"Don't tell me, poor you, having to spend the day with Lindsey Ryan. Do you know how many women, and men for that matter, would trade places with you in a heartbeat?" She rubbed her thumb and forefinger together like a tiny violin. "Listen hard for my nonexistent sympathy."

Dale bit back the harsh response that rose to her lips. Bianca was only teasing and she didn't mean anything by it. The worst thing she could do was let her or anyone else know how much Lindsey had gotten under her skin. "She's okay, I guess."

"You guess?" Bianca bent closer. "Seriously, is she as totally badass in person as she is on TV?"

Badass. Not the word she would have used to describe Lindsey. Smart, engaging, well-spoken, but badass? She hadn't seen enough of her on TV to know if Bianca's characterization was accurate, but the questions she'd asked Chief Turner seemed designed to foster a tiger-like reputation. Even the producer had seemed a bit thrown when Lindsey strayed from the script. And speaking of that producer, what was her deal? Dale hadn't missed the possessive way she led Lindsey around. Something about the way she touched her, the glances she gave, signaled more than a work relationship.

Shit. Why did she care? Just a few more days and she should be able to escape the whole crew for good. She shook out of her musings to find Bianca staring at her with a playful grin. "What?"

"Nothing."

It wasn't nothing, but she wasn't in the mood to hear what Bianca had to say unless it was about work. "Okay, you called this little powwow. What's up?"

"I have an idea, but Peyton's not going to like it, so you're going to have to talk her into it or we have to go behind her back."

Grateful for the change in subject, Dale said, "Spill."

"I think it's time we stopped trying to hunt down Sergio Vargas and get him to come to us."

"And how do you propose we do that?"

"We have the perfect bait. His sister. Sophia."

"Lily's mother?" When Bianca nodded, Dale smacked her hand down on the table. When several of the other patrons looked their way, she waved them off and whispered to Bianca. "Don't let me ever hear you refer to her as bait again. Do you understand me?"

Bianca nodded, looking appropriately contrite. "Sorry. Bad choice of words, but the theory's sound. I've been thinking about this a lot. We get her to go see Arturo in jail and imply that she can help him. I haven't thought it all through, but she could tell him something to get his curiosity piqued. I have no doubt Arturo can get word to Sergio, and we'll just follow the trail from there."

"Except what happens when they figure out Sophia did this for us? What happens when they hack her into a bunch of tiny pieces and leave them for her daughter to find? What do you think Peyton will say then? Aren't you forgetting that we already have one witness under protection because we tried to use her for bait and it backfired?"

"It didn't backfire entirely—we have Arturo Vargas in custody, and it wouldn't have happened without Carmen's help." Bianca referred to one of the defendants they'd managed to flip in exchange for leniency on her case. "I respect Peyton as much as you do, but she's not in a position to make the hard calls on this. We may have to do it for her."

Bianca had a point. Whichever way she turned, Peyton was conflicted. Her brother, her lover, her lover's mother—all of them stood between her and the tough choices that had to be made to break this case. She trusted Peyton with her life, but Peyton's loyalty meant they all paid a price, and that price was the inability to do what needed to be done, to hell with the cost. She knew what it was like to have something personal at stake, but her case was different. Her desire to find and punish the assholes behind Maria's killing wasn't a roadblock. It was a catalyst. She didn't like going behind Peyton's back, but the idea of catching Sergio Vargas was a strong incentive to do just that.

"Okay, but we need to come up with a solid plan since, in your own words, you haven't quite thought this through." Dale rubbed her forehead as she considered how to proceed. "Get me transcripts of all the phone calls Arturo has made so far, and let's tailor something believable for Sophia to offer. Whatever we do has to be ironclad because we're only going to get one shot at this. If it goes wrong, Sergio will go deep underground and we may never see him again."

"I'll have something to you by morning. Where should we meet?"

Dale drummed her fingers on the table. She'd committed to meet Lindsey and her team the next morning at Lindsey's hotel to go over logistics for some additional interviews they planned to do later in the week. She'd rather chew nails than spend the valuable time she should be spending tracking down Vargas sitting around babysitting this fake news reporting. She couldn't risk meeting with Bianca at the courthouse again, and if Bianca showed up at her office, Diego would be suspicious.

"You have other plans in the morning?" Bianca asked.

"Actually, I do, but I guess we could meet later." But she didn't want to meet later. If they were going to make this work, they needed to jump on it and fast. She cast about for a convenient solution, and bam, one appeared. "Wait a minute, I've got the perfect place in mind."

❖

Lindsey carried two drinks over to the table in the bar where Elaina was waiting. She didn't have time to set the glasses on the table before Elaina started in. "What was the deal with you grilling the chief today?"

"Maybe I'm dying of boredom." She slid into the booth and took a deep swallow of the expensive scotch she'd ordered on the network's dime. She might be spending her days drowning in mediocrity, but that didn't mean she couldn't enjoy the complexity of a good whisky.

"You know you're being punished, right?" Elaina said in a know-it-all tone. "Even if Larry didn't tell you as much, lots of people paid a price for the stunt you pulled with General Tyson."

"Nobody pays a price when the truth is told except the ones who tried to hide it in the first place."

"Are you really that naive? You had full access to Tyson and his team, and instead of doing the so-called substantive story you claim to be famous for, you chose to publicly embarrass him. Your little stunt shut down access for dozens of other reporters who are just trying to do their jobs."

"Give me a break. First of all, the network you've sworn allegiance to couldn't air that footage fast enough. Their ratings skyrocketed. It wasn't until the conservative backlash started that anyone, including Larry, had any second thoughts about the piece. Tyson is a douche and I'm not a bit sorry he showed his true colors. The only thing I'm sorry about is being stuck on this job, but once I pay this penance, I'll be back out in the field reporting on real news instead of glorified PR stunts."

"That's what you think this story is?"

"Don't you? You really think any good comes from these once in a while displays of community involvement? I'd bet every penny I have in the bank that not one of the DEA or local cops believe this

Take-Back day has ever accomplished anything in the real war on drugs, as if there really is such a thing. You think people are going to show up carrying bricks of cocaine or baggies of heroin? The drugs that are killing people will never stop as long as there's money to be made. Did you know the Medellin Cartel made so much money in Colombia they couldn't even launder it all? They had to start burying it in fields. A farmer found some by accident when he was plowing. Did he take it to the police? No, he knew it had to be Cartel money and he went straight to them out of fear for his life."

"We're not in Colombia, Lindsey."

Elaina's condescending tone set her on edge. "Not yet. Mark my words, the Texas Mexican Mafia, the Zetas—they're all here and working hard to make sure that changes. As long as the DEA is focused on all show and no substance projects like this one, the bad guys have a fighting chance." She raised her glass and took another deep swallow, bracing for Elaina's next parry.

"I always liked your passion."

Lindsey laughed at Elaina's response to her diatribe. "Until it got in the way of your career."

"Not fair. There's no room in your life for anything but your work. If I'd asked you not to go back to Afghanistan, would you have stayed?"

Lindsey started to point out that Elaina hadn't asked. Elaina had only been annoyed that she was once again disrupting their normal lives in the city where bouts of work were sandwiched between dinners and parties designed to have them rubbing elbows with the in-crowd. To Elaina these events were networking, but to her they were a chore she could hardly wait to have done. Just like this conversation. "Let's talk about this another time. I'm exhausted." She swirled the last bit of scotch in her glass and downed it to signal the end of the conversation. When she stood up, Elaina stepped out of the booth.

"I'm tired too. Let's go."

They didn't speak in the elevator. Lindsey was certain Elaina was waiting for her to own up to her part in the demise of their relationship, but she wasn't interested in rehashing it. They'd wanted different things, and to her, the things Elaina had wanted were too shallow to merit a second look. Maybe she'd judged too harshly. Maybe she was judging too harshly now, about Elaina, about this assignment.

When the elevator dinged, they both walked out. Elaina's door was just down the hall from hers and they reached it first. She was several feet away before she heard Elaina cursing as she rummaged through her purse.

"Damn."

"What's up?"

"I can't find my key. I bet I left it in the room." Elaina glanced back at the elevator. "It's such a trek back to the front desk. I don't suppose you'd mind if I called them from your room?"

Lindsey searched Elaina's face for any signs she was trying to ignite some past flame, but she saw nothing to cause alarm. She could suggest Elaina call the front desk from her cell, but it seemed rude to make her wait in the hall. "Sure. Come on." She led the way a few doors down to her room and invited Elaina in. "Help yourself to the phone. I'll be right back."

She walked into the spacious bathroom and shut the door behind her. The bathtub was huge and featured spa jets and a basket full of essential oils. A hot bath was exactly what she needed after a stressful day. Funny how she considered the day stressful in light of the kind of days she'd been used to on her last assignment where long, hot baths were an unheard of luxury. Did burger-loving Dale take bubble baths?

The thought came out of nowhere, but she reveled in the idea of Dale Nelson, stretched out in the tub, patches of muscled flesh showing through billowing foam. Damn. Maybe she'd downed that scotch too quickly. As soon as Elaina left, she'd run herself a bath and indulge in a little harmless fantasy. She set out a towel and robe and then brushed her teeth and hair. Finally, she decided she'd allowed Elaina enough time to take care of her business.

When she walked out, she was surprised to find Elaina sitting at her desk. For a second, she was suspicious, and her gaze swept the area to see if anything was out of place before she decided she was making too much of it. Too long on the job made her question everything. She pointed at the phone. "Everything okay?"

"Yes. I'm supposed to meet them at my door, but I was waiting for you to come out so I could say good night." Elaina stood up and stepped close. "So, I guess this is good night."

Her voice was a whisper, and the question in her eyes signaled she was open to staying. She was a beautiful woman, no doubt, but if that were enough, they would still be a couple. Lindsey squeezed her hand, but then stepped back to put some distance between them. As she moved away, Elaina's expression changed, but Lindsey couldn't quite tell if it was sadness or relief. Didn't matter either way. They wanted different things, and right now all she wanted was to be alone with her fantasies.

CHAPTER TEN

The next morning, Dale strode into the lobby of the Anatole and was surprised to find Bianca already there.

"Tell me there's somewhere nearby where I can get something to eat," Bianca said as she approached.

"Sure. There's one of those coffee bar things." Dale pointed to an area around the corner from the lobby. "Over there."

"Thank goodness. I could eat a dozen bagels right now."

Dale walked her to the coffee bar and watched with amusement as Bianca ordered the largest cup of coffee they had and a giant bear claw. Once they sat down, she said, "Wow, you really are hungry. I didn't mean to get in the middle of your breakfast time with this meeting. Besides, you're early."

Bianca took a huge bite of the pastry and washed it down with her complicated coffee concoction before responding. "I've been here for thirty minutes, but I didn't want to leave the lobby in case I missed seeing you. This place is huge. I dropped my daughter off at school an hour ago. She kills me with her early morning track practice. Why did I have to spawn a sporting child instead of a bookworm like me?"

Dale did a double take. "You have a daughter? How old is she?"

Bianca smiled indulgently. "Yes, I have a daughter. She's eleven. Just started the seventh grade—skipped a grade because she's smart in addition to being athletic. And I don't keep stuff like this," she held up the remains of the pastry, "at home since it would be setting a bad example about a nutritious breakfast. Go ahead, tell me I'm too young-looking to be a mother of an almost teenager."

"Well, you are." Dale felt the slow creep of a blush as she paid the compliment, but her discomfort came from embarrassment, not attraction. "It's just you're always available whenever we need you, night or day, and…" She stopped when she realized she sounded stupid for assuming that just because Bianca had a child, she wouldn't be able to handle anything the job threw her way.

"I know. And before you ask, I'm a single parent. I'm just lucky to have a mother who lives down the street and has nothing better to do than indulge her granddaughter's hectic schedule. And Emma loves her *abuela*, so it's good they get to spend so much time together, but if you try to schedule something during a track meet, watch out."

Dale held both hands in the air. "I'm sufficiently scared. Sorry. I was just surprised, is all."

"I better not catch you treating me differently. I spend a lot of time with my daughter, but I want Emma to grow up understanding how important a good career is, especially this one. If I have to be somewhere during family time, she'll know I'm working to make a better life for all of us."

"You won't get any flack from me. Hell, I'm impressed. I'm not sure I could handle a kid on my own."

"You could. It's amazing what you can do for family. Did you and Maria ever talk about having children?"

The question brought Dale up short. Not because of the subject, but because hardly anyone ever talked to her about her relationship with Maria anymore—like the subject was encased in glass, too fragile for close inspection. Yet, Peyton had brought her up the other day, and here Bianca was bringing her up again.

Maria had talked about making a family once they were more settled in their careers, but settling in for both of them was more like diving in, and at the time of Maria's death, they had been completely immersed. Someday, they'd have a family. But someday had never come, and Dale didn't plan to dream those dreams again.

"Sorry. That was none of my business."

"It's okay. We did talk about it, but never did anything about it. I like kids."

"I love Emma, but I'm not sure I would've chosen to have a child. It was more a bad prom night decision than a life plan. I've grown up a lot since then, and I have Emma to thank for my ability to be self-sufficient."

"So, no stepdad material in the dating pool?"

"Like I have time to date. Besides, if I was looking, which I'm not, it would be for a step*mom*."

Dale smiled. She'd pegged Bianca for family from the get-go, and it was nice to know her instincts were spot on. "Well, let me know when you're looking again and I'll keep an eye out."

"Right, because you meet all kinds of criminals in your daily life that I'm just dying to date. Speaking of criminals, want to hear my plan?"

Dale listened while Bianca outlined her ideas for what she'd nicknamed the Sergio Trap.

"I checked the transcripts of Arturo's jail calls," Bianca said. "He's not stupid, but he's not a rocket scientist either. They're using some of the same code they were using with Gantry. Talking about oil field equipment and drilling rights."

"Which really means drug distribution and money laundering."

"Exactly. I don't know about you, but I think they're worried about how they're going to launder funds now that Gantry's under a microscope."

Bianca handed her a few sheets of paper, and Dale skimmed the transcribed lines. If her off-the-cuff translation of Arturo's double-speak was spot-on, then she was right. Arturo was reaching out to various contacts to find a source to launder the money they were still making on the outside. While he was smart enough not to call Sergio directly, Dale was certain Arturo was using his lieutenants to communicate with his brother.

"So, what do we do with this?"

"We give him what he wants. Or rather Sophia does."

"You lost me. Say again?"

"Here's the cover. Sophia visits Arturo in jail. Tells him that she's having trouble making the ranch payments, plays the weak woman card. She can say Gantry has been supporting her through the years—which is partly true—and now that he's in trouble, the money has dried up. Who else is she to turn to except her family?"

Dale mentally replayed what she knew about Lily's mother and her tenuous relationship with her brothers, but she couldn't quite connect the dots. "How does Sophia's need for help get Sergio out of his jam about laundering money?"

"Sophia's ranch is the perfect place for them to funnel money. She specializes in breeding quarter horses so her business gets a bump and no one's the wiser, because that champion stud of hers just won the Futurity."

"Okay, but wait. Isn't that race like a million dollar purse? Arturo's going to wonder why she needs money after a win that big."

"Even big money goes fast, and with no more regular income from Gantry, she's in a bind making the mortgage. She just added a new barn and a bunch of new horses, which she wouldn't have done if she'd known her primary lending source was going to dry up." Bianca dusted her hands in the air like it was a done deal. "That's the story she'll give Arturo, anyway."

"You sure you just thought this up last night?"

"I don't sleep much."

"I guess not."

"So, what do you think?"

Dale drummed her fingers on the table while she sorted through Bianca's plan. "So you think Sergio is going to show up on Sophia's doorstep and do this handshake deal with her? And then what? Sophia starts laundering piles of cash? What if someone working the investigation into Arturo gets wind that Sergio is working with Sophia? If our plan is off the books, how's she going to stay out of trouble?"

"I've got that covered."

Bianca looked confident, but Dale was anything but. "I might need to know a little more than that."

"Tanner Cohen, the FBI agent who's working the case, can help us. She's good people. I think we need to bring her on board. She can be trusted and this would help her too. She wants to shut down the

Vargases' operation as much as anyone, and she's just been working it from a different angle. Trust me, she's not at all happy with the way Gellar is barreling toward indictments without making sure every angle is covered. He seems way more concerned about taking down Cyrus Gantry than prosecuting either of the Vargas brothers."

Bianca was right. Whenever Gellar had been present at a task force meeting, he'd practically frothed at the mouth when Gantry's name was mentioned. She hadn't given it a second thought before, having written it off to zealous prosecution, but if others had noticed and questioned his approach, she wondered if there was more to it. "And Tanner disagrees with his strategy?"

"I've heard rumblings to that effect."

"Okay, bring Tanner to the meeting at the ranch tonight and I'll take it from there."

"You think that's a better idea than letting Peyton know first?"

"Sometimes it's better to ask forgiveness than permission," Dale said. "Pretty sure this is one of those times." As she spoke she noticed Bianca staring at something over her shoulder, and she was certain Bianca hadn't heard a word she'd said. She waved a hand in front of her face. "Hey, your coffee wear off or did you fall into a sugar coma after eating that monster bear claw?"

Bianca shook her head and smiled, her eyes still trained on whatever was behind her. "Don't look now, but Lindsey Ryan is on her way over here, and she is way more gorgeous in person than on TV."

Like anyone who was told not to look, the desire to look filled Dale's every conscious cell. If she turned around right now, would she see casual Lindsey with the shorts and hoodie, maybe on her way back from the gym? Or on-camera Lindsey, dressed in a suit, sleek and dangerous? Either would be a welcome sight, and she had mixed feelings about that revelation. What she should be thinking about was not how Lindsey looked this morning, but about how she was going to explain Bianca's presence. Good thing she had already cooked up a story. She whispered to Bianca, "Hey, your mouth's hanging open. Don't worry. I'll introduce you, but if she asks about why you're here, let me handle it. Just go along with me, okay?"

Bianca nodded, her mouth now closed, but firmly fixed in a smile. Satisfied that Bianca would soon resolve her starstruck trance, Dale turned in her chair. No shorts, no hoodie, just another killer suit and a dazzling smile. For a second, Dale worried her own mouth might be hanging open. Lindsey Ryan, network ready, was stunning, and even she wasn't immune to the pull of her attraction.

❖

Lindsey watched Dale huddle with the woman across from her for a few minutes, trying to get a read on the situation. She checked her watch. She was a few minutes early, but curiosity got the better of her so she strolled over to find out who had captured Dale's attention. As she approached, the beautiful Latina looked up and met her eyes and then burst into a deep red blush. Odd. What in the hell were she and Dale talking about that caused such embarrassment at the prospect of being caught?

She was still a few feet away when Dale finally turned and met her eyes. Shaded mystery there, as always, but did she detect a hint of interest, welcoming her to come closer? She kept her smile in place and strode the final few steps to their table. "Good morning."

Dale stood and motioned for her to take her seat, and then walked over to one of the empty tables and snagged another chair. In the few seconds she was gone, Lindsey introduced herself to the other woman while she sized her up. "Lindsey Ryan. And you are?"

The woman opened and closed her mouth twice without saying anything before Dale returned and came to her rescue. "This is Bianca Cruz. She's an AUSA for the Northern District. I was enlisting her help with some of the programming for the Take-Back event." Dale laughed. "She might be a little starstruck."

"More than a little," Bianca said as she stuck out her hand. "Your coverage of the war was riveting, and your interview with General Tyson was brave and relevant and fierce."

Lindsey felt the heat of a blush flood through her. "Thanks. Not everyone agrees with that last thing."

"Well, I do. My daughter does too. She wrote a report about the troop drawdown for her social studies class, and she mentioned the interview as an example of how exposing the truth is the only way to effect change."

"Wow, and here I thought I was just pumping up the ratings." She glanced at Dale who had the good sense to appear slightly embarrassed. When she looked back at Bianca, she caught her looking between them like she was trying to figure out the inside joke. "Some folks think ratings are all I, or anyone else in my industry, care about."

"I can't speak for everyone, but I don't know many people who would risk their lives just to get a good story," Bianca said. "Tell me about Afghanistan. Was it really as dangerous as it seems?"

Lindsey could feel Dale's eyes on her, and she hesitated. Dale hadn't been in combat, not officially anyway, but she had been in the thick of things. She'd earned a Navy Cross, the highest commendation a Marine could earn, and she was one of only a few women ever to do so. The only thing Lindsey knew for sure was that whatever danger she'd encountered in the Middle East, it had visited Dale tenfold. "I felt safe the whole time I was there, but then again I was in good company. The folks in the units I was assigned to were a pretty tough lot, as I'm sure were most of the troops who'd been there for any length of time."

She kept her eyes focused on Dale as she spoke, wanting desperately to know what she thought about this whole conversation, but Dale gazed into the distance, looking as if her mind was anywhere but here. Lindsey had seen similar disconnects when she'd spoken with other soldiers. Most of them didn't like talking about the dangers of the war, if they spoke about it at all, and she imagined Dale was no exception. She'd been able to do her best reporting only while she was among them, capturing everything in real time. Being in the thick of the action was her best platform, and the realization gave her an idea. "Hey, what do you say we ditch the schedule today and you show me the seedier side of this area—you know, where the really bad stuff happens?"

"You have a death wish or something?" Dale asked.

"Legitimate question considering the circumstances, but no. I think it would give me some good context for the story to see the rough edges of the city, and then show people who don't think they can relate, how to contribute to the cause just by making sure the drugs in their medicine cabinets don't fall into the wrong hands."

She delivered the hastily concocted explanation and hoped it wasn't so transparent as to send Dale packing. What she really wanted was to see Dale in her element, hunting for bad guys, letting her actions speak for her.

"What's your producer going to say about that?" Dale made a show of looking around like Elaina would pop up out of thin air.

"Got a note from her this morning. She's off working on something else until this afternoon. It's just me and the rest of the team." When she'd received Elaina's message, Lindsey had been annoyed that Elaina had ditched her for the day, but now she was glad for the chance to interact with Dale without some prewritten agenda driving their every move. "So, are you up for it?"

Dale exchanged an unreadable look with Bianca. *Please say yes, please say yes.*

"Sure," Dale said. "Why not?" She stood up. "Go get your pals and let's head out. I'll meet you out front. I'll be doing the driving today."

Lindsey watched Dale and Bianca walk away before she glanced at her notes about the Take-Back program agenda. Bianca Cruz wasn't listed anywhere on the program. Maybe she was a late addition. Or maybe she was here for some other reason and maybe that reason had nothing to do with work and everything to do with the handsome woman who had just promised to show her a little danger.

❖

"Can you pull over there? I'm jonesing for a Coke in the worst way."

Dale looked in the rearview mirror at Alice aka Coke-a-holic. "Not a great place for a roadstop."

"I'm not asking to bed down for the day. I just need to run in and buy a drink. Seriously, I'll be back in under five."

Tito's Stop and Shop on Sylvan Road was well known for providing a little bit of everything for everyone from the eight-liner machines and adult movies in the back of the store to more hardcore options, like hookers and crack dealers roaming the aisles. Letting Alice or anyone else from the crew wander around inside was a bad idea. Dale started to say so when she felt a hand on her shoulder and looked over to see Lindsey's pleading eyes.

"How about we all go? Strength in numbers, right?"

She should shake her head and speed off to find another place where they could satisfy their caffeine fix, but she couldn't say no to those eyes. "Fine, but no wandering off. And no cameras."

"Deal." Lindsey barely had the one word out of her mouth before she was out of the truck, stretching her arms over her head. Dale watched, transfixed, for a moment, but when Lindsey started toward the doors to Tito's, she shut off the engine and hopped out of the truck to join her with Alice and Jed following close behind.

Once they were inside, Alice and Jed took off toward the cold drink case that lined the back wall, and Lindsey made a beeline for the candy aisle. Dale cast a quick glance toward the back of the store and followed Lindsey. By the time she reached her, Lindsey had a Snickers in one hand and a Payday in the other. "Can't make up your mind?"

Lindsey flashed her TV perfect smile. "Don't plan to. Isn't that the beauty of being an adult? Not having to choose?"

"Hmmm. Sounds like the exact opposite of being an adult."

Lindsey grabbed a third candy bar from the shelf, a Hershey's Almond this time, and stepped close. "You're telling me you think it's better to pick just one of these than to have a taste of all three?"

Dale looked at the shelves, the floor, anywhere but Lindsey's eyes, convinced they were no longer talking about candy, but unsure how to navigate this minefield of a conversation.

Lindsey, however, was clearly not done, and she waggled the candy bars under her nose. "Which one would you pick, Agent?"

Dale put her hand up and grasped all three of the choices Lindsey held. As her hand gripped the candy, she met Lindsey's eyes. They were full of questions, and Dale knew they had nothing to do with candy and everything to do with the smoldering arousal she felt simmering between them. She couldn't engage. Or could she? The list of reasons why she shouldn't ticked through her mind—allegiance to the job, the fact she hadn't flirted with any woman besides Maria in over a decade, and her dedication to Maria's memory—but none of the reasons had the power to quell her body's reaction to the flirtatious banter from the smart, beautiful woman standing in front of her.

You may not be able to control your body's response, but you can control what you do about it. She looked down at her hand still wrapped around Lindsey's, both of them clutching the candy bars and each other, and without meeting Lindsey's eyes, let go. "Payday."

"What?" Lindsey's voice was a husky whisper, and when she looked up, her eyes had a faraway sheen.

"I pick the Payday. You're buying, right?"

Lindsey nodded. "Sure, sure. You want something to drink?"

Before she had a chance to respond, Dale heard a shout. She whipped around, looking for the source of the outburst. The rotund cashier was sitting on a stool behind the counter, mauling his way through a glazed donut the size of his head. Satisfied no one was trying to rob the till, Dale kept looking for the source of the commotion while she listened to a string of disembodied outbursts.

"Not going!"

"I wasn't asking. I was telling. Let's not ruin everyone else's day over this."

"Get away from me!"

A loud yelp and then "Holy hell, that hurt!"

"Put away that gun! I'm not going!"

The yells were coming from the back of the store, where Alice and Jed had gone. Where she'd stopped watching while she flirted or whatever with Lindsey. Damn. Dale craned her neck, but she didn't see any sign of Alice or Jed. She grabbed Lindsey around the waist and propelled her toward the front of the store. She needed to get her out of here and then assess the situation.

As they moved, Lindsey struggled against her, and she whispered in her ear. "You need to go. Trust me." She felt Lindsey relax against her, but at that moment, the cashier opened his mouth, bits of donut spewing into the air with each word.

"Somebody better pay for those candy bars!"

Dale ignored him and pushed Lindsey out the door. Satisfied Lindsey was safe for now, she drew her gun and stepped carefully back through the store. She stopped every few steps and glanced at the mirrors along the side wall, trying to spot the source of the commotion. She was two-thirds of the way down the aisle when she spied the characters at the center of the drama. A tall, broad-shouldered woman with hair that looked like she cut it herself had a large revolver pointed at a scrawny woman who had to be at least eighty years old. The older woman was screaming her head off, which wasn't helping the situation at all. Dale ducked into the next aisle to get a better position, and then she stood up straight, her gun pointed directly at the younger woman's chest. "Federal officer. Drop your weapon."

The woman met her eyes and her expression was full of fierce indignation. "The hell I will."

Lindsey held her breath as she watched the exchange a few feet from where Dale was standing. She'd gone outside as Dale directed and found Alice and Jed waiting on them at the truck. She'd been so busy flirting with Dale, she hadn't noticed them leave. Satisfied they were okay, she'd snuck back into the store. She told herself she was back inside because whatever was happening was newsworthy, but the real reason was fear for Dale's safety, although now that Dale was in a standoff with a crazy person, she wasn't sure what in the hell she could do about it.

"I'm giving you one last chance," Dale said. "Put your gun down."

"Or what? Are you going to arrest her?" The woman shook her free arm in the air and Lindsey spotted trails of blood trickling down her forearm. "She stabbed me with a can opener I'm pretty sure she doesn't plan to pay for. I suggest you let me take care of it."

Lindsey was at enough of an angle to see the perplexed expression on Dale's face. Dale maintained her position, but her tone shifted from full-on authoritative to reasonably curious. "Are you on the job?"

The woman shook her head. "Not a chance, but this one's got a warrant. Don't be fooled by the screaming granny act. She hightailed it on a half dozen robbery charges. I don't mind a few scratches for a bounty this size, but no way am I handing her over to you without getting my share."

The older woman was hunched over and shivering, like she was expecting to be gunned down at any moment. Dale lowered her gun, and Lindsey watched as she walked over to the gun wielder. "You have paperwork?"

"Back pocket."

Dale reached into her back pocket and pulled out a folded sheet of paper. She scanned the page. "You sure this is her?"

"Seriously? I've been tailing her for weeks. This is the first time I've got her somewhere we weren't surrounded by a bunch of other geriatrics. Believe it or not, I'm not interested in scaring old people to death." She looked at her arm. "Although I might be inclined to change my mind after this one."

Dale refolded the paper and handed it back to the woman. "Agent Dale Nelson. What's your name?"

"Luca Bennett."

Dale cocked her head when the other woman said her name. "Bounty hunter?"

"Guilty as charged. Before you go judging, you should know I've done favors for some of your fed friends. You know, stuff they didn't want to mess with." She reached her free hand toward her pocket. "If you want to see my license, it's in my wallet."

Dale waved her off. "Nah, I believe you. Just wish you could've done this outside."

"You and me both. Granny's a little feistier than you'd think."

"You want some help?"

"I got it. Besides, it looks like you have someone waiting for you."

Luca pointed in Lindsey's direction and Dale swung around too fast for her to get out of sight. Caught defying orders, Lindsey offered a weak smile and waved, but her attempt at levity didn't dispel Dale's frown. She followed Dale out of the store, more captivated by what had just happened than concerned about whether Dale was angry with her.

"So, what was that? You're just going to let that vigilante hold a gun on that old woman? Is that how you do things in Texas? Old West justice style?"

Dale pulled up short, and when she turned around, her face was a steely mask. "I told you to wait outside."

"Seriously, that's all you have to say? Some scraggly character holds a woman at gunpoint in a convenience store and the best you can do is ask her if she needs help?" Lindsey didn't know whether to be angry or annoyed at the casual manner in which Dale blew off her questions.

"What went on in there doesn't concern you."

"Oh, so now you're in charge of what concerns me? I wasn't aware that was part of your assignment."

"Part of my assignment is to make sure you get your story without getting hurt. You could've been shot."

"You had everything under control. I was fine."

"You don't know that. Things can change in an instant. Just because you think you're safe, doesn't mean you are. It's stupid to put yourself in a dangerous situation."

Dale's words were delivered in a sharp staccato, and her eyes burned with anger. Lindsey stopped deflecting and got right back in her face. "If that woman was so dangerous, then why did you let her keep her gun? Sounds to me like you may have overreacted. Everyone is fine."

"Everyone may be fine, but that's just dumb luck. You could've been shot, all because you want something titillating for your 'news' story. We're done with this little sideshow. I'm taking you and your crew back to the hotel. Get in the truck."

Lindsey purposely hung back as Dale stalked off toward the truck. Dale might be furious, but she was angry too. Dale thought she was trying to find fodder for a story and that wasn't it at all. As she walked toward the others, she muttered her thoughts under her breath.

Dale whipped around. "What did you say?"

"Nothing."

"You have something to say to me, at least have the guts to say it to my face."

Lindsey paused and considered, but only one thought she felt like sharing came to mind, and she blurted out the words that summed up exactly why she'd gone back into the shop. Not news, not curiosity—no, it was something else entirely, and the realization surprised her. "It could've been you."

"What?"

"You. You could've been shot."

Dale held her gaze, and in the span of seconds, a mix of emotions cycled through her expression. Remorse, resignation, regret. She opened her mouth as if to say something, but instead she just shook her head. "Let's go."

Lindsey climbed into the backseat of the truck and once again avoided Alice's and Jed's curious stares. She was a ball of emotions and didn't feel like sharing any of them with anyone. What she needed to do was get a handle on herself. She was here to do a story, not flirt with an attractive woman, especially not one as infuriating as Dale Nelson. Her only job was to be professional and deliver this candy-ass puff piece that the network wanted. Then she could go back to Manhattan and resume the life she'd had before she'd chucked it all away to go overseas. Lord knows there were plenty of attractive, willing women in New York without the baggage of Agent Dale Nelson.

CHAPTER ELEVEN

Lindsey pounded her fist on Elaina's door, ducking the dirty looks from the room service waiter walking toward her. She was about to give up when the door swung open and Elaina whispered, "Why the hell are you trying to beat my door down?"

"If you'd answer your damn phone, maybe you'd know."

The sound of a throat clearing interrupted their tiff, and Lindsey turned to see the room service waiter standing behind her. "Yes?"

"Service for Ms. Beall," he said.

Lindsey did a mock bow and flourish. "By all means." She followed him into the room and sank into one of the chairs. "So, Ms. Beall, what are we having? I had no idea today was stay at the hotel and be pampered day. If I had, I would've scheduled a massage. What's for dinner?"

Elaina ignored her while she signed the room service check. When the waiter left the room, she pointed at the bottle of red wine. "Would you like a glass?"

"I'd rather have some answers. You have any of those?"

Elaina took an infuriatingly long amount of time to pour herself some wine. She took a sip and smacked her lips in approval. "What do you want to know?"

"Where were you all day? The rest of us were working. I get that this assignment is totally beneath your pay grade—mine too, but at least I'm showing up and doing my part."

Instead of answering, Elaina poured another glass and handed it over. "Try this. It's amazing."

Lindsey shook her head, but she took the glass and swallowed a healthy portion. The wine was fantastic.

"Complex, right?"

"It is. It's very good, but I'm hoping we can talk about more than wine."

"Absolutely." Elaina settled onto the couch. "In addition to discovering this excellent wine, I've spent the day working on your story."

"Oh, really?"

"Yes. I met with Hector Diego, the division chief for the Dallas office of the DEA. I explained to him that our piece about the Take-Back program was likely to generate more interest if we had a human interest hook, something more titillating than the collection of medicine cabinet discards and Just Say No programs for local school children. After a bit of convincing, he agreed with my assessment."

Lindsey heard the undercurrent in Elaina's voice and briefly wondered what method she'd used to convince Dale's boss to beef up the story. "So, are you going to tell me what you cooked up or am I supposed to guess?"

"Did you happen to know that Agent Nelson is not only a decorated Marine, but her now-dead wife was an assistant United States attorney who prosecuted drug cases?"

"Matter of fact, I do. I guess you think that just because I think a story is silly, I don't do my research. Really, Elaina, I would think you know me better than that. The better question is why wasn't it in the research the network gave you?"

She shrugged. "I guess the writers didn't get the significance of the angle since it was buried in the research materials. Besides, I'm not sure they planned to assign her to this project until we showed up. Anyway, I talked to Diego about it and he agreed. We parallel the story about Agent Nelson's loss to her continued work to take down the organized drug trade. Show how this initiative is a piece of the overall picture. It's the perfect human interest angle."

Of course it was and it had been her idea in the first place. Lindsey flashed to the memory of Elaina sitting at her desk when she'd come out of the bathroom the other night. She'd bet all the money in all the world that Elaina had read her notes about Dale and this original idea was the fruit of her spy mission. She started to call Elaina out, but decided not to bother since she agreed with the outcome. Only one thing needed to be sorted out. "Is Agent Nelson on board with being interviewed?"

"She will be."

"What's that supposed to mean?"

"I'm sure her boss will have a talk with her and she'll understand that the better the ratings the show has, the better chance this story will have to cast a good light on the agency overall."

Lindsey balked at the explanation. She was torn, but she couldn't help but point out the negatives from Dale's perspective. "First of all, she's a widow. Her wife died under horrible circumstances, and for all we know she's still grieving. Her buy-in is critical if we're going to put her life front and center. Second, what if what she has to say doesn't cast a good light on the agency? Maybe she harbors ill will for her superiors because of the shooting. For all we know, she holds a grudge that they weren't able to protect her."

"And you should know, we kind of got into it today. I'm not entirely sure she'll open up to me no matter what the circumstances."

She waited for Elaina to respond, but she seemed way more interested in getting to the bottom of her glass than answering the questions she'd posed.

Finally, Elaina drained the last drop of wine and set her glass aside. "Well, look at you. Lindsey Ryan, ace reporter, returns from Afghanistan and goes all sweet and soft. What's the deal? You can attack generals in charge of thousands of troops, but you can't get one little DEA agent to open up to you without worrying about hurting her feelings? Please. You made a deal with Larry. If you want the network to fund your missions of truth in the future, you make this chump story a riveting, tearjerker piece that has everyone thinking the DEA is the savior of modern mankind. Got it?"

Lindsey stood. She had made a deal with Larry and her job depended on it. As much as she cherished the freedom to choose the topics of her reporting, she knew that network backing was the reason she was able to dig deep on many of the stories she chose to pursue. If the network, in the form of Elaina, had a specific agenda here, that was their problem. At least now one of her problems was solved. If Dale was to be the subject of this story, she was clearly off limits personally. She wouldn't waste any more energy chasing the strong pull of attraction that appeared every time she was near. She had one task and one task only—explore the Dale Nelson angle, and she would go wherever it led. No matter what.

Suddenly, she knew exactly how she'd spend the rest of her evening.

❖

Dale barely waited for Lindsey's crew to clear the truck before she peeled out of the Anatole parking lot, tires screeching on the pavement. She'd dutifully carted them to the day's worth of appointments at the mayor's office and to watch one of the local cops interact with a group of school kids, and she'd watched with growing impatience as Lindsey handled the interview with kid gloves, completely at odds with the way she'd grilled her about the way she'd handled the bounty hunter back at the convenience store.

Like Lindsey knew jack shit about life in her world. Now that they were out of her hair for the afternoon, she couldn't tell if she was more angry or frustrated, but she did know she was relieved to be out from under Lindsey's glaring inspection. For half a second, she considered showing up at the office and telling Diego he needed to find someone else to play babysitter.

And then what? If Diego granted her request, which wasn't likely, he'd load her up with new cases. Truth was, working with the film crew gave her more flexibility to work on the Vargas case. While Lindsey was busy glad-handing the mayor, she'd been able to do some checking on Tanner Cohen. The general consensus held she was a stand-up agent, by the book, but willing to think outside the box. She hoped Bianca's instincts about including Tanner in their off-the-record enterprise were well founded.

She drove the short distance to her apartment and parked on the street. She had a reserved space in the garage, but hated the fact she had to twist and turn her oversized truck down four levels to get to it and back out. She bypassed the elevator and took the stairs. She hadn't been able to go to the gym since the gunshot wound, and she was hyper aware of how out of shape she felt. The long, slow climb up the seven flights provided a nice, slow burn, but when she finally reached her door, she was starving. The fridge was a lonely place, home to random takeout condiments, a half a carton of eggs, and some milk long past its expiration date. She couldn't remember the last time she'd been to the grocery store—she'd picked up the eggs at the convenience store down the street one day when she was craving something that reminded her of the breakfasts she and Maria used to share. Her version of huevos rancheros hadn't come close to the original, and tonight she didn't even bother, instead scrambling three eggs and eating them right out of the skillet.

The forecast called for a drop in temperature, so she combed her closet for a jacket and tugged it on before heading back out to her truck. The drive to Peyton's ranch was about forty-five minutes on a normal day, but traffic was heavier than usual. She spent the time examining Bianca's plan for flaws. There were plenty of possible obstacles, but no strategy was perfect. They had to take some major risks if they wanted to catch Sergio and, in her view, the risk was worth the potential reward. When she finally reached the turnoff to the ranch, she was fully prepared to convince Peyton they had a solid plan.

As her truck rumbled down the drive, she saw Bianca turn in behind her. When they reached the house, she waited for Bianca and Tanner to get out of the car before stepping down to greet them. She shook Tanner's outstretched hand, pleased at the strong grip. "Dale Nelson, DEA."

"Tanner Cohen. No need for the introduction. Pretty sure everyone knows who you are."

Dale eyed Tanner closely, searching for a hidden meaning to her words, but finally decided Tanner was just sucking up to a more experienced agent. Good. Deference could come in handy. "Cruz already talk to you about what we have planned?"

Tanner nodded. "She did. I think it's doable. If Ms. Valencia is on board with it, then I am too."

Dale clasped her shoulder. "Actually, the first hurdle is AUSA Davis, but you let me worry about that part. The most important thing you can do tonight is listen. Let Cruz and I pave the way. Got it?"

Tanner nodded and they made their way from the vehicles to the porch just as Peyton walked out the front door.

"What the hell is she doing here?"

Dale stopped, surprised by the sharp edge to Peyton's question. She shot a glance at Bianca who looked like she wished she could melt into the ground. "Hey, Peyton, we brought some extra help."

Peyton turned to Bianca. "Isn't this the agent who executed the warrant on Cyrus's office?"

"She was one of the agents that was there," Bianca said. "But she wasn't aware of the circumstances. Now she's the lead agent working with Mr. Gellar on the case."

"Dale, Bianca, I'd like to talk to you inside," Peyton said. "Agent Cohen, I'm sorry to be inhospitable, but if you could wait on the porch, we'll be right back." She didn't wait for an answer before she stalked off into the house. Dale motioned to Bianca to follow and she brought up the rear. When they were inside, Peyton pulled up short in the entryway and turned to face them. "Not cool, bringing someone else here. This is my home. Lily is here, and that woman was one of the agents that grilled her about her father's business dealings. I get that we probably need to work with her, but at the office, in court. Anywhere but here."

Bianca started to respond, but Dale broke in first. "It was my idea. We have a plan that involves Agent Cohen, and we thought it would be best to talk to you both at the same time about it."

Peyton shook her head. "I'm afraid any new plans need to be put on hold for now. I need your help. Sophia came over this afternoon and she's here now. She received a threat. Against Lily. Graphic and violent. I was hoping we could spend tonight's card game focused on that instead of the rest of the case."

Dale looked at Bianca who nodded. "I'm sorry to hear that, Peyton, but actually that kind of fits right in with what we were thinking. If Sophia's here, we'd like to talk to her. If you really have an objection to Agent Cohen, we'll figure something else out, but Cruz here thinks she can be trusted."

"Tanner Cohen?"

Everyone turned at the sound of Lily's voice. Dale hadn't heard her enter the room, but she was standing in the doorway to the living room, dressed in riding clothes. She waited for Peyton to answer.

"Yes," Peyton said. "But don't worry; she's leaving."

Lily stepped forward and slid her arm around Peyton's waist. "I remember her. Two agents asked me questions at my father's office. One of them was a complete jerk and the other was very kind. I think Tanner's good people, Peyton. Trust your friends."

Dale watched as Peyton turned into Lily's arms and searched her face like she was looking for guidance. She remembered the strong pull of a beautiful woman, and the power they could wield over the ones that loved them. She'd have done anything for Maria. If only she'd been able to trade places with her that fateful morning.

"Okay," Peyton said. "If you two vouch for her, bring her in."

A few minutes later, Mary arrived and they all congregated around the kitchen table, cards dealt and chips stacked to keep up the appearances of a heated poker game. Peyton started the meeting by having Sophia explain what had happened. As Dale listened to her account of returning to the house to find a threat painted in blood on her front door, she couldn't help but look between the woman and her daughter, Lily. The resemblance was striking, and she was probably seeing in Sophia how Lily would look in twenty years.

"What did the message say?" Dale asked. She directed her question to Sophia who grasped her daughter's hand before answering.

"It said: Muerta de los Lily. Death to Lily."

"Nothing else?"

"Did it need to be more specific?" Peyton said. "It's pretty clear to me they are targeting anyone having anything to do with Cyrus."

Dale cracked her knuckles as she considered how to respond without pissing Peyton off. "I guess I'm just wondering what the 'or what' is. I mean, why just death to Lily? Seems like Sergio might have a request, and then if he were denied, he would threaten to hurt the one thing that would be most precious to the person he was asking the favor from. In this case, he came to Sophia. My read is he wants something from her and that will be the next communication." She looked over at Bianca who nodded. "In that regard, Cruz and I have a plan." She laid out the plan Bianca had concocted. "I'll confess we came here tonight ready to tell you this idea, and I was a little skeptical, but now I'm convinced it's the best way to lure Sergio out of hiding."

Sophia didn't hesitate. "I'll do it."

Dale spotted Peyton shaking her head, but she ignored her for the moment and turned to Tanner. "Cohen, you on board with this? We're going to need your help. If Ms. Valencia is going to be a CI, you're going to have to shield her from prosecution. Only the folks around this table can know what's really going on, and it may take a while for her to earn Sergio's trust."

She watched while Tanner looked around the table, like she was sizing up the group. She had to realize they were all top-notch talent, and if they were bucking the system, then there was a damn good reason for it. Finally, Tanner's gaze rested on Peyton and she said, "I'm in if Peyton's in."

It was exactly the right thing to say since it showed deference and insight into the dynamics of the group. All eyes were focused on Peyton now, but she spoke only to Sophia. "We might not be able to protect you. We'll have to leave the threat you just received unreported because it won't make sense that you're visiting Arturo in jail if he just threatened you. If he doesn't believe your story, he will have no choice but to eliminate you." She turned to Lily. "Or you. Do you realize what they are asking me to do? Both of your lives could be in grave danger."

"Our lives are already in danger, but this is a chance to act instead of hide from it," Lily said. "If you believe in these people, then so do I. I'm betting Sophia feels the same way."

"I do," Sophia said. "Peyton, you must know that no one is better acquainted with the cruelty of my brothers than me. I know the risk and I accept it." She directed her next words to Dale. "Everything I have ever done has been to protect my daughter, and that will not change now. Just tell me what to do."

Dale and Bianca described the specifics of the plan. Sophia would go to see Arturo the following day at the Seagoville Federal Detention Center outside of Dallas. She'd describe her troubles and give him enough vague details to get him to put her in touch with Sergio. And then they would wait. Peyton asked Dale to be in charge of keeping an eye on Sophia to make sure nothing happened to her.

"Can you dodge your Hollywood film crew long enough to stay on top of things?" Peyton asked Dale.

"They're from New York, and yes. There's nothing I'd rather do." She meant it. Lindsey Ryan was trouble, but all she needed to do was stick to the script and soon they'd be gone. Back to New York where they'd piece together the most boring piece of PR in history. The Take-Back Initiative event was on Saturday, and she couldn't imagine they would be here longer than that.

She experienced a twinge of regret at the realization. In another time, another place, under other circumstances, she would've wanted to explore the attraction, but letting Lindsey get close seemed as much a betrayal as an impossibility. Her focus was best left to her work where she knew what she was doing and could tally the results. Being around Lindsey left her feeling out of her element.

An hour later, she drove the graveled road out of the ranch, deep in thought. The next day's itinerary for Lindsey's crew was fairly light, but she still needed a ready excuse to get away to accompany Sophia to the prison in the morning. She wasn't going inside with her, only keeping an eye out to make sure they weren't followed either coming or going. She'd promised Peyton she'd keep her safe, and she fully intended to keep that promise.

When she reached the highway, she spotted a car pull out of the gully on the side of the road and drive off in the opposite direction. There was nothing particularly odd about the car itself—it was a dark colored sedan with Texas plates, but she experienced a twinge of recognition. That and the fact that it had been parked by the turnoff to the ranch had her thinking. She stared into the rearview mirror and jotted down the plate number on the pad of paper she kept in the console. As the car faded out of sight, she called DPD officer Andrea DeJesus.

"DeJesus, here."

"Andrea, it's Dale Nelson. I was hoping you might be able to do me a favor."

"For you, anything."

Dale did her best to ignore the sexy undercurrent in Andrea's voice, but the memory of Lindsey's words echoed in her ears: *Careful, you're making her blush.* Maybe this wasn't such a good idea, but she didn't want to wait to find out who had been lurking around the Davis ranch, especially since she'd promised Peyton she would protect her family. "It's probably nothing, but I was hoping you could run a plate. It's for a friend, so if you don't feel comfortable doing it, I totally understand."

"Say no more. Give it to me."

Dale read off the plate number.

"Got it. Call you right back."

Dale had only driven a few more miles when her phone rang. "Nelson."

"I got the info," Andrea said, "but it's not real helpful. It's a rental car. Registered to Enterprise. I can run it down further if you have a little time."

Dale considered taking advantage of the request, but the tone of Andrea's voice signaled she might be sending the wrong message if she asked for more favors. "No, that's okay. It's probably nothing. Thanks for your help."

"I'm here anytime you need me. *Anytime.*"

Dale winced at the not so subtle emphasis in Andrea's tone, but she kept her voice calm and got off the phone as quickly as possible. She was probably just being paranoid, about the car, about Andrea's flirting, about everything. She'd been on edge all week and, as much as she didn't want to admit it, her moods had started shifting with the appearance of Lindsey Ryan. Swinging from excited to annoyed and back again, she didn't understand how this woman could hold such a strong sway over her feelings. Just a few more days and

Lindsey would be gone, and then she wouldn't have to worry about it anymore. Even that revelation gave her mixed feelings, and she needed something to distract her. The plan to lure Sergio out of hiding couldn't have come at a better time.

❖

"Do you think she spotted us?" Alice asked.

Lindsey looked back and watched the taillights of Dale's truck fade into the distance. "She probably saw the car for sure, but I doubt she realizes it's us. Why would she? We're in the middle of nowhere."

After she'd left Elaina's room, Lindsey had phoned a contact the network used to dig up background information who was known for his discretion. She'd asked him to prepare a dossier on Dale. If Dale was going to be the hook for this story, she wanted to know everything: her family, her friends—past and present, what she did for fun. Within an hour, she had her hands on some preliminary information, but the rest would take some time. On a whim, she'd told Alice to grab her equipment and they drove to the address the investigator had given her for Dale's home.

Dale's apartment building was older and nondescript, but it was clean and it appeared to be well maintained. The individual units were only accessible through two locked security doors, and one of those doors was located in a tenant only parking garage. They'd circled the building a couple of times to get a feel for the place when Lindsey had spotted Dale's truck parked on the street. "I bet she plans to go out again."

"What do you want to do?" Alice asked.

Following Dale around town felt like borderline stalking, but Lindsey was compelled to know more about her, although she wasn't entirely convinced she was only digging for the sake of the story.

Maybe they should go back to the hotel. She could wait for the file from the investigator and learn what she needed from the paperwork. She had been about to tell Alice that when she saw Dale walk out the door of the building and head to her truck. She ducked down in her seat and made a snap decision. "Let's see where she goes."

Following Dale's truck out to the country might have been a stupid move, but she'd managed to gather a lot of information during the trip. An Internet search of county records revealed her destination was a piece of property called the Circle Six Ranch, owned by Raymond and Helen Davis. When she dug a little deeper, she discovered Raymond and Helen had a daughter named Peyton who was an assistant United States Attorney, working in the Northern District. She also discovered Peyton was engaged in a lawsuit against her brother Neil and Gantry Oil—a temporary injunction having to do with drilling rights at the ranch.

On its own, what she'd learned wasn't much, but on a hunch she had her contact run the plate of the car that had turned into the ranch right after Dale. The sportster belonged to Bianca Cruz, the AUSA they'd met that morning, and she didn't think it was a coincidence that a DEA agent was meeting with two AUSAs outside of the office. When she'd shared her hunch with Alice, she'd suggested they wait for a while.

Now it was an hour later, and Lindsey was certain Dale had spotted their car. As they raced down the road, she could only hope the dark night hid their identity.

"What now?" Alice asked.

"Good question." Lindsey considered her options. She wanted to find out everything she could about Bianca Cruz and Peyton Davis, but it was pretty unlikely they would be able to mine resources until the next day. Which left Dale as the only subject of her curiosity left to explore. She made a split-second decision. "I need you to drop me off on your way back to the hotel."

CHAPTER TWELVE

Dale unlocked her apartment and walked the few feet to the kitchen where she fished in the fridge for a beer. She'd have one and then try to sleep since she'd have to be up early the next day to put the plan they'd hatched into motion. She was halfway through the bottle when she heard a knock on the door. The clock on the stove read nine p.m.—late for an unexpected visitor. When she peered out the viewfinder and saw Lindsey Ryan, unexpected was an understatement.

It was late and she was tired, but she couldn't deny the surge of anticipation at the sight of Lindsey standing outside her door. She'd changed out of the suit she'd worn earlier and was dressed in dark jeans and a rich looking burgundy V-neck sweater. Probably cashmere, probably designer. She shook her head. Her law enforcement training meant she was acutely aware of descriptive details, but lately it seemed she was obsessed with every facet of Lindsey's appearance, and it had nothing to do with her work. She schooled her features into what she hoped was a nonchalant expression.

Lindsey's hand was raised to knock again, and she looked startled when Dale opened the door. "What's the matter?" Dale asked. "Some late night filming emergency?"

"If I said yes, would you invite me in to talk about it?"

She was definitely quick on her feet, and Dale made a mental note to be careful. Lindsey's ability to improvise might be admirable on screen but could pose a problem if she decided to turn her investigating skills to something other than the story her network had assigned. She glanced back inside her apartment. Except for the day she'd been released from the hospital, she hadn't spent much time here during the past few weeks, so the place was relatively clean and uncluttered, but the real reason for her hesitation was not knowing the true reason for Lindsey's visit. Curiosity won out and she swung the door wide. "I'm having a beer. Join me?"

"A beer would be great. Thanks."

Dale pulled another bottle from the fridge and twisted the cap off before handing it over. She watched, transfixed, as Lindsey took a long pull and then wiped her mouth with the back of her hand. The simple act was so unassuming and so completely sexy, and she couldn't help but like her more. "Thirsty?"

"Actually yes. PR is hard work."

Lindsey's tone carried a slight edge of sarcasm, and Dale figured she was trying to provoke a reaction. Since she had no idea where Lindsey was headed or why she was here, she kept her response even. "I imagine it is. Especially if it means you have to make night visits to your contact. I assume you're here about the story, right?"

Now it was Lindsey's turn to maintain composure. Dale could almost see her mind ticking through the options: tell the truth, make up a story, or settle for something in between. When Lindsey's features finally settled, Dale was convinced she was going to dissemble.

"Yes, it's the story."

"And it couldn't wait until tomorrow?"

"I suppose it could, but I didn't want to wait. I didn't want to take a chance on catching you off guard tomorrow."

Dale's antennae went up and she struggled to keep the edge out of her voice as she asked, "Any particular reason I should have my guard up?"

Lindsey cocked her head like she was trying to assess hidden meaning behind Dale's question, but Dale gave her nothing. Lindsey had shown up here, at her home, for no real reason she could discern. The very fact Lindsey knew where she lived was disturbing enough, but now she was implying there was some reason she should be worried about the story. All her training dictated she should be on alert, but her instincts also told her she would get more information by letting her guard down. She settled on diversion as a way to get the most out of this encounter. "Would you like to have a seat?"

"Sure. Lead the way."

Dale led Lindsey the few steps from the kitchen to the living room where a plain tan couch and matching chair comprised the only real furniture in the place. Her television was mounted on the wall and two folding TV tables were the only other accessories in the room. She watched Lindsey's eyes sweep the room, certain she was noting every detail of her ascetic lifestyle, and she tried not to care what Lindsey thought even as she felt the need to explain. "I have a lot of stuff in storage. Not sure how long I'm staying here."

"I get it. I put all my stuff in storage and sublet my place when I went overseas. Now I'm home, but I don't have a home."

She got that Lindsey was only making small talk, but it wasn't the same. Lindsey going to Afghanistan was a choice. When she'd left the home that had turned into a crime scene, it had been a necessity. The crime scene techs had spent several days after the shooting combing through every inch of the house and yard, looking for clues about Maria's killers. Dale had spent those nights at Mary's house. Mary was the only one she'd trusted to witness her breakdown that had occurred in spurts, in between answering questions about Maria's enemies and planning her funeral.

Five days later, when the cops were done and Maria was buried, Dale had returned to the house and packed the bare minimum she would need to start her new life as a widow, devoted to her work and nothing else. Having visitors, especially ones as inquisitive and unsettling as Lindsey Ryan, had never figured into her planning, and she felt agitated. "Are you going to tell me why you're really here or are we going to dance around the subject until you can no longer pretend you were just in the neighborhood?"

If Lindsey was put off by the abrupt question, she didn't show it. She took her time with another long pull of her beer before saying, "I can't tell if it's me you don't like or if it's my occupation."

"I don't have a problem with reporters." She didn't. Even the ones who'd swarmed her when she'd left her house the day of Maria's murder.

"So, it's just me."

It was just her, but Dale didn't want to admit that it wasn't about like or dislike. It was the way her body went on high alert every time Lindsey walked into the room. The way her heart raced and her mind pulsed. When she was with Lindsey, she felt like she was coming out of her skin. Even when Lindsey had been grilling her about how she'd handled the confrontation with the bounty hunter, she'd been electrified.

And that was it. Lindsey sparked something. Something she hadn't felt since Maria died. Alive.

The questions she asked, the buttons she pushed—as antagonizing as Lindsey was, she penetrated the wall of disinterest that she'd hidden behind over the past year, and the realization was both enlightening and frightening at the same time. She stepped carefully around the pitfalls of Lindsey's question, deflecting as best she could. "I work with reporters all the time. It's part of the job. Tell me what you need and I'll tell you anything I can."

Lindsey finished her beer and set the bottle on the TV tray beside the couch. Earlier, she'd considered Elaina's interference a favor, a way to draw a distinction between Dale, the liaison whose role constituted a gray area of conflict, and Dale, the subject who was clearly off limits, but now that the lines should be clear, they were anything but.

Coming here tonight had been a mistake. She leaned forward, balancing her elbows on her knees and clasping her hands together as she steeled herself for Dale's reaction to what she was about to say. "So, here's the deal. We're tweaking things a bit and we're going to make you the centerpiece of the story. Special Agent works hard to put away drug lords. Suffers the ultimate sacrifice." She delivered the message clearly and concisely and waited for Dale's reaction. She expected anger, but she was prepared for anything. Or so she thought.

"You're kidding, right?" The crack of inflection in Dale's voice signaled she was truly incredulous.

"No."

"Not going to happen."

"It's a done deal. I got word from my producer tonight. She talked to your boss about it today." She watched and waited for Dale to stand, hit something, yell, but she was met with stony silence. She waited it out for a few long minutes. "Would you like to talk about it?"

"No."

"I guess it's going to be a short interview." Lindsey smiled to soften the mood, but Dale offered nothing in return. "Seriously, there're no cameras rolling now. You can talk to me."

Her plea was met with silence. She should give up. She'd been misreading signals from Dale since the moment they met, and now that Dale was the subject of her piece, she was acting like a child who wanted what she couldn't have. She'd never had to beg for an interview before. Cajole, promise, but never beg, and she wouldn't be reduced to begging now. She stood up, intending to leave, but Dale's words stopped her before she could take a step.

"Don't you already have everything you need?"

Dale's voice held a slight edge of accusation, but there was something else there as well. Resignation, maybe? Lindsey sat back down. "I'm not sure I understand what you mean."

"The first morning, when I picked you up at your hotel room. You'd already found out everything you could about me. My entire life was splashed across your computer screen."

Damn. She thought she'd been so clever, hiding the evidence of her intrusion, but Dale had known all along that she'd been digging into her past. "Why didn't you say anything?"

"Really? What did you expect me to say? Hey, did you hear about how my wife was gunned down on our front lawn while she was picking up the paper?" Dale sprang out of her seat and began pacing. "Maybe you're so used to rummaging through the pain of other people's lives, you're immune to it, but…"

Dale's words trailed off and she leaned against the kitchen counter. Lindsey crossed the room and stood a foot way, watching her face for a sign. Should she push the point or let it go? She could handle Dale's anger; she was skilled in sparring with subjects. But Dale hadn't sounded angry—she'd sounded defeated. Lindsey had wrestled many interviewees to defeat before, but this was different. Her heart told her to comfort Dale, but her instincts screamed for her to keep her distance. She settled on simple. "I'm sorry. I'll do everything I can to make this as painless as possible, portray your loss with honor and respect. I have a job to do, but I'll do my best not to let it get in the way." She placed her hand on Dale's arm as she spoke, unsettled by the rush of excitement that washed over her at this simplest of touches.

Dale raised her head and her eyes were dark and piercing. "It already has."

CHAPTER THIRTEEN

The next morning, Dale parked her truck in front of a diner on the service road to Highway 175 at six a.m. She'd chosen the location because of its proximity to the Seagoville Federal Detention Center, one exit farther south. She cut the engine and spent a few minutes scouring the parking lot for any signs she'd been followed. It was a dark, damp morning, and it matched her mood perfectly. Glad to see she was the first to arrive, she used her time to reflect on Lindsey's visit to her apartment the night before.

She'd tossed and turned all night, sorting through her scattered thoughts that ranged from wondering how Lindsey had found out where she lived to why she'd chosen to show up late in the evening to deliver the bad news that Diego had sold her out in the name of PR. Lindsey had seemed almost regretful, like it wasn't her idea to make her the focus of her story, like she would make a different choice if she could, but Dale knew that couldn't be true. Surely a reporter with Lindsey's clout called her own shots.

Like you? She struck her palm against the steering wheel. Dammit. She was a fucking federal agent, yet she was spending her days working as a tour guide for a press crew instead of using her skills for what she was trained to do. She didn't buy the line Diego had handed her about how she'd been sidelined because of her injury. He'd had no problem with her staying on the job when they were hot on the heels of the Vargas brothers. No, his change of heart was a direct result of Gellar's decision to disband the task force, but it still didn't make sense. Task force or no task force, Sergio Vargas and his lieutenants were still on the loose, not to mention hundreds of other members of the Zeta and other active cartels, yet she was stuck working on a program that would have virtually no effect on the war on drugs.

Even Lindsey Ryan got it. Her pointed questions had made it clear she thought the Take-Back initiative was a waste of time and resources. So why was she here covering the event?

She didn't get it, but what she didn't get more was the way her body betrayed her every time she laid eyes on Lindsey. She recalled the way Bianca had reacted yesterday morning, when she'd met Lindsey at the hotel—starstruck and in awe of Lindsey's physical beauty. She couldn't blame her. Lindsey was stunning, but she'd had a completely different reaction when they'd first met. Not starstruck, but startled. Not in awe, but definitely attracted, and not just physically. Lindsey's confidence, her refusal to be intimidated, and her dogged resolve stirred feelings she'd thought were long dead. Feelings she wasn't at all sure she was prepared to experience again.

A sharp rap on the window snapped her out of her thoughts, and she looked over to see Bianca standing next to her truck. She shook off her decidedly non-business thoughts and motioned for her to open the door.

"I need a step stool to get in this thing," Bianca said as she climbed into the passenger seat. "You haul cattle in your spare time?"

"Spare time?" Dale shook her head and smiled. "Sorry, I'm not familiar with the concept. Care to explain?"

"You and me both." She looked around. "I'm guessing Sophia isn't here yet."

"Not yet." Dale glanced first at her phone and then out the window, surveying the parking lot. The plan they'd hatched was for Mary and a local cop they trusted to follow Sophia to this diner where they would go over the details of Sophia's visit to Seagoville one more time. Sophia would need to get to the detention center around seven a.m. to get in line with the rest of the relatives and friends visiting inmates. With their credentials, they could have arranged for her to visit during off hours, but that might have caused Arturo to become suspicious, and they needed this plan to go off without a hitch if they had any chance of catching Sergio before they got caught running this clandestine operation.

"I was going to wait until they got here to spring this on you," Bianca said, "but…"

Bianca looked like she was about to burst, and Dale rolled her hand in the air. "Keep talking."

"I reached out to a friend on the staff at Seagoville. I've arranged for you to be in the security booth so you can listen in on Sophia's visit with Arturo in real time instead of waiting to hear what she has to say about it after."

Dale cocked her head. She was impressed at Bianca's move, but curious about what prompted it. "You worried she might not tell us everything?"

"Look, I get that we're supposed to handle anything to do with Lily with kid gloves because of Peyton, but Sophia spent her entire life hiding who she was from her only child. As a mother, I find that a bit hard to swallow, no matter what the circumstances. I'm not saying she's in league with her brothers, but wouldn't you rather hear their conversation and evaluate it yourself?"

Dale couldn't deny Bianca's instincts were right. She would always rather judge a situation firsthand if she had the opportunity. "Okay. How's this going to work?"

Bianca handed her a folded piece of paper. "Go now. This will get you through to the staff parking and entrance. They'll set you up. I'll wait here. Mary and I can brief Sophia." She glanced at her watch. "I've got a hearing at nine and I'll catch up with you after."

Dale took the paper from Bianca and shoved it in her pocket. As she did, she felt the vibration of her cell phone, and she pulled it out and glanced at the screen. Diego. He was probably calling to tell her he'd sold her out to Lindsey's crew. She hit ignore and let it go to voice mail. She was too angry to talk to him now and she wasn't about to let anything, including Lindsey Ryan, get in the way of the plan she and the rest of the unofficial task force had set into motion.

❖

"Well, where is she?"

Lindsey struggled against the urge to strangle the impatience out of Elaina's voice. She'd called Dale's cell three times so far this morning, and each time the call had gone directly to voice mail. It was nine thirty, and they were expected at the local network affiliate where a full film crew was on standby to assist with the taping. "I don't know. She's a cop. Maybe she's doing something a little more important than sharing the very worst moments of her personal life for us to show to millions of strangers."

Elaina frowned. "Her superior assured me she would be available. Maybe I'll just call him and let him know his employee can't be bothered to cooperate with us."

Lindsey cringed at Elaina's pretentious use of the word "superior" and scrambled to think of a way to prevent Elaina from making good on her threat. She was frustrated too, and she didn't honestly think Dale had a legitimate reason for blowing her off, but she couldn't with good conscience trace her aggravation to the fact Dale was ignoring her calls. No, the source of her frustration was the conflicted feelings that lingered after her awkward encounter with Dale the night before. She shouldn't have gone to Dale's apartment. Doing so had been a clear signal she was more interested than she should be—a sign of weakness, both personally and professionally. And then there was the inexplicable emptiness she'd felt standing outside, waiting for an Uber after Dale had asked her to leave. She'd been given a hook for this story that had some teeth to it, but she'd been left feeling like she was losing out and she didn't get it. All she knew was she wanted to distract Elaina from Dale until she knew more about what was really going on.

She injected her voice with what she knew was just the right amount of persuasion to get Elaina to acquiesce. "Call the station and ask them to reschedule for this afternoon. I'll take Alice and Jed and we'll go shoot some scene intros at a few places I think will work for after break openers. I'm sure that whatever Agent Nelson is doing will be wrapped up by this afternoon. I'll make sure of it. I promise."

Elaina gave her a probing stare as if trying to figure out if she had an ulterior motive, but Lindsey maintained what she hoped was an earnest expression. "Fine. Maybe I'll go with you."

As the field producer, Elaina had every right to accompany them, but Lindsey had plans that didn't involve Elaina tagging along. She had to talk her out of going without raising her suspicions. She slipped an arm through Elaina's. "I'm sure you have more important things to do than scope out scenery. In fact, I prepared some questions for Agent Nelson, and I'd love it if you would review them and make sure I haven't missed anything." The lie was hard to swallow, but it worked like a charm.

"Good point," Elaina said. "I've already started a list of areas you should cover. I'll work up some specific questions to help you out."

Lindsey smiled and gritted her teeth to keep from telling Elaina what she could do with her list of questions. "That would be amazing. I'll call you when we get back."

Thirty minutes later, she was in the local station van with Alice and Jed. She filled Jed in on their adventure in the country the night before.

"Are you planning to drive out there again in broad daylight?" Jed asked.

"Not likely. Hell, we almost got caught there last night, but I'd like to see what we can find out about the other people who were there. In addition to Peyton Davis, a car belonging to AUSA Bianca Cruz and one other car left the ranch before Dale." She pulled out a couple of articles she'd printed from the Internet. "Here's what I found out about Peyton so far. She's involved in a relationship with Lily Gantry who just happens to be an oil heiress, but more importantly, her father is a Cyrus Gantry whose offices were recently raided by the feds."

"Okay, but what does any of this have to do with Dale Nelson and the DEA?" Alice asked.

"I don't know, but I do think it's weird that Dale's boss plucks her off a two-year-old task force investigation into the cartel to be our tour guide. Top that off with the fact that Dale was meeting with two AUSAs, and what I bet was some other federal agent at night, far from any of their offices. Something's going on and someone is going to great lengths to keep it secret. If my hunch is right, there's a way meatier story here than a bring us your prescription drugs program or dredging up the painful past of a DEA agent."

She took a deep breath and scanned Alice's and Jed's faces to see if they were with her or if they thought she was crazy. Jed was the first to speak. "Okay, I'm in. I've always had a hankering to be a Hardy boy. Not sure how my skills are going to help you unearth the truth, but I'll do what I can."

Lindsey smiled. "Thanks. If nothing else, you're providing cover for me to get this done without Elaina finding out what we're up to." She turned to Alice. "You in?"

Alice hesitated, and Lindsey prompted her to speak her mind.

"I get that you and Elaina have history, and she can be a bit of a..."

"Bitch?"

"Your word, but yeah, something like that," she said. "But is there some other reason you're not looping her in on all of this?"

Lindsey nodded. "Fair question. Elaina's working her own agenda on this piece, and I'm sure it's right in line with what the network wants: safe and sympathetic. If I tell her what I'm doing, she'll shut it down before we have a chance to see if this develops into anything."

"Fine, I'm in. Where should we start?"

"I called the US attorney's office this morning and found out AUSA Bianca Cruz has a hearing this morning." She consulted the notes on her phone. "Judge Niven's court. It was scheduled for nine o'clock, but the court clerk was kind enough to let me know that the judge had another pressing matter that meant his entire docket had been delayed. If we head there now, we might be able to catch her."

Alice smiled. "You really like to dive in, don't you?"

"No better way to get to the bottom of things."

❖

Dale sat in the booth and watched the friends and families of inmates assemble in the visitation room. Sophia was in the second group that entered the room. Unlike many of the other visitors, she looked composed and didn't appear to be overly curious about the room. Dale had been to this unit many times in the past to talk to defendants and snitches, but not from this vantage point. "How do I hear what's going on?"

"There are mics all around the room," the guard who'd introduced himself as Leo, told her. He pointed out a set of headphones on the counter in front of her. "Put those on and we can direct what mic you're getting input from once you see your mark. It won't be perfect, but you should be able to get a good idea of what's going on."

Dale put the headphones on and listened to the murmur of voices in the room. She'd debated figuring out a way to get Sophia to meet with Arturo in one of the plexiglass cubicles normally used for attorney-client meetings, but she'd decided that might arouse suspicion. She looked at the closed circuit screens that gave them a view of every angle in the room. Two of the walls were lined with vending machines featuring everything from candy and chips to soups and burritos. Visitors were allowed to bring in up to thirty dollars in quarters to purchase food for the inmates to consume during the visit, and she knew many of the inmates looked forward to the vending machine food more than the fellowship of their family.

A few minutes later, a line of men in orange jumpsuits filed into the room, accompanied by prison guards. She spotted Arturo Vargas right away. He looked around the room for a moment before his eyes finally settled on Sophia, and Dale caught just a hint of surprise in his eyes. She held her breath as she waited for his reaction. There was a chance he would refuse to see her.

She watched Sophia stride across the room. When she was within a foot of Arturo, she reached out both hands. One, two, three seconds passed, and finally Arturo grasped her hands and pulled her close. Dale saw them exchange whispered conversation as they hugged until a guard in the room barked at them to separate. Arturo shot the guard a feral grin before he and Sophia took a seat in the far corner of the room.

"They're over there," Dale said to the guard in the booth. "Can you hook me up?"

"Got it." He flipped a few switches on the control panel in front of him. "You should be able to hear them now."

Dale listened closely, filtering out the surrounding noise until she heard Sophia's voice. She gave the guard a thumbs-up and focused on the conversation between Sophia and her brother.

"You look surprised to see me," Sophia said.

"Do you blame me?" Arturo asked. "You've spent a lifetime betraying our good family name. First by giving birth to a bastard and then you set up your blood family with the feds. Surprise doesn't begin to cover what I feel."

"I was young and foolish. Surely, you wouldn't hold that against me for my entire life?"

"Your youth doesn't explain away recent events."

"You're in here because you showed up at my ranch, tried to steal my prize stallion, and threatened my daughter. I stood up against you to protect what is mine. What would you have done in my place?"

"Don't pretend to compare our places in the world. You chose the life of a kept woman while Sergio and I earn our way. The daughter you speak of isn't family—she will always belong to another world."

"That may be true, but she's my blood as much as you are, and I would do anything to keep her safe." She paused and stared hard at Arturo. "That's why I'm here. If you will guarantee her safety, I have a way we can help each other."

Dale watched Arturo glance around the room. Sophia was following their instructions about being purposely vague regarding the recent threats against Lily, since they believed Arturo was less likely to go along with her plan about the money if she hammered him on the subject. Plus any mention of violence in this not very private place could pique the interest of one of the guards. So far, Sophia sounded sincere to her ears, but she had no idea if her sociopath brother was buying what she had to say. The true test would come in a moment.

"I'm listening," Arturo said.

"My ranch is in dire financial straits. Recent events…" Sophia paused and cleared her throat. "Events I believe you are very much aware of have caused my usual funding sources to become unavailable."

"So? You have a winning horse and the opportunity to stud him for much money."

"Do you know how much it costs to operate the ranch? The purse Queen's Ransom won was spent before he earned it."

Arturo steepled his fingers and stared at a distant point on the wall as if he were completely disinterested in the conversation. "What do you want from me?"

"I thought we could help each other. I have a reputable business, but I need cash. You may need a reputable business to handle your cash. Don't make me say more."

At that moment, several other people settled into chairs near Sophia and Arturo, and the noise level grew. Dale strained to hang on to the threads of the conversation. When Arturo responded, his words were measured and his tone even.

"Don't worry," he said. "I have no desire to hear more from you. How dare you come here and try and entice me with problems of your own making. If you wanted to be a part of this family, you should have thought about that before you went to bed with him. You want help, you should go see him."

He stood up and Sophia followed suit. Then, to Dale's surprise, Arturo pulled Sophia into his arms. The embrace lasted several seconds before he broke away and walked toward one of the guards. Sophia looked down at the table as Arturo left the room.

"What the hell?"

The guard in the booth looked over at her. "What's up?"

"I'm not sure." She pointed at the screen that showed Sophia still seated at the table. "Are these units recording?"

"Yep."

"Any chance you could play back the last few minutes for me?"

"Sure, but it'll just be a visual. Sound is recorded separately." When she nodded, he reached over and flipped a few switches and the screen scrambled as the tape rewound.

She stopped him after about a minute. "Right there. Let it play from there." He showed her how to replay the tape and went back to his duties. Dale watched the final exchange between Arturo and Sophia again. First their back and forth with words, and then a moment later, their unexpected embrace. She replayed it three times before she caught the subtle hand signal from Arturo, delivered as he stood to leave. He'd motioned for her to come closer, and Dale was certain their hug was a cover for another whispered exchange.

Their arrangement had been for Sophia to leave on her own and meet up with Mary at the diner where they'd gathered that morning. Mary was supposed to do the debrief and fill them in later, but Dale knew she had to get to her as soon as possible. She let the tape play out to avoid drawing attention to the screen that had caught her attention, and she thanked the guards for their help and left. When she reached her truck, she picked up her phone and saw at least five missed calls from Diego and Lindsey, but she ignored them all and dialed Mary's number. When the call went straight to voice mail, she decided to take matters into her own hands.

CHAPTER FOURTEEN

Once they passed through security on the first floor of the federal building, Lindsey located the directory and ran her finger along the lines until she found the floor for Judge Niven's court. "Eight." She motioned to Alice and Jed. "Let's go."

When they emerged from the elevator on the eighth floor, Lindsey looked around for another sign to direct them to the courtroom.

"Excuse me, miss?"

She turned to the voice and spotted two older men dressed in charcoal gray slacks and blue blazers standing next to a metal detector just like the one they'd passed through downstairs. "Hi, we're looking for Judge Niven's court."

"What's your business here this morning?"

It had been a while since a story had led her to federal court, but the intricacies slowly came back to her. She pulled out her press pass. "We're just here to observe this morning's proceedings." She gestured to Jed and Alice. "They're with me." She watched as the taller man eyeballed Alice's and Jed's casual attire and then scanned her credentials.

He pulled out a plastic tray from underneath the desk. "I'll need to see everyone's ID, and phones and any other recording devices go in here. You can collect them when you leave."

Damn, she'd forgotten that little detail. What if Dale called her back? She was wrestling with what to do when a large group of people starting walking toward them, on the other side of the ID-checking, phone-grabbing gatekeepers who were holding her up. She recognized the man in the lead as Herschel Gellar, the US attorney. He was flanked by a tall, androgynous woman dressed in a suit that didn't quite hide the fact she was carrying a gun, and following close behind them were reporters calling out questions as Gellar strode down the hall. They were headed toward the elevators, and for a second she was torn between pursuing her original idea of looking for Bianca and following this press circus wherever it led.

She caught Alice's eye and made a snap judgment. "You two, go with them. I'll catch up with you in a bit." She handed over her phone and ID and waited impatiently for the marshal to check her in. A few minutes later, she slipped into Niven's courtroom and took a seat in the back row.

Bianca was at the podium, and Lindsey took the opportunity to assess the young attorney. She argued her position a little too fervently, but she appeared to be smart and well-versed in the facts. Experience would make her less eager and more jaded, but for now Lindsey planned to use her youth and inexperience to her advantage.

The hearing lasted the better part of an hour as each side called several witnesses in an attempt to convince the judge to suppress certain evidence in an upcoming trial. By the time it was over, Lindsey had a good feel for the best way to approach Bianca, and she lingered in the courtroom until Bianca was almost out the door.

"Ms. Cruz?"

Bianca turned toward her, and instantly, her face lit up with recognition. "Lindsey Ryan? What in the world are you doing here?"

Lindsey flashed what she hoped was a winning smile. "Hoping I could buy you a cup of coffee? Please tell me you have a well-deserved break coming after that beast of a hearing."

Bianca smiled. "Is this about the Take-Back Initiative?"

"In a way, yes. I'd love to get your perspective on the event." Lindsey delivered the half lie and hoped she sounded convincing. "Is there a place close where we could talk?"

Bianca hesitated for a moment, but then she acquiesced. "Sure. Let's take a walk."

Lindsey followed Bianca to the marshal's desk and retrieved her phone, and then the two of them rode down to the first floor. During the elevator ride, Lindsey glanced at her phone, but there was still no return call from Dale. She looked up and caught Bianca smiling.

"Busy day?" she asked.

"Always. I'm sure you understand."

"I do, but then I'm not in the limelight every day like you are. Must be different, always having to be camera ready."

"You'd be surprised how much of my job is pure drudge. Fact-checking, research. My on-camera time is only a sliver of the job. But, hey, how about you? I bet you wind up on camera with some of the cases you handle."

"Rarely. Federal judges almost never let cameras in the courtroom, and the office usually lets a spokesperson handle the press so we don't have to try to field questions on our own." Bianca's hand flew to her mouth and her face reddened. "Sorry, I didn't mean that exactly the way it sounded."

Lindsey offered up what she hoped was a bright and disarming smile. "I kinda think you did, but I won't tell. I get it. It's important to craft the message, and most agencies have people assigned to do just that." She paused for a minute and then whispered, "Although your boss probably doesn't like to go through a spokesperson."

Bianca's face wrinkled into a frown. "Peyton?"

Lindsey filed Bianca's response under things she would examine later and told a little white lie. "I'm not sure I know who that is. I was talking about Herschel Gellar."

"Oh. My boss's boss." She grinned. "You might be right about that. Good hunch."

"It was more than a hunch. I saw him wading through a pool of reporters on his way downstairs when I was on my way in to see you."

The elevator door pinged, and they stepped out into the lobby where Herschel Gellar was holding forth, still surrounded by reporters with Alice and Jed on the periphery. Bianca edged away from the crowd and Lindsey followed, although her instincts were divided on whether she would get better information watching Gellar or talking to Bianca. When they stepped out of the building, she tossed out a casual remark to get Bianca talking. "He likes to talk. Has he always been like that?"

Before Bianca could respond, another voice beat her to it. "Herschel Gellar would light himself on fire if it meant he could get time on camera."

Lindsey whirled around and sucked in a breath. Instead of her usual jeans and T-shirt, Dale was wearing gray wool slacks and a pale blue, button down shirt. Shiny black alligator boots replaced the Ropers she usually wore, and her normally ruffled hair was combed into some semblance of order. She looked delicious.

"Wow. Look at you, all dressed up." The words tumbled out before she could stop them, and Lindsey risked a quick glance at Bianca's face to see if she'd registered anything off. But Bianca didn't seem to be paying any attention to her; instead, she was mouthing words at Dale. Lindsey looked back and forth between them and said, "Am I interrupting something?"

Bianca's face flushed red and Dale pulled her aside, tossing a simple, "We'll be right back," over her shoulder as they walked a good distance away. Lindsey watched their conversation, punctuated by various hand gestures, but as hard as she tried, she couldn't hear a word they were saying, which, though frustrating, left her free to stare unabashedly at Dale.

She looked camera-ready. Had she had a change of heart about doing the interview? If so, why hadn't she returned one of the dozen calls or texts from this morning? She glanced at her phone. If Dale was ready and willing, she should get in touch with Alice and Jed right now, but a wave of caution flooded her brain and kept her from thumbing the words to summon them.

The minute she sat across from Dale with the camera trained on them, any chance this smoldering attraction might spark into something more meaningful would be extinguished. She shouldn't care, and the list of reasons why was exponential, but the top two were the biggies: Dale was a widow, still grieving her loss, and Lindsey had never let her personal life get in between her and a story. She'd never regretted the latter before, but right now she couldn't help but feel a stinging sense of loss.

Dale had a hunch Lindsey was staring at them, and when she turned back around, her suspicion was confirmed. The brief jump of exhilaration she'd felt when Lindsey had commented on her appearance had leveled out and now she was on alert. "What's she doing here?" she asked Bianca.

"I'm not sure. I think I was about to find out when you dragged me away. Did this morning go as planned? Any idea when you know who will be meeting up with the other you know who?"

Dale shook her head at Bianca's attempt to be clandestine. "On the surface, it looked and sounded like Arturo rejected Sophia out of hand."

"But?"

"But I think there was more to it than that. He said something to her at the end of her visit that I couldn't hear, and she's MIA. She didn't show at the diner, and Mary hasn't heard from her and our calls are going to voice mail. I was hoping you'd heard something. I've been trying to reach you."

"Oh crap." Bianca pulled her phone out of her briefcase and looked at the screen. "I had it off because I was in court, and then..."

"And then you got distracted by a reporter."

"She's pretty distracting. Emphasis on pretty."

Dale couldn't help but glance over her shoulder at Lindsey who was pretending not to try to listen in to their conversation. Pretty wasn't the word she'd use. Lindsey was storm and shadows. Dangerously attractive, yet like many dangerous things, her allure was strong. "Be careful. You can't let her get too close."

Bianca raised an eyebrow, but didn't question the warning. "So, what's the plan to track down Sophia?"

"Mary's working on it. I don't think it's a good idea for us to show up at Sophia's place in case she's being watched." She jerked her chin in Lindsey's direction. "I'm supposed to spend the rest of the day selling my soul for a news cycle, but I want to fill Peyton in."

"She's at the ranch today. Pretty sure Lily's there with her."

"Thanks for the warning about that. At some point we're going to have to take off the gloves and start fighting anyone who is working against us. No matter who they are related to."

"Agreed, but I think I'll let you get things started. I'm headed back to the office." Bianca cast a wistful expression at Lindsey. "Tell Wondergirl I'm sorry I had to run."

Dale watched Bianca duck back inside the building and then turned to face Lindsey.

"Are you going to run off everyone I need to talk to or just the important ones?" Lindsey asked.

"Whatever you needed to ask her, you can ask me."

"Really. Are you sure about that?"

Dale detected the undercurrent of disbelief. She knew she'd given Lindsey plenty of reason to doubt she'd be cooperative, but maybe it was time to surrender. She could give the interview, answer all the questions Lindsey or anyone else had about Maria, and be done with it, once and for all. She could almost hear Maria telling her it was the most expedient, painless thing to do. "I'm sure, but here's the thing. I have something I have to do today. Let's have dinner tonight. You can ask me anything you want and, if you think it's newsworthy, I'll give you the on-camera interview after the event tomorrow." She offered what she hoped was a humble expression. "I'll be less distracted then. Deal?"

Lindsey narrowed her eyes for a minute like she expected Dale to yank away the generous offer she'd just extended, but then her features settled into one of her famous broadcast smiles. "Deal."

After settling on a place to meet for dinner, Dale walked to her truck. She should be focused on finding Sophia and figuring out if she was really on board with the plan to catch Sergio or if she was trying to play them, but all she could think about was Lindsey and whether she ever used that smile for personal use.

CHAPTER FIFTEEN

W hat's the plan?" Alice asked.
Lindsey looked up from her iPad and fumbled for a response. They'd just left the courthouse, and she had nothing for her efforts other than a tacit agreement from Dale to relay her story. And a dinner date.

No, it wasn't a date. A date was personal, a lead-in to something more intimate. Dale's story might be intimate, but it wasn't going to lead to more. Not with her anyway. She shouldn't care, but she did.

Alice and Jed hadn't fared much better. All they'd been able to glean from listening to Herschel Gellar's press junket was that he planned to exile Cyrus Gantry to the gates of hell for using his business as a cover for drug money. He'd said it a dozen different ways, but it all came down to the same grandstanding promise to impose loads of prison time and lots of restitution.

The whole thing seemed off. Gellar had practically frothed at the mouth when it came to Gantry. Seemed like he'd focus his vitriol on the violent drug lords instead of the otherwise upstanding businessman. Lindsey had a sense there was something else at play, and she wondered if last night's out in the country law enforcement meeting had anything to do with it.

They spent the rest of the morning doing what Lindsey called filler work—necessary, but boring. They filmed shots at various venues with Lindsey doing the back from break spots that would be aired after the show returned from commercial breaks. When they'd arrived at the studio at noon, Elaina was apoplectic when she learned Dale wasn't going to show up.

"She'll give the interview after the event tomorrow," Lindsey said.

"What if she changes her mind?"

"She won't." Lindsey injected her voice with all the confidence she could muster, but Elaina's question planted a tiny seed of doubt. What if Dale was putting her off, thinking that once tomorrow's event was over, she could duck the obligation without fallout?

She knew Dale didn't want to do the interview, but she didn't think Dale would break a promise. Lindsey smiled as she remembered one of those promises was dinner tonight, and she got so lost in the fantasy of what might happen if it weren't a work thing that she had to ask Elaina to repeat her next comment.

"I was thinking tonight we could go over the interview questions," Elaina said. "I could order room service and we could work in my room."

Lindsey recognized the tone in her voice and the glint in her eyes. A stint of late nights on location spent "working in the room" had been the genesis of their relationship. Did Elaina think they could just pick up where they left off or was she looking for a no-strings attached fling? Either way, Lindsey wasn't interested. If she were going to break her rule about mixing work with pleasure it wasn't going to be with her ex, but she didn't want to hurt her feelings either. "Actually, since tomorrow's going to be a long day, I think I'll just spend tonight putting my thoughts together and we can talk after the event, but before I interview Agent Nelson. Okay?"

It wasn't a complete lie. Dale had said she would answer any of her questions at dinner, and she could think of no better prep for an on camera interview than full disclosure.

❖

Dale didn't call before she drove out to the ranch. She didn't want to believe that Lily or Peyton were sheltering Sophia, but her instincts told her it was better to be cautious. People were funny when it came to family. When the door opened in response to her knock, she didn't recognize the face of the young man that answered, but she knew he had to be a Davis. He was a younger, male version of Peyton. "May I help you?"

"Dale Nelson. I'm here to see Peyton."

"Hi, I'm Zach, Peyton's brother. Come on in. You thirsty?"

Dale strode into the house. "Sure. Water's fine." She followed him to the kitchen and waited while he fetched a metal tumbler from the cabinet and filled it with cold water from a pitcher in the fridge. "Thanks," she said when he handed it to her. "You look a lot more like your sister than Neil."

"True. We get along a lot better too. You're the agent who arrested Neil, aren't you?"

"Arrested is a strong word. Let's just say I found him in a bit of trouble. It's not like he's in jail or anything." She downed the rest of her water. "What's he up to lately?"

Zach grinned. "Working his ass off. Dad has him doing double duty. Probably to keep him out of Peyton's hair."

"How is your dad?"

The smile dimmed. "Not great, but he's happy to be here at home. We have a nurse come by every couple of days, which he doesn't like, but to be honest, I'm not sure he remembers her once she leaves."

Dale nodded. She couldn't imagine watching one of her parents dying a slow death, let alone having to deal with the added challenge of Alzheimer's. "He's lucky to have family to take care of him and a nice place to be."

"We do the best we can, considering everything."

He didn't have to say more. "Probably helps to have your sister back in town," Dale said.

Peyton strode into the room at that moment. "Don't answer that, Zach," she said with a smile. "Whatever you say, she'll hold it against me."

"Don't worry, sis. I've got your back." He looked between them. "I suppose you have important things to discuss, and I have an appointment with a horse. See you later. Nice to meet you, Dale."

After he cleared the room, Dale asked, "Where have you been hiding him?"

"Mom sent him to check out some stud horses in New Mexico. I think she was just trying to keep him out of the way with everything that's going on. He's always been a big fan of Neil's, and now he's not really sure what to think."

"Got it. This whole ordeal has been hard on your family. And Lily's." She cleared her throat to segue into the reason for her visit. "Speaking of which, I need to talk to you about our plan."

"I called Bianca and she said she didn't think Arturo went for it."

"I told her to tell you that."

"Come again?"

"I watched the whole exchange. Arturo did tell Sophia to get lost, loud enough for everyone to hear, but then he whispered something to her and she's suddenly AWOL. I don't suppose you've spoken with her?"

Dale didn't have to wait long for a reaction. Peyton shoved back from the table and stood. "What are you implying?"

"Not a damn thing, but here's the deal. They had a conversation that no one else could hear and she's ducking our calls."

"Maybe she's in trouble. Did you ever think about that?"

"Actually, that's the first thing I thought so I sent Mary to check things out. Sophia's at her ranch and going about her business like nothing ever happened."

"Why didn't Mary ask her what's going on?"

"Because I told her to keep her distance and report any unusual activity. We may not be the only ones with eyes on her. If my hunch is right, I bet Sergio has someone watching her ranch."

"So, now you're spying on Lily's mother after she did what you asked."

"If she wasn't Lily's mother would you even care?"

Peyton's expression was pained. "I'm sorry. You're right. I guess the lines are getting a bit blurred. Do you want me to try and reach her?"

"No, let's just keep an eye on her for the next twenty-four hours and see if anything develops. I only came out here to give you a chance to come clean if you have the inside scoop." Dale grinned. "I guess those blurry lines are contagious."

"Thanks, pal. If I hear from Sophia, you'll be the first one I tell. Okay?"

Dale stood up. "Okay, but don't let Lily go out there."

"Not a chance."

"How's Lily handling all of this?"

"Better than me. She's made of steel."

"I'm glad you found each other. Sorry it's so complicated."

"The things that are worth it usually are."

Dale played Peyton's words over in her head on the way back to Dallas. Life with Maria had been complicated at first as they negotiated the uncertain terrain of careers that came with an element of danger. But as time progressed, the strength of their bond made even the most complex situations seem surmountable when they tackled them together. She couldn't even imagine a new relationship. She'd probably spend all her time trying to replicate what she'd had while the other person tried to build something from scratch.

She knew all this thinking about a new relationship was prompted by her undeniable attraction to Lindsey, but she also knew attraction didn't a marriage make. Lindsey would finish up her story tomorrow and head back to New York where she belonged. She, on the other hand, would stay right here and keep doing the same old things. Eventually, she would be content with memories to comfort her for the rest of her life.

Lindsey tossed the dress on the bed and pulled another from her hotel room closet. She was supposed to meet Dale at the restaurant in thirty minutes, and she was running out of options. A knock on the door blasted her ability to think clearly. She cinched the tie of her robe and walked over to look out the peephole to see Alice waiting outside. She swung open the door. "Whatcha need?"

"Elaina said you'll be taping with Dale after the event tomorrow. Do you plan to do it onsite or back at the studio?"

"What do you recommend?"

Alice glanced at the pile of clothes on the bed. "Hot date?"

"What?"

"You're not one of those I have to wear the perfect thing for the camera girls, so I figured this clothing volcano must be due to a hot date."

"Well, you'd be wrong."

"Right. Let me guess. You'll be dining with a certain Special Agent Nelson this evening."

"I'm conducting a pre-interview over dinner. You know, to be disarming." Lindsey tried not to flinch at her own disingenuousness.

"Pre-interview. Is that what you're calling it?" Alice shrugged. "Fine. She's totally not my type, but there's something about her. She's all mysterious and law-and-order. Makes you want to get under her skin."

Lindsey looked away to hide the smile on her face. Alice had nailed it. Almost. She didn't want to get under Dale's skin; she wanted to rub up against it. But that wouldn't be happening. Not tonight, not ever. She'd get her tell-all tale tomorrow, and on Sunday she and the rest of the crew would be on a plane, back to New York.

New York, where she no longer had a place to live. A flash of melancholy told her it might be time to find a new home. She couldn't toss her sublet out for another six months, but she could find something new. Something more permanent than the one-room loft she'd used as a stopover on her way in and out of town for the past couple of years, a place that looked very much like Dale's apartment.

Dale. Lindsey looked at her watch. She was blowing through her get-ready time and Alice was standing there staring at her, waiting. "What did you just say?"

"I said I recommend doing the interview on location. Jed and I already scoped it out and found a few places that would work. I assume you want kind of an intimate feel, but realistic."

Right. The interview. She dreaded dragging Dale through the experience—a sure sign she was going soft. When this week had started, she was all about the story, and now she was letting her personal feelings get in the way. Dale Nelson was just one of many people she'd interviewed who had experienced tragedy. Now that she was committed to telling Dale's story, she had a duty to dig deep, to be impartial. Or fake it as best she could. For now she settled on faking it.

"On location it is. Now, I've got to run. I'll see you bright and early tomorrow morning."

The minute Alice left the room, Lindsey grabbed the dress on top of the pile on her bed, refusing to agonize over the decision any longer. What she was wearing tonight was the least of her worries. Her primary mission was to get as close to the facts as possible while still keeping her distance. The way her heart beat faster every time Dale walked into the room, she'd need every ounce of skill she possessed to strike that balance.

Dale was explaining to the hostess at Bob's Steak and Chophouse that she was still waiting for the rest of her party when she felt a tap on her shoulder. She turned to find Lindsey standing behind her, dressed in a stunning green dress that made her hazel eyes sparkle and pop.

Whoa. Trained as she was to notice the most minute details about a person's appearance, sparkling eyes had never been an attribute she'd included in her reports on the job. Meeting Lindsey like this, after hours, at a restaurant, with no escape plan was probably a very bad idea.

"You look nice," Lindsey said.

"I'm wearing the same clothes I had on this morning."

Lindsey looked her up and down. "Yes, and you look as good in them now as you did this morning."

"I guess jeans and T-shirts aren't your thing." Dale wished she could bite back the question. Why should she care about what Lindsey thought about her wardrobe?

"Not true. You're one of those people who look good in everything, but I have to admit the black T-shirt, Levi's, and boots ensemble is my personal favorite."

Dale felt the heat of a blush curl up her neck. Okay, so she cared, but she shouldn't. Time to steer this conversation in a different direction. She signaled to the hostess that she was ready to be seated, and the next few minutes spent walking to the table and looking through the menu were a welcome reprieve.

"What's good here?" Lindsey asked.

"Steak."

"How about the fish?"

Dale put her menu down. "Steak. You're in a landlocked city. The waiter will tell you they fly the fish in fresh daily, but fish weren't meant to fly. You want fish, you go to the ocean. You come to Texas, you order beef. It's easy."

"I suppose it's a good thing I'm not a vegetarian."

"Actually, the sides here are amazing, so you'd be safe."

"Should we order some wine?"

"You're buying. Order what you want."

"Why are you making this hard? You know I'm asking if you want some."

Dale set her menu down. She did want wine, lots of it. Anything to reduce the anxiety that was making her crazy. "I'll have a glass of whatever you're having."

Lindsey cocked her head. "I can't tell if you're being agreeable because you feel agreeable or if you're just trying to get through this as quickly as possible."

Dale couldn't help but smile at Lindsey's keen insight. "With your sharp mind, maybe you should be a federal agent."

"Not a chance."

"That's pretty definitive."

Before Lindsey could respond, their waiter came by to take their orders. They both ordered steaks, and Lindsey spent a few minutes quizzing the waiter about the wine list. When he finally left, Dale was ready to move on to other subjects, but Lindsey jumped right back into the conversation where they'd left off.

"Not that there's anything wrong with what you do," Lindsey said. "But don't you have a lot of rules? I'm kind of allergic to too many rules."

"Is that why you got called back from Afghanistan?"

"Someone's done her homework."

Dale shifted in her seat. She had. In the couple of hours before she'd shown up at the restaurant, she'd spent some time looking at reruns of *Spotlight America* to see coverage of the time that Lindsey was embedded with Army and Marine Corps units, and something had happened that she hadn't counted on. She'd been impressed. Lindsey had a knack for getting the soldiers to open up and share the emotions that accompanied their experiences in a way that appeared effortless for both the interviewer and interviewee.

But then Dale watched the coverage of the time Lindsey had spent with General Tyson. Lindsey had spared no effort to portray Tyson as a ruthless bastard, completely disloyal to the president who'd appointed him. "I've watched some of your reports from Afghanistan."

"I sense you have an opinion about my work. Care to share your impressions?"

Dale started to brush her off, but Lindsey's earnest expression told her she really wanted to know. "Okay. Well, it seems to me for all your talk about objective journalism, you inject a lot of your own opinion into your stories."

"Is that so?"

Was that a hint of defensiveness she heard? Dale decided to ignore it. Lindsey had asked the question and she was going to get an answer for no other reason than Dale wanted to know the why behind it. "Yes. You oppose the war, but you respect the soldiers who are there to fight. You delve into their personal stories and relay them with compassion. But when it came to General Tyson, you were ruthless. You didn't even try to cast him in a positive light. You don't approve of his aggressive style and desire to keep us engaged in the region and you made it clear in every frame of that interview."

The waiter returned at that moment with the bottle of wine. Dale watched impatiently while he poured a small portion into

Lindsey's glass. She was anxious to hear Lindsey's response, but Lindsey seemed to be stalling. She swirled the wine in her glass and held it up to the light before taking a drink and swishing it around in her mouth. Finally, Lindsey smiled her approval at the waiter and he poured them each a glass, but before he could leave, she said, "Do you mind if I ask you a question that has absolutely nothing to do with the food or wine?"

He raised an eyebrow. "Sounds intriguing."

"First off, what's your name?"

"Jonas."

"Okay, Jonas. What's your opinion about the troop drawdown in Afghanistan? Is it happening fast enough or should we keep a presence there for the indefinite future?"

Dale sighed. "I'm sure Jonas has better things to do than debate you on international relations."

"Let's hear what his opinion is before we decide if there's going to be a debate. Jonas?"

"I think it's time for our troops to come home. Hell, everyone I know thinks the same thing. I mean—hey, aren't you Lindsey Ryan? I watch you on TV all the time. I love your show."

His voice rose with his last remark, and several patrons at nearby tables turned to look their way. Lindsey did her best to hide a grimace, but she had only herself to blame for letting an intimate evening with Dale turn into a very public display. While she fumbled for what to say, she saw Dale crook her finger and motion for Jonas to come closer.

"Jonas, she is definitely the Lindsey Ryan you see on TV, but she's having a rare night off and we're relying on you to ensure our privacy." Dale handed him a folded bill. "I know you'll do a great job."

Jonas glanced at the bill in his hand. "Absolutely, Ms. Ryan. Not to worry." And then he was gone.

"I thought he'd never leave," Dale said.

"You're just mad that he agreed with me."

"Nine out of ten people would say they want all the troops to come home, but they don't understand the intricacies of the situation.

You know as well as I do how unstable the region is when we're not there and it's not a simple matter of pulling out. Besides, your pal Jonas was stumbling all over himself from the first moment he saw you. He would have agreed with anything you said."

"Too bad I don't have that affect on you." Lindsey wanted to pull the words back the moment she spoke, but now that they were out there, she waited eagerly for Dale's response.

"If you didn't, this whole process might be a hell of a lot easier."

Dale delivered the words and immediately picked up her wine glass and took a deep drink. Was her hand shaking slightly? Lindsey played the words back in her head several times to make sure she'd heard correctly. Had Dale just admitted she was attracted to her or had she misunderstood?

Ask her, dammit. Lindsey locked eyes with Dale, but she didn't ask for clarification. She couldn't. If she did, then this conversation was sure to take a completely different direction than its intended purpose.

The irony wasn't lost on her. She was here to ask personal questions, but this line of questioning was completely off limits if she wanted to get the story she came for. Whatever she said next would set the course for what lay ahead: giving in to the attraction between them or giving her all to deliver a hard-hitting human interest piece. She knew what she wanted, but she didn't know how to choose, so she did what she knew best and stuck with the story. "Tell me about Maria Escobar."

A few beats of silence passed between them, and then Dale took a deep breath. "Tell me what you want to know."

She wasn't going to make this easy. "Tell me how you met."

A smile flickered across Dale's face and then settled into an earnest expression. "We met in the service. She was the prosecutor and I was her key witness. I'd arrested a private for driving while intoxicated."

"I guess that professional conflict didn't keep you from forming a personal relationship."

"Is that a question?" Dale asked.

"Maybe it was just an observation." Lindsey didn't like where this was going, but she'd started it, so it was up to her to get things back on track. "I assume you started dating later, you know, after you were no longer her key witness."

"Sure, that sounds right."

Lindsey heard a ringing sound and watched as Dale reached under the table and pulled her phone out of her pocket. "Do you need to get that?"

Dale frowned at the screen and touched it with her thumb. "No. Sorry, I thought I'd put it on vibrate." She set the phone facedown next to her wine glass and folded her hands on the table. "Next question."

This wasn't working. Dale was poised and ready, like she'd prepped to tell all the details of her personal life, but the preparation robbed the telling of any vibrancy. When they got around to filming tomorrow, the result would be a dried up version of Dale's story of loss, devoid of emotion unless she could figure out a way to catch her off guard. The truth was she didn't want to talk about Dale's past at all, not right now anyway. Not while they were enjoying a nice dinner that had started to feel an awfully lot like a date.

Jonas showed up at that moment to deliver their food, and they spent the next several minutes engaged in conversation about regular dinner table topics like their favorite foods, what they liked to read and watch on TV. When they were done and the plates were cleared, Jonas reappeared to ask if they wanted dessert. Lindsey deferred to Dale.

"I couldn't eat another bite, but if you'd like to keep talking how about we take a walk?"

After they settled the bill, they walked outside. The restaurant was in the convention center hotel, and there didn't appear to be much going on on that side of downtown after dark. Lindsey caught Dale looking at her high-heeled boots. "You like my boots?"

"I was just wondering how comfortable they are."

"Trust me, I've walked miles in these babies. I won't slow you down."

For the next few moments they walked in silence through the dark, cool night. A few blocks away from the hotel, Dale switched to the curb side of the street and looped their arms together. Lindsey saw the reason a few feet away as they came up on a huddle of homeless men on the opposite sidewalk, but when Dale continued to hold her arm for the rest of the walk, she wondered if the gallant touch meant something more.

"Do you have more questions?" Dale asked.

She did have a ton of questions prepared for the interview tomorrow, but right now, leaning into Dale's side, walking the streets like lovers enjoying a nighttime stroll, she didn't want to ask any of them. If she was going to ask questions they were going to be things she wanted to know. "Why did you decide to become a DEA agent?"

"Not a very interesting story."

They came to a park and Dale motioned to a bench. Lindsey sat down next to her and said, "Tell me anyway."

"I come from a family of cops. It was kind of expected."

"But you like it."

"Yes. What about you?" Dale asked. "Why did you become a reporter?"

"There are a bunch of reasons, but one is that I like to tell people's stories."

"Even when they don't want you to?"

"Are we talking about you?" Lindsey asked.

"Not necessarily. Forget I said that. What are the other reasons?"

Dale shifted on the bench and stretched her arm along the back of the seat. When she turned toward her, the light from the nearby lamppost illuminated her smile and her full, luscious, kissable lips. Suddenly, the night was no longer cool, and Lindsey lost the train of the conversation because all she could think about was the press of Dale's hand against her back and how much she wanted to kiss her. "Reasons?"

"The other reasons you wanted to become a reporter?"

Okay, she could do this. "You'll laugh."

"I won't."

"You will because it sounds corny."

"Tell me."

"To root out the truth." Lindsey watched as a flicker of a grin crossed Dale's lips. "See, you're laughing."

Dale held her hand to her chest. "I'm not. I swear. Okay, maybe a little. So, here's a test. What are you thinking right now—tell me the truth."

Lindsey wavered. She shouldn't. Dale was a subject. She didn't mix business with pleasure. But here they were, sitting on a park bench, talking about the kind of things she imagined real people talked about on a first date. She knew the next step, even if she knew she shouldn't take it. Before she could think it to death, she leaned in and touched her lips to Dale's.

They were as soft and firm as she'd imagined, and she swooned as Dale pulled her closer and deepened the kiss. She had no idea how much time passed before they broke for breath, but when they did, she was heady with want.

Dale's phone buzzed again. She didn't take it out of her pocket, but she stood and extended her hand. "We should get back," she said.

Lindsey took her hand and held it as they walked back to the restaurant. She wanted to ask more questions, but all she could think about was the kiss. She shouldn't have done it, but now that she had, she wanted another. Maybe she could invite Dale back to her room for a drink. No, that was a bad idea. If Elaina saw them, she'd go ballistic. They could go to Dale's place. Her mind whirred with possibilities, but they all ended with more kissing.

They were back at the valet stand. Dale handed her ticket to the valet. "Do you need a cab?" she asked.

Now was the moment. She started to say, no, I want to go home with you, but Dale's phone buzzed again. She watched while Dale pulled it out of her pocket and her eyes moved across the screen. "Is something wrong?"

Dale looked up, and her face was an unreadable mask. "I have to go."

Lindsey saw the valet pull up in Dale's truck, and she felt the tender passion of their evening slipping away. She reached for Dale's arm. "Take me with you."

Dale stepped back. "Not a chance," she said, and this time her voice had a distinct edge.

Lindsey watched helplessly as Dale climbed into her truck and sped away. She had no idea what had just happened. She replayed the last few minutes in her mind, over and over, but all she came up with was a few key facts—Dale was pissed off, she'd begged Dale to stay, and Dale had refused—none of which boded well for whatever was going to happen the next day.

"Is everything okay?"

Lindsey looked up to see the valet standing next to her. She asked for a cab and prayed it came quickly. Whatever had happened between her and Dale tonight was over. It was time to stop wanting things she couldn't have and focus on doing her job.

❖

Dale sped away from the restaurant, more angry with herself than Lindsey. She'd lost her focus, and she needed to know what kind of damage she caused. She glanced at the text she'd received again. *The car you asked about was rented by Spotlight America.* Damn. She punched a number into her phone. Andrea DeJesus picked up on the first ring.

"Dale, you got my text?"

"I did, but I wanted to hear it directly from you."

"Okay, well, I did some checking around about that plate you called in."

"And?"

"Enterprise rented it to Elaina Beall. She's the producer for that piece I gave the interview for earlier this week. You know, *Spotlight America*? Remember, down at the police station earlier this week?"

Dale remembered all right, but all she cared about now was why a car rented by the producer who was working with Lindsey had turned up at Peyton's ranch. "Do you have a copy of the paperwork?"

"No, but I'm sure I can get it."

"Don't. I was just curious," Dale said, struggling to keep her voice even. "I appreciate the heads up, but I'm sure it's nothing."

She was lying, but she had no desire to involve Andrea more. She was certain she'd led Lindsey and maybe her entire crew, to Peyton's doorstep no doubt looking for a juicy story. Several events from the last few days flashed through her mind stoking her suspicion, including Lindsey showing up at her apartment the night she'd spotted the car outside the ranch and Lindsey poking around the federal courthouse the morning Gellar was in court on Cyrus Gantry's case. For all she knew the coverage of tomorrow's Take-Back event was a cover to allow Lindsey and her team to poke around and see if they could find a salacious scandal to garner higher ratings.

She could barely contain her anger, and most of it was directed at herself for putting the task force work in jeopardy. Whatever this was between her and Lindsey had caused her to drop her guard, but it wouldn't happen again. Not a chance.

CHAPTER SIXTEEN

Lindsey stared at her face in the mirror and wondered if there was enough makeup in the world to cover the bags under her eyes. She'd finally given up on sleep at five a.m. and ordered coffee from room service which had only served to make her jittery.

The programming portion of the Take-Back event was scheduled for three o'clock, so she had all day to dread it. Most of her interviews were already in the can, and today was mostly about capturing some live moments for the show, including the cornerstone interview with Dale. Any time now, Elaina was going to knock on her door to go over the questions she'd prepared, and Lindsey would have to admit Dale wasn't going to show up.

As if she'd summoned it, she heard a few sharp knocks and looked through the peephole to see Alice standing outside. She swung open the door. "Come in. Thank God it's you."

"You look like hell."

"You're supposed to tell me you can put some special gel on the camera to make me look amazing."

"I can only do so much."

"You're a big help."

Alice made a show of looking around. "So, I guess your hot date went well. She still here?"

Lindsey threw a towel at her. "No hot date and no one was here last night."

"Right."

"I'm serious. In fact, serious is all I have right now. I'm pretty sure Dale isn't showing up today."

"We don't need her to cover the event," Alice said, her tone unconcerned. "It sounds like it's going to be a glorified school assembly."

"I'm talking about for the exclusive interview after."

"What happened?"

"I'm not sure. I took her to dinner and I started asking questions I should've held for the interview, but I didn't want to catch her completely off guard. Maybe it was too much. Anyway, I thought everything was going great, but then she got a text and she couldn't ditch me fast enough."

"She got a text? Duh, it was probably work."

Lindsey knew that was the easiest explanation, but she couldn't help but think it was something more. Dale's tone, her entire demeanor had signaled she was angry, and the anger was directed at her.

She'd let her personal feelings get in the way of her reporting, and now she had no story. Not one with any meat anyway. When Elaina found out Dale had bailed, she was going to throw a fit. She could deal with Elaina's anger, but she wasn't in the mood for a call from Larry and threats to her autonomy to investigate other stories.

Maybe there was a solution to this. "Hey, you have time to do a little digging with me before we head downtown? I still think there's another, more important story, based on what we saw at Peyton Davis's ranch, and I want to run down some leads. See if you can get Jed to run interference with Elaina while we check it out."

"Sure. I don't have a lot of setup to do because the local studio is doing most of the legwork for the event. My only job is to get you on tape. I'll go get my stuff and be right back."

Lindsey smiled. She was back on track. She'd get her story in spite of Dale.

❖

"I'm not doing it." Dale paced Diego's office and slammed her fist into her palm to emphasize the point.

"Look," he said. "I get it. You've sacrificed more than most. If it wasn't really important, I'd say to hell with them, but I need you to do this interview. Do it and you'll get a letter in your jacket."

"Since when does the agency offer bribes to get agents to talk to the press?"

"It's not a bribe. Can you sit down for a minute? You're giving me a headache with all the walking around."

Dale compromised by standing still, but she had too much pent up energy to take a seat. She'd been keyed up since she'd left Lindsey the night before. Instead of going home, she'd driven out to the Circle Six and done a couple of loops around the property in her truck. She didn't have a clue what she expected to find, but she needed some reassurance that no one was spying on Peyton. The exercise had been in vain because she didn't feel better for not finding anyone. The absence of a threat didn't mean it wasn't real.

She'd finally managed to get a couple of hours of restless sleep, and she'd woken up resolved to take control of things. She called Diego to let him know she had to meet with him this morning, and she'd shown up with a head full of questions and a heart full of mixed emotions. "I don't get why this interview is so important."

"It's a trade-off."

"Come again?"

"You give them some heart-wrenching story about your life, and Operation Discreet is off limits. They won't ask about it. They won't mention it. It's like it never happened."

And just like that, she realized she was being sacrificed for the good of the agency, and her lifetime of duty meant they expected her to go along without question. Once upon a time, their expectation would have been spot-on, but she was beginning to tire of the politics that got in the way of good police work. "That's bullshit. That story broke months ago. Why would they even want to resurrect it now? If you're going to sell me out at least get something good in return."

"Dale, it wasn't me. I'm just passing along the directive. If you decide not to go along, I get it, but I can't promise I can protect you from the fallout."

The only fallout she cared about was the pain of having to sit across from Lindsey Ryan and bare her soul. Last night when she'd been on the precipice of asking Lindsey back to her place, but the text from DeJesus had erected steel walls around her heart. Now that she knew Lindsey had her own secret agendas, Dale wouldn't trust her with a grocery list.

She glanced at her watch, eight o'clock. DEA agents and local cops were staked out at various community centers around the metroplex getting ready to collect prescription discards. The ceremony commemorating the event was scheduled for three p.m. If she gave in, her interview for *Spotlight America* would take place immediately after. The time would fly by, but the reality was she had hours to make her decision. "I've got some stuff to do. I'll see you downtown."

She didn't wait for his protests. What was he going to do—threaten her more?

Back in her car, she dialed Mary's number.

She answered on the first ring. "Hey, Nelson, aren't you supposed to be babysitting today?"

"Today and every day. I've got some free time this morning. Can we meet?"

"Sure, but you may not want to make the drive. I'm staked out on Sophia's ranch—just relieved one of the local cops I bribed into helping. Still not a word from her."

A stakeout sounded like exactly what she needed to pass the time. "Text me your location and I'll see you there."

The drive to Valencia Acres took the better part of an hour. Dale zoomed by the turnoff from the highway and drove a mile down the road, following Mary's directions, almost missing the second turnoff that was surrounded by a dense thicket. She drove the rocky, dirt road about fifty feet before she spotted Mary's SUV and parked right up against it, cursing the tree branches that were scraping the sides of her truck. She jumped down and was looking for the bridle path Mary had told her to follow when she heard a loud whisper and looked up to see Mary standing a few feet away.

"I thought I was supposed to meet you near the horse stables."

"I got tired of waiting on your sorry ass. Besides, Sophia's out riding so I doubled back here to meet you."

"I wish we could put a real team on this job. She might be meeting someone about Sergio. Hell, she might be meeting Sergio."

"Or she could be just going for a ride. Pretty sure she does that most days."

"I know you think I'm being overly suspicious, but I wish you could've seen her with Arturo yesterday. There was some connection there. One he didn't want anyone to notice. If nothing happened then why didn't she show up at the diner or return any of our calls?"

Mary shrugged. "I don't know, but I can tell you that it's been a dead zone around here. Aside from a hay delivery, not a lot of action here at the OK Corral. If you stay here long you'll probably fall asleep before your big interview."

"Not too sure that's going to happen." Dale kicked some dirt with the toe of her boot. "I had a meeting with Diego this morning. Basically, he told me if I don't give the interview it could be bad for the agency and there might be consequences."

Mary put a hand on her shoulder. "Fuck him. Pretty sure you've already suffered the worst consequences. He can't make you do it."

He couldn't, but he had appealed to the one thing she'd always been able to rely on. Duty. Her whole life she'd let the obligations of duty invade her personal life, but she owed no duty to Lindsey and *Spotlight America*, and she was beginning to wonder how much allegiance she owed to the job.

"I bet she's back from her ride now," Mary said. "You ready to check things out?"

"You bet." Work, real work. That's what she needed to get past this feeling that she didn't have control over her own destiny.

Dale followed Mary along the wooded path until the barn rose into sight. She'd been at the property the day Arturo had held Sophia and Lily at gunpoint. Based on what she'd seen then, she found it hard to believe Sophia would willingly conspire with Arturo outside of the job they'd sent her to do, but she'd seen stranger things. Family had a way of making people form strange alliances.

Mary pulled out a pair of binoculars and handed them to her. "You can get a pretty good view of the horse stables and the front porch of the house from here. If you look to the left, you'll see her car. She's got a pickup too, but she only uses it on the property."

"How're we going to know if she's back from her ride?"

Mary pointed to the building that housed the stables. "She changed into riding boots outside and left her tennis shoes sitting right outside the door. They're still there, aren't they?"

Dale looked through the strong lens and confirmed the tennis shoes were still in place. "You should be a detective."

"I'm thinking about it." Mary leaned against a tree and folded her arms. "You know, if you were a good friend, you would've brought me breakfast. I've been up since—"

Mary's voice became a dull roar against the backdrop of what Dale was seeing through the binoculars. The front door to the house opened and three people walked out. Sophia, Lindsey, and Lindsey's cameraman, Alice. She made a zip it motion with one hand, pointed in the direction of the house, and motioned for Mary to look through the binoculars. Even without the aid of the lens, she could see that Lindsey and Sophia were engaged in an animated conversation, arms gesturing, but their voices didn't carry.

"What the hell are they doing out here?" Mary asked.

"Fuck if I know, but I'm going to find out."

Dale started to walk toward the house, but Mary grabbed her arm. "Let's think about this. If you go barreling up there, what's it going to look like to anyone who might be watching?"

"I don't care."

"Yes, you do. You can question Lindsey about it later, but if Sergio's people are watching and you get in the middle of this, we'll blow any chance we have of him reaching out to Sophia."

Dale seethed, but she knew Mary was right. How in the world did Lindsey wind up here, questioning Sophia? More importantly, how had she not seen this coming? She debated telling Mary that she believed Lindsey had staked out Peyton's ranch earlier in the week. Mary was her friend and her colleague and she deserved to know, but she didn't know for sure that it had been Lindsey in the car that night. Although what she was seeing now seemed to confirm they were all being followed.

"Looks like they're leaving," Mary said.

Dale watched Lindsey and Alice walking away from the house toward the driveway while she came up with a plan. "I don't get it. Where's their car?"

"Maybe they walked in from the road."

"If I head back out now, I might be able to make it back around to the front drive so I can at least follow them. No telling where they're headed next."

"Go, now. Let me know what you find out."

Dale crashed through the woods on the way back to her truck. Part of her wished she'd confided in Mary, and not just about what DeJesus had told her. But telling Mary she'd almost fallen for Lindsey Ryan would somehow make it real. And it wasn't. The fleeting attraction was just that, fleeting, and it was gone for good. The only thing she wanted from Lindsey now was some answers.

❖

"Pull over here and let's look up the county tax records for this area," Lindsey said.

"Does everyone in Texas live out in the woods?" Alice asked.

Lindsey laughed. After they'd left the hotel, they'd gone to the home of Agent Mary Lovelace, owner of the other car they'd seen the night they lurked outside of the Circle Six Ranch. On the way, Lindsey shared the hodgepodge of facts she's managed to gather so far about the players they'd seen gathered at the Circle Six ranch earlier in the week.

While they discussed their next step, the garage door opened. Lovelace's car pulled out and turned down the street and they followed. The drive into the country had been challenging, but luckily, there were quite a few cars on the road that helped mask the fact they were tailing a federal agent. At least Lindsey hoped that was the case. Alice seemed oblivious to the danger, and with every mile, she'd conveyed her disbelief that anyone would choose to live so far from the city.

Lovelace pulled off the road and they'd whizzed on by, doubling back to see if they could get any information about who she was headed to see. Alice had spotted a sign for Valencia Acres just up the road from where Lovelace had turned off.

Lindsey paged through the local county appraisal district site on her iPad. "These aren't woods. These are ranches. And this particular ranch is owned by VA Enterprises."

"Well, that's informative."

"Hang on. I'm signing onto LexisNexis, but the connection out here's pretty slow." Lindsey tapped her fingers on the console as she waited for the page to load. She couldn't help but wonder what Dale was doing right now. Was she sleeping in because she planned to blow off meeting up with them at the Take-Back event, or was she back to doing the real work she'd been prevented from doing while she escorted them around?

She wished she could have a do-over, but she wasn't sure what exactly she'd done wrong. Dale had consented to the interview. Surely she had to know that tough, personal questions were part of it, but Lindsey would give anything if she hadn't been the one asking them.

"You find anything yet?"

Lindsey shook away the endless what-if thoughts and focused on the screen. A few keystrokes later, she found the names of the principals for Valencia Acres. Sophia Valencia owned the majority of the quarter horse breeding ranch, but someone named Jade Vargas owned thirty percent of the property. She took a screenshot of the information and then Googled Sophia Valencia's name. The first thing she found was a tiny news article in the local paper that mentioned the arrest of Arturo Vargas, a Zeta Cartel leader. The arrest had occurred here at the ranch, and Sophia had been shot during an altercation with Vargas. More searching told her Arturo Vargas was currently incarcerated at the Seagoville Federal Detention Center awaiting probable indictment on federal drug charges. Mentioned in the same story was Cyrus Gantry who was believed to have laundered money for Arturo and his brother Sergio, who had yet to be apprehended.

"Holy shit."

"What?" Alice asked.

Lindsey gave her a capsule summary. "I don't know what all this means, but Cyrus Gantry is Lily Gantry's father, and Lily is in a relationship with Peyton Davis, the woman whose ranch we stalked the other night."

"She's the AUSA who worked on the task force?"

"One of them. The other one is Bianca Cruz, the one we went to see at the courthouse yesterday."

"Okay, so what do we do with all this?"

Lindsey mentally ticked through a list of options. They could drive back to town and she could spend a few hours on the computer, trying to connect the dots. Or she could march up to the front door of Valencia Acres and ask some questions. The first plan would probably net some solid information about the whos and whats at play, but the second method was a better way to get a feel for whether there was a real story here or just a string of coincidences. There was no substitute for asking questions while you were staring a subject in the face. "Let's pay a little visit to the ranch."

Alice pulled back onto the road, and Lindsey navigated them back to the turn-in for Valencia Acres. They drove down the long, winding drive lined with tall pine trees until a cluster of pale yellow buildings came into sight.

Lindsey pointed to a turnout to the right. "Let's park over here and walk the rest of the way in. No sense giving whoever is here too much notice that we're coming."

As they walked along the gravel road, Lindsey noted the surroundings that included a two-story house with a wide, wraparound porch flanked by a barn and another building, probably the horse stables. The grounds were well tended and beautifully landscaped with containers full of mums, pansies, and winter cabbage. Whoever lived here cared about the place, or at least they cared about keeping up appearances.

They were a few feet from the house when Lindsey registered the clomp of hoofbeats and turned to see a woman on a gorgeous white horse galloping toward them. She stopped in place. "Follow my lead," she said to Alice.

The woman reined in her ride and walked the horse over to them. The rider was beautiful, with dark hair, tan skin, and coal black eyes full of questions. Lindsey did her best to be disarming. "That's a beautiful horse. Is he available for stud?"

The woman dismounted. "He is not, but I have others who are." She looked around, her eyes darting back and forth while she switched the reins from hand to hand. "Most people looking for breeding services arrive in a car, and some even have appointments."

Despite her attempt to look in control, the woman was nervous, apprehensive, and Lindsey sensed it was about more than the fact they'd showed up without an appointment. She had two choices: set the woman's mind at ease or keep her off-kilter and use the element of surprise to her advantage. "You're Sophia Valencia, right? What's your relationship to Lily Gantry?"

It was a shot in the dark, but it hit its mark. The woman paled, and she gripped the horse's reins tightly in her fist. For a second, Lindsey was convinced she was going to order them to leave so she was surprised when the woman pointed to the residence and said, "Go to the house. Wait for me there."

She didn't wait for them to respond before she walked to the stables and led her horse inside. Lindsey watched her walk away and then motioned to Alice to follow her to the house. They waited on the front porch.

"What's next?" Alice asked.

"I don't know, but I do know she's jittery about something. Did you see the way she acted when I asked her about Lily? I'm just thankful she didn't toss us out."

"Shhh, here she comes."

The woman shut the door to the stables and walked across the yard toward them. Lindsey took the time to size her up. She was tall and graceful and dressed in jodhpurs and sleek black riding boots. She looked the part of a gentrified horsewoman. Lindsey was certain this woman was Sophia Valencia, owner of the ranch.

"Come inside," the woman said, holding open the door. When they hesitated, the woman's voice growled with urgency. "Now."

Lindsey was the first in the door, and she took a moment to observe her surroundings. Hardwood floors, vaulted ceilings, muted colors—the interior was classic, well-kept, and beautiful. Like its owner. She waited until the woman had shut the door behind them before she tried again. "Sophia?"

"Yes. Who are you?"

"My name is Lindsey Ryan." She pointed to Alice. "This is my colleague, Alice Jordan. We're working on a story for *Spotlight America*. I want to ask you some questions about Arturo Vargas."

Sophia frowned. "You asked me about Lily. Why?"

"Well, I'd like to know more about her too. You know, to round out the story. My sources say you were shot during the altercation with Arturo. Are you okay?"

"Who sent you?"

"No one sent me. Your name came up when I was investigating this story." Lindsey dug a pen and notepad out of her bag. She didn't need to take notes, but she figured it would lend some legitimacy to her questions.

"If you want to know about my brothers, you will have to talk to them," Sophia said in a dismissive tone. "I'm not interested in airing our family laundry in public, and if that's what you're after, I think it's time for you to leave."

Brothers? What? Was Sophia Valencia related to Arturo and Sergio Vargas? Did that make Sophia a criminal too? Deciding Sophia's patience would only tolerate one more question, she lobbed a big one. "Does AUSA Peyton Davis know her girlfriend was here at the same time you were involved in a shootout with your brother?"

Sophia was in motion before Lindsey finished her sentence. She stomped to the door and yanked it open. "Get out."

Lindsey held up a hand. She'd struck a nerve, and she desperately wanted to trace the source of Sophia's sudden hostility. "I'm sorry. I didn't mean to make you angry. Let's start over."

Sophia's only response was to walk out onto her porch and wave for them to follow. Out of options, Lindsey and Alice left the house, but Lindsey gave it one last shot. "I'll be honest. I'm working on a story involving the DEA, and that's what led me to your door. I don't have all the facts, but I'd like to give an accurate reporting about what's going on. I have to talk to everyone involved. If you consent to an interview, I promise I'll be fair in how I convey your side of the story."

Sophia stared at her for a minute, and Lindsey had a feeling she was weighing her request, vague as it was. But then Sophia's eyes narrowed and she knew she'd figured wrong.

"I think you're bluffing. I think you're trying to put my family in danger." She waved her arms. "I want you to leave my property now and don't come back. Ever."

That was it. As Lindsey walked with Alice back to the car, she could feel Sophia's eyes on them the entire way. Sophia's refusal to talk had lit Lindsey's curiosity on fire. She was walking away without answers now, but she was more determined than ever to puzzle the pieces of this complicated story together.

CHAPTER SEVENTEEN

Dale drove the highway outside of Valencia Acres several times, but there was no sign of Lindsey or the car she'd seen the other night.

She slammed her hand against the steering wheel. This was ridiculous. Why was Lindsey even out here? Had she been following the members of the task force when she wasn't working on her piece for the show? Was the story about the Take-Back Initiative a cover for some deep throat investigation of the task force?

Too many questions and she didn't know how to go about finding the answers.

That wasn't true. She knew exactly how to find the answers. Same way she always did—go to the source. While she might not know where to find the source at this very minute, she did know where she would be in a few hours. *Guess I'm going to be at the event today after all.*

Resigned to her plan, she pulled out her cell and called Mary who answered on the first ring. "I can't find them."

"Well, they didn't show back up out here, but something else strange happened after you left."

Dale gripped the steering wheel tighter. "Talk."

"I snuck out by the stables to see if I could tell where they'd parked. Sophia came back out and spent about ten minutes on the phone speaking in very heated Spanish."

"You happen to catch any of it?"

"Not much besides the curse words. I took French in college."

"Way to be useful," Dale said. "So, tell me why you think the phone call was strange."

"Partly hunch and partly because while she was on the phone, I spotted a truck on the ridge behind the property. Trained the binoculars on it. Didn't recognize the driver, but he was on the phone. When Sophia hung up, he did too and then he took off."

Dale replayed what Mary had just said a couple of times to process the information. "Okay, so we assume this guy saw everything including Lindsey and Alice showing up on Sophia's doorstep. Probably one of Sergio's guys and he called to find out who the hell Sophia was talking to. Do you think he saw you?"

"I hope not. I was careful, but I guess he could have. I wish we could put more people on this."

"Me too, but we're it for now. I'm headed back into town to find Lindsey and figure out what she's up to, and I've got a plan to make things easier for us to keep track of her. I think it's time someone confronts Sophia about exactly what went down at the prison yesterday. You mind calling Peyton and filling her in? She's going to want to be part of that conversation."

"Deal. Let me know what you find out."

"Will do." Dale hung up and tossed her cell phone into the seat. She'd need to go home and change before showing up downtown. She'd be back in Dallas in less than an hour, but if she wanted to catch Lindsey before things started she'd have to hurry. She raced the oversized engine in her truck and flew down the highway as she struggled to process everything that had happened.

Lindsey Ryan could not be a more frustrating woman. There were moments when she seemed incredibly open, but her antics over the past few days made it clear she had a hidden agenda and little regard for who got hurt in the process. Including herself. She'd marched up to Sophia's door likely having no clue that one of Sergio Vargas's henchmen was watching her every move. If Sergio thought Sophia was talking to the press or the police, there was no telling what he might do, but it would certainly derail their plan to draw him out in the open.

Dale spent the rest of the drive planning exactly what she would say to Lindsey when she saw her. Her goal was to strike a careful balance between providing just enough detail to warn her off without telling her too much. Perhaps letting Lindsey know she'd decided to do the interview would be enough of a distraction.

She'd finally come to the conclusion it was time for her to tell Maria's story. The interview would be the final piece to laying her wife to rest, a way to honor her memory. She knew in her heart Maria would want her to find closure. She'd been hanging on to what had been as a way to shut out what could be. Although her simmering attraction to Lindsey could never amount to anything more, she felt alive for the first time since Maria's death, and she was determined not to slip back into the shadows.

❖

"Where have you been?"

Lindsey looked up to see Elaina rushing toward her. She and Alice had slipped into the city hall building moments ago and run into Jed who warned them Elaina was on the warpath. He and Elaina had arrived about thirty minutes before, and now that Elaina had spotted her, she'd been doing her best to act like she'd been there the whole time. She could tell by the look on Elaina's face she wasn't buying it. She dreaded her reaction when she found out Dale wasn't going to show up.

"I was checking out a few things," Lindsey said. "Why, did you need me?"

"We were supposed to go over your interview notes, but we'll have to wait. The mayor and several city councilmen are here, and we've got a spot for you to do some sit-downs with them before the outside ceremony gets underway. Alice is already setting up."

Lindsey sighed in relief at the reprieve. She had a little while longer before she had to break her news. Maybe by then she'd have some more information about Sophia Valencia. On the drive back from Valencia Acres, she'd called Burt, the network investigator, and given him every shred of information she'd found about Lily Gantry, Sophia Valencia, and Arturo and Sergio Vargas and instructed him to use all his resources to find more. She was convinced there was a story among the scattered collection of facts she'd gathered so far, and she was determined to root it out. She had to admit appeasing Elaina with a new and bigger story wasn't her only goal. A break in this investigation might give her added insight into Dale, not to mention an opportunity to talk to her again, even if as an adversary.

"Agent Nelson, nice to see you again."

Lindsey whirled in her chair and saw Dale standing directly behind her, so close she was surprised she hadn't known she was there. Lindsey watched while Elaina enthusiastically shook Dale's hand. Dale's smile was tight and forced, but Lindsey wondered if anyone else noticed. She also wondered if anyone noticed how hot she looked. She was wearing a charcoal gray suit, a jet-black shirt, and the same shiny black boots she'd sported yesterday. Dale looked dark and sleek, and she certainly looked like she planned to be on camera. Had she changed her mind about the interview?

Dale flicked a glance in her direction and then turned back to Elaina. "Nice to see you too. I was hoping I could get a few minutes with Ms. Ryan before things get started."

"Yes," Lindsey said.

"Actually, no." Elaina pointed in the direction of the stage. "We have a few people waiting and we need to get to them quickly. I promise we'll all have time to talk before you go on camera. You look great, by the way."

Lindsey watched the exchange carefully, wishing she'd been the one to tell Dale how great she looked, but Dale didn't react to the compliment. In fact, the only emotion Lindsey registered was a flicker of disappointment on Dale's face, but it disappeared quickly, replaced by a mask of nonchalance.

"Okay then," Dale said. "Ms. Ryan, where will you be during the ceremony?"

Elaina jumped in before Lindsey could answer. "Jed can fill you in. He's right over there." She pointed to an area to the right of the stage and nudged Lindsey along. "We'll see you later."

Lindsey didn't even try to hide her annoyance at being led around. "I wanted to talk to her."

"Who wouldn't? She's even more gorgeous all dressed up."

Lindsey seethed at the way Elaina objectified Dale. Of course, she'd been doing the exact same thing a moment ago, but it felt different because she appreciated other things about Dale like her strength, her resilience, and her dedication. Things Elaina didn't know a damn thing about.

She looked over her shoulder. Dale was watching her walk away, her eyes trained on her arm that was firmly in Elaina's grasp. While Dale was still watching, she shrugged out of Elaina's grip, but Dale's expression didn't change. The slight frown, the piercing eyes—she looked angry. But she was here, and that was a major step toward mending the rift between them. For a second, Lindsey forgot all about the interview, the late night meetings, and her encounter with Sophia Valencia, and she wanted nothing more than to have met Dale under other circumstances where they could explore the attraction between them without secrets and hidden agendas.

Dale stood in the wings and watched. For all the pomp and circumstance, the ceremony was pretty boring. The mayor, Diego, and a few other local dignitaries all gave speeches talking about the dangers of drug use and commending the citizens of Dallas for doing their part to combat the problem.

Bullshit. As long as greedy, ruthless gangsters like Sergio Vargas remained free, there would always be a drug problem, and the damage they caused made the thousands of pounds of prescription drugs collected today seem like candy medicine in comparison. With campaigns like these, no wonder regular citizens didn't appreciate the extent of the real threat. Even Lindsey didn't seem to understand the danger. If she did, she wouldn't go crashing around town, stirring up trouble.

Or maybe she did understand the danger and simply chose to ignore it. Dale shook her head. If that was the case, then she was better off staying as far away from Lindsey as possible. Dale wasn't afraid of danger. She put herself in harm's way on a daily basis, but she did it for a higher purpose, unlike Lindsey who rushed into danger, here and in Afghanistan, for TV ratings. What she did was reckless and brash.

Dale checked her watch. It was almost four, and the ceremony would be over soon. She looked over at Jed, the soundman on Lindsey's team. He was eyeing her with a curious expression. She raised her eyebrows and he waved her over.

"Yes?" she asked.

"I just got word the order of the program changed and Herschel Gellar may not be here. Do you know anything about that?"

Dale shook her head. Gellar had been scheduled to give a speech right before the class of fifth graders who'd just graduated from the DARE program sang "America the Beautiful," she assumed to show how talented non drug users could be. She wasn't surprised he'd bailed on the obligation, but she was surprised that he'd give up an opportunity to hog some press time. Whatever it was that kept him away must be pretty damn important. "No idea, sorry."

"No problem," Jed said. "Just need to make a couple of adjustments for the kids' song, and I was going to wait until after his speech. Thanks."

"What's the plan after the ceremony ends? Are you going to be interviewing anyone else?"

"You mean besides you? Elaina arranged for some of the kids to stick around so Lindsey can do a quick spot with them. She mentioned she might try to get it done backstage while the closing remarks are happening."

They both looked toward the stage as the emcee announced Richards Elementary's fifth grade DARE class, and watched as a group of about twenty ten-year-olds filed onto the stage. They were all dressed up for the occasion, and Dale couldn't help but smile as they belted out the song with gusto.

When they started the last verse, she moved toward the back of the stage. She wanted to catch Lindsey alone for a minute before the ceremony broke up and the madness started, and this might be her only opportunity. She spotted Alice and Elaina engaged in a heated discussion, and she approached them quietly to try to overhear.

"The school bus will make for a better backdrop," Elaina said.

"We've already got a setup in the building. We'll get a much better picture inside. Besides, who knows how many takes we'll have to shoot before we get clear sound. It didn't matter so much with the ceremony since we're going to cut it down to clips, but talking to the kids should be quick, and you're probably going to want to use the whole thing. Remember, you've got another important interview scheduled."

Jed and Lindsey walked up and Jed asked, "What about sound?"

"Elaina wants to move the interview with the kids outside by the school bus," Alice said.

"Actually, I think that's a great idea," Lindsey said. She turned to Jed. "What do you think?"

"We can probably make it work, but if you get any planes overhead, it's going to put you way off schedule for your other interview."

At that moment, Lindsey looked over and met Dale's gaze. Dale was surprised since she didn't think Lindsey realized she was standing there. She watched her for a moment, trying to get a read on Lindsey's expression. Resignation, relief? Before she could figure it out, Lindsey looked back toward her crew. "Let's do it. The kids should be coming out right about now."

The music came to an end and the kids filed backstage. Elaina walked over to the group and wrangled two of the kids from the crowd and had a conversation with the adult who was with them. While she arranged the details of the shoot, Lindsey came over to stand next to Dale.

"I'm surprised you're here," Lindsey said.

"Me too."

"You don't have to do this, you know."

"I know."

"I'll make it as painless as possible."

The words were like oil on a fire, and Dale fought to keep her anger under control. She knew Lindsey was talking about her personal interview, but she wanted to shout that if Lindsey really wanted to make things painless, she would stop running around on her own investigating behind the task force.

This wasn't the time or place. She had a plan to keep Lindsey under control and she'd stick to the plan. Right now, she just needed to get through the questions Lindsey had in store for her.

Elaina called for Lindsey, and she offered Dale a pained smile before joining Elaina and the rest of the crew to walk outside by the school bus that was parked near the water feature in front of city hall. Dale pulled out her phone and sent Mary a text. *Anything new?*

She waited for a minute and then a new text appeared on her screen. *No. Talked to Peyton. She's coming out here this evening. Hopefully, we'll get to the bottom of things then.*

Keep me posted. Dale pocketed her phone. She could hear the closing remarks being made on stage. In a little while, she'd be the one in the spotlight, and she couldn't wait to get it over with.

"Tell me one of the most important things you learned from working with the Dallas Police officers in the DARE program."

Lindsey stood next to the bus with a kid on either side, Carolina and Emilio. This final piece of the Take-Back Initiative symbolized exactly how pointless it all was. The kids were cute, all dressed up in their Sunday best, and they would likely recite whatever line Elaina had fed them to make it seem like the Just Say No program at their school was really having an impact, but Lindsey knew better. Elaina had picked the minority kids for optics, but they were still upper middle class, from a private school no less, and didn't represent the type of kids who were more susceptible to the kind of street drugs that were responsible for most violent crime. She couldn't wait to finish this interview so she could resume her quest to figure out what was going on with the Vargas investigation and why a group of agents and AUSAs seemed to be handling it on the sly.

Except one of those agents was Dale, and the closer she got to her, the closer she wanted to get, despite the fact Dale had made it perfectly clear she didn't want anything to do with her. But she'd shown up today.

Lindsey glanced in Dale's direction and hoped her presence was a sign they could move past the differences between them.

In the meantime, the kids finished rambling. She asked them a couple of follow-up questions about today's event and wrapped it up when Elaina finally signaled they were done.

"Can I get your autograph?" Carolina asked.

"Me too," Emilio chimed in.

"Sure." The request was cute and she didn't mind at all, but she didn't have anything to write on. Lindsey looked over at Elaina, but she'd buttonholed Dale again, and she couldn't get her attention. She turned to Alice who'd walked over to join them. "Do you know if we have any press kits in the car?"

"I think so. You want me to get them?"

"No, I can do it." Lindsey took the keys from Alice and motioned to the kids. "Follow me. My pal Alice will let your teacher know we'll be right back."

The street next to city hall was shut down for the festivities, but because of their role, the local cops had let them park just inside the barricade. Lindsey led the kids toward the car while Carolina, who'd seemed shy at first, peppered her with questions the whole way.

"What kind of grades do you need to make to be a reporter? My dad says reporters don't make any money, but I don't care. I think it would be fun. Did you major in journalism in college?"

Before Lindsey could answer, Emilio chimed in with, "I bet she makes a lot of money. She's on TV and she's famous. You went to war, right? What was it like?"

Lindsey unlocked the car and started rummaging around in the trunk. "Tell you what. Let me get your autographs, and on the way back to your bus I'll answer as many questions as you can think of."

She located Elaina's briefcase, tugged it open, and combed through contents looking for copies of the eight-by-ten glossies she'd autographed for some of the locals who'd asked. She found them in a file folder marked PR, but they were behind a bunch of random photographs that she recognized as her story notes. She pulled them out of the folder and took a closer look. Someone had taken pictures of the notes she'd written while she was researching Dale and her wife's death. What was Elaina doing with these? If she wanted copies of her notes, why not just ask?

A loud shout behind her yanked her attention from the photos. She turned with the folder in her grip in time to see two men in black masks advancing on them with automatic weapons. One of them pointed his gun at the lone DPD officer who had been assigned to make sure traffic didn't break through the barricade, and the other had his weapon trained on her and the kids. She dropped the folder onto the ground and whispered, "Run! Yell 'fire'! Go!" She pushed the kids away from her and ran toward the man to draw his attention away from them.

She risked a glance at the school bus, but her crew was on the other side of it and it blocked her view. When she looked back, the man waved at something behind her. She whirled in time to see the other man disarm the police officer and strike him over the head with his own gun. He met her eyes and lifted his weapon. She was trapped. She knew it; they knew it.

"You will come with us. Now. No talking."

Lindsey held up her hands. "Please. Whatever you want."

Her plea was met with the muzzle of the gun jabbed into her side. "I said no talking. Come. Now."

Fear heightened all of her senses. She'd seen, close up, the power of an automatic weapon and she knew she had no chance of escaping their fire. She'd have to figure out some other way to escape. She had no idea what was going on, but the next thing she knew they forced her into a large cage in the back of a waiting van on the other side of the barricade.

Determined to find out a way out of this, she fought back her fright and catalogued her limited options. Her cell phone was in her bag backstage. Without a way to call for help, she focused on remembering each turn the van made while a litany of regrets coursed through her mind. Not coming clean to Dale about what she'd been doing the past couple of days and not confessing that she cared about her were at the top of that list.

CHAPTER EIGHTEEN

Dale was pacing near the school bus when she felt her phone buzz in her pocket. She checked the screen. Peyton. She considered letting it go to voice mail. She knew Peyton probably wanted to discuss what was going on with Sophia. She did too, but right now she was more focused on getting in a mental head space to face Lindsey and answer her hard questions. Ultimately, she decided it would be easier to take Peyton's call. "Hey, Peyton, what's up?"

"I talked to Sophia."

"Good."

"It was a pretty one-sided conversation, but I figure she's worried someone might be listening in on her end."

Dale spotted a Dallas cop sprinting by the school bus. She tracked his path and watched as he skidded to a stop directly in front of Elaina who was standing backstage talking to the mayor and Diego.

"Are you there?" Peyton asked.

The cop was animated, waving both hands in the air. Diego looked around and started shouting at several of the other DEA agents who were present for the event, pointing toward the school bus. Dale's stomach churned and her heart started thumping wildly. She whipped around, but couldn't see the source of the commotion. "Peyton, I have to go."

She started to disconnect the call, but Peyton yelled, "Wait!"

"Seriously, I have to go."

"Just a sec. Arturo did tell Sophia something. Something that scared her, but he didn't threaten her and neither did Sergio. He told her someone working with us was the source of the threat. We should meet. Just the core group. Leave Tanner out of it for now."

Out of the corner of her eye, Dale saw more cops, coming from the other side of the stage. She recognized some of them—they'd been in the audience earlier. They were all headed her way. She saw Elaina and Alice running after them, and a growing sense of panic spurred her to start walking, faster and faster until she broke into a run. She'd barely registered Peyton's words, but she offered a rote "sounds good" and shoved the phone back in her pocket.

Dale rounded the corner of the school bus and pulled up short. A crowd of uniformed cops were gathered on the portion of the street next to city hall that had been blocked off. She pulled out her badge and pushed her way into the center of the crowd until she spotted Diego. "What's going on?"

"Not sure yet. A DPD officer got pistol-whipped. He's coming to, but he's fuzzy about what happened. Says some guys in black masks toting automatic weapons came up on him and some other folks. They knocked him out and that's all he remembers."

What the cop described didn't make any sense. Guys with masks and guns show up, assault a cop, and then what? Where were they now? Dale replayed the words over in her head. There was a clue there.

"Has somebody talked to the kids?"

Dale's head snapped in the direction of the voice, but she didn't recognize the man who'd spoken. She started to ask him what he was talking about when she heard a sharp cry and looked around for the source of the sound.

The two kids from the program were huddled over to the side with Andrea DeJesus. Elaina and Alice were standing a few feet from a car, and a uniformed officer she didn't recognize was yelling at them to step back. She catalogued the details of the scene in slow motion. A dark four-door sedan. The trunk of the car was open. A brown folder lay on the ground behind the trunk, its contents spilled out on the pavement.

She shoved past Diego and strode toward the car, every step a heavy, weighted agony against the background of the cop yelling at her to step back. She ignored him as she made her way to the children, but she froze when she saw the papers fanned out on the cement.

One, two, three, four, five. Five photographs of Lindsey, smiling and glamorous. Dale's skin felt tight and suffocating and she fought for breath. She heard someone shouting and looked up from the photos into Elaina's face. Her mouth was moving, but Dale had to struggle to make out the words. When she finally understood what she was saying she realized Elaina was telling her what she already knew.

"Lindsey's gone. We have to find her."

❖

Lindsey hated not being able to see. The van had stopped just outside of downtown, and one of the men had opened the cage, strapped a zip tie around her wrists, and tied a black cloth around her head. She heard murmured voices and, after a few minutes, they took off driving again.

The darkness heightened her other senses but did nothing to diminish her fear. Sour sweat burned her nostrils, and her ears pounded with the sound of heavy metal banging from the van's speakers. The van that was taking her farther and farther away from downtown. Away from Alice, Jed, and Elaina. And Dale. How long would it be before any of them noticed she was gone? She hoped Carolina and Emilio would run for help, but in their panicked state would they remember anything about what they'd seen?

She shoved aside her fear and searched her memory for details of the training she'd received before she went to Afghanistan. The network had made sure she'd received instruction in how to handle being taken hostage before she went overseas. She'd been lucky not to have to use the techniques they'd taught her, but she prayed her training would come in handy now.

The things she remembered right off the bat were to develop a relationship with the captors and convince them you're interested in telling all sides of a story. She'd have to ignore the no talking rule to accomplish either of these.

"My name is Lindsey Ryan. I'm a reporter for *Spotlight America*. If you have a message you want to get out to the world, anything at all, I can help you. I know lots of important people."

"No talking."

The words were delivered with a grunt, but the voice sounded more apathetic than angry. She sifted through her thoughts to remember what else she'd learned. Make it personal—tell the captors personal details about yourself to appeal to their humanity. Played back in the middle of a real situation, these tips were starting to feel pretty stupid. Guys with assault rifles didn't exactly strike her as the warm and fuzzy types who wanted to hear about her personal life. Of course they'd had the opportunity to kill that cop and the kids and they hadn't, so maybe there was a chance they valued at least some human life.

The problem was she couldn't think of anything to tell them. The trainers had said tell them about your family, your loved ones, and your interests. Lindsey didn't think a story about her single life as a solitary reporter who spent every waking moment working and was estranged from her family would be especially appealing. She spent her life telling other people's stories never giving a thought to building a life of her own. She had no family to come home to, no place to live, no one to miss her if she didn't live through whatever happened next.

Well, she couldn't change any of that right now, but she could do her damnedest to make sure she lived so she could make different choices with the rest of her life. In the meantime, she didn't think they'd kill her while they were driving. She'd spend the next however long counting the turns and plotting her future, starting by making a plan to get out of this mess.

❖

Dale pushed Elaina aside and ran over to the kids.

"I taught their DARE program," Andrea said, her voice animated. "They ran straight to me. They saw it all go down."

Dale hunched over so she could look the kids in the eyes and searched her memory for their names. "Carolina, Emilio, you guys sure are brave. Do you know where Lindsey is? Can you tell me what you saw?"

Emilio was pale and shaking, but Carolina was amped up. "We're not brave. Lindsey went right for them, but she told us to run and we did. They had on black ski masks and they had guns. Not handguns, but rifles. Black ones. The kind that keep firing, you know, that you don't have to reload."

Dale breathed deep as the image of Lindsey running toward danger cast an ugly shadow across her mind. "Okay. Did they say anything?"

"Not that I could hear."

"Think hard for me. Did you see anything else?"

Carolina shook her head, but Emilio piped up. "They got in a van. Dark blue. I looked back for a sec, and I saw them put her in the back."

Dale stood up and put her hands on their shoulders. "Great job, guys. Thanks." She motioned to DeJesus to follow her, and they walked a couple of steps away. "They say anything else before I got here?"

"No. They were in shock. I'm surprised you got them to talk at all. What do you need me to do?"

"Stay with them." Dale didn't wait for a response. Her mind was racing as she considered what to do next. The answer was right in front of her, tickling her subconscious. She just needed to focus. The tracking device! She'd never anticipated these would be the circumstances under which she'd use what she learned, but she offered up a silent thanks to the universe for happenstance.

She ran back over to the crowd of law enforcement around the car and found Diego. "We need to talk." She motioned for him to join her a few feet away and spoke fast. "I have a confession to make. You're going to be pissed, but I need you to yell at me later, not now."

Diego grimaced. "Spill."

"I put a tracker in Lindsey's jacket."

She held back a flinch as she waited for his response. To his credit, he didn't say anything, but his eyes got wide and then his face settled into a scowl. She started talking quickly to ward off his anger. "I'll explain why I did it later, but right now it's the best chance we have of finding her." She pulled out her phone and opened the GPS app tied to the device she'd attached to Lindsey's jacket when she'd arrived at the event. "They have about a fifteen-minute head start and they're headed north on I-35. I know an agent who's working on a case in that part of town." She waited for his response, but she wouldn't wait long.

"Go, but keep your phone line open. I'm going to notify SRT that we have a situation and have them contact you for details. Do not, I repeat, do not approach on your own. You do and I'll be more than pissed. You'll be out of a job. Understood?"

She didn't answer because she was already on the move. Lindsey was in danger, and Dale didn't give a damn about anything else.

Chapter Nineteen

Dale sped down the highway, her eyes moving between the road and the red dot on her phone that she held tightly pressed against the steering wheel. Not wanting to risk a second away from the screen that was tracking Lindsey's movements, she used voice commands to dial Mary's number.

The phone rang four times and she was about to disconnect when Mary's voice came through the line. "Hey, Nelson, miss me?"

Dale didn't waste a second. "Where are you right this minute?"

"Headed to the Circle Six. Peyton's right behind me." Mary's tone was serious now, like she could tell something was up.

"I need you to take a detour. I'm on I-35. I just drove past the Corinth exit. Can you get to me quick?"

"Absolutely. We're just north of there, on the service road near Lake Dallas. Tell me what you need."

Dale did a quick mental calculation and changed her mind. "Change of plans. Stay put and I'll be right there." She clicked off the line and stepped hard on the gas. At ninety miles an hour, she was flying by the other vehicles on the road, and she'd already decided if a state trooper lit up near her she was going to fly on by. She might get to Lindsey faster if she had a lights and sirens escort.

Lindsey. Just a few hours ago, she couldn't wait to be rid of her and now she was racing to her rescue. Who had taken her and why? She had a ton of questions, but the logistics and purpose behind Lindsey's abduction weren't at the forefront. If she was being honest, the biggest question was why the news of Lindsey's abduction sent her reeling. From the moment she'd learned Lindsey had been taken, she knew without a doubt she would do everything in her power to find and protect her, and she also knew the compulsion was more than duty, it was…

She hit the steering wheel with her palm. Dammit. She wasn't ready to put a name to her feelings. She might never be. The best thing she could do right now was ignore emotion and focus on coming up with a plan before the red dot on her phone stopped moving.

The sign for Lake Dallas came into view, and she roared across three lanes of traffic to make the exit. As she merged onto the service road, she saw Mary and Peyton standing behind Mary's Jeep at the gas station on the corner. Mary had a large canvas bag labeled ATF on her shoulder.

Dale swerved into the parking lot, stopped directly behind them, and lowered her window. "Get in!"

They'd barely shut the doors before she took off again. She handed her phone to Mary. "Watch that red dot and tell me where it goes. Lindsey Ryan was abducted by at least two armed guys. They shoved her into the back of a dark blue van and that red dot is going to lead us to them."

"On it," Mary said. "How did we manage to get tracking on them?"

"I planted a tracker on Lindsey at the event today. I figured it was time she got a taste of her own medicine." Dale looked back at Peyton. "Don't start with the lectures about warrants and shit. She and her camera crew were staking out your ranch earlier in the week, and she showed up at Sophia's this morning. I don't know what she's up to, but she obviously wasn't going to stop, so we had to have a way to keep an eye on her."

"So you decided to take off after these armed men all on your own?"

Peyton sounded incredulous, but Dale ignored the question. There was only one explanation for her reckless behavior, but talking about it would be a waste of energy. Peyton's question did remind her about something else though. "Mary, will you call Diego? He's supposed to have SRT get in contact with me, and I want to keep my phone free if I can. Give him your number and they can get in touch with you."

Dale listened to the one-sided conversation while Mary described where they were and told Diego that based on the map, they were about fifteen minutes behind the van. What followed next were a few "okays" and "uh-huhs" and she was about to tell Mary how to transmit the information on her phone about Lindsey's location to the special response team, when Mary exclaimed "two hours?"

"Put the phone on speaker," Dale said, resisting the urge to grab it out of Mary's hand. When she heard Diego's voice, she practically yelled. "Are you saying you can't get SRT scrambled for two hours?"

"We've got a team in cars headed your way now, but the chopper is grounded. We've got one on the way from DPD SWAT, but it's going to take a little time to get it outfitted."

"Not acceptable."

"Dale, I'm doing the best I can. Just hang tight. You promised you wouldn't go in on your own."

Mary waved her hand and pointed at Dale's phone. She held it up and Dale saw that the red dot had moved to the right. It was off the highway now, and turning right. Dale whispered, "Find me the exit." And then louder, "Diego, gotta go. They just turned off the highway."

Before she hung up, she heard him say again, "Remember, you promised."

He needn't have worried. She glanced at Mary and Peyton. She'd keep her promise—she wasn't going in alone.

Nothing she said the entire drive elicited a response, and Lindsey was beginning to wonder if there was a point in continuing to try. As far as she could tell, they'd been driving at a pretty steady clip in a straight line for a long time, but they'd just slowed down and made a right turn. If she had to guess, she'd say they'd been on the highway. Resigned to silence, she was left with just her thoughts.

Elaina was probably having an aneurism right about now. Hopefully, Carolina and Emilio had made it safely back to the crowd at the event and were able to relay what had happened. If not, and Elaina and the rest of her crew were in the dark, Elaina probably thought she'd gotten tired of doing the network's bidding and had bailed on the interview with Dale.

Which led her to wonder what Dale was thinking. Had she stuck around, ready to answer questions or had she left the event and written this entire episode off to a bad day at the office? She had no doubt Dale resented the intrusion into her life, but she'd been intrigued too. She'd known it for a fact at dinner last night until something caused her to do a one-eighty.

There was a good chance she'd probably never see Dale again even if she survived this episode of her life, but on the off chance she came out of this unscathed, she started a mental bucket list—an exercise she'd always considered a bit silly because if a person wanted to do something, they should just do it and not wait until they were at the end of life to check things off the list. She'd climbed mountains, jumped out of planes, traveled the world, learned new languages, and gotten paid handsomely for the privilege. Other people's bucket lists would pale in comparison to the things she'd experienced as a matter of course, but she couldn't help but feel empty because she'd had no one to share her life.

Even with Elaina, all the fulfilling moments she'd had had been alone. They hadn't shared the same interests, the same passions. They'd simply mistaken the intersection of their careers as a reason to couple up, and they'd been at odds from the start. Elaina had never understood Lindsey's unwillingness to compromise her work for what the network deemed palatable, and Lindsey would never concede that compromise was a necessary evil.

Of course, she'd compromised when she'd taken this particular assignment. She was only here, in Dallas and in this van, because she'd thrown a bone to the network in exchange for having control over the type of news she wanted to cover. How poetic that her first compromise might be her last.

The van jerked right again, and she braced against the side of the cage to keep from sliding. They were no longer on a paved road, and she felt every bump and bounce of the uneven terrain. She had a feeling they were nearing their destination, wherever that might be. Now was the time to add something new, something meaningful to the bucket list, but her mind was paralyzed with dread at what might happen next, and she couldn't manage to put words to her dreams.

The van braked to a halt, and she heard the men inside clanking the lock on the cage that held her. Rough hands grabbed her and pulled her forward. She stayed in a crouch until she felt a gust of cool breeze and felt herself lifted in the air.

She had a split second to make a choice. Docile and disarming hadn't worked so far. She didn't have a clue where they were or what kind of opposition she was facing, but if she was going to try to escape, right now seemed like the perfect opportunity. She bent her knees, leaned back as far as she could, and swung both feet forward as hard as she could.

She heard a loud grunt before she hit the ground, flat on her back. She rolled away from the noise and struggled to get up, but with her hands still tied tight behind her, she couldn't get purchase. She heard a deep voice yelling in Spanish asking what happened and another voice answered saying he was taking care of it. Next thing she knew, she was yanked to her feet and marched away.

A few minutes later, she heard the sound of a creaking door. The ground became level and the air smelled like hay. She listened carefully, but didn't hear any distinct sounds other than the snips of conversation between the men and the sound of their breathing.

They came to a stop and a hand pushed down on her shoulder. "Sit."

He didn't wait for her to comply, instead forcing her into a chair. It was cold and hard. She wondered if they were going to tie her to it. She'd read somewhere that you should try to relax if someone was tying you up—that doing so would put some slack in the bindings. She took a few deep breaths and willed herself to

CARSEN TAITE

remain calm and loose, but not being able to see only fueled her anxiety.

Escape hadn't worked, so she was back to plan one: engage the captors. She didn't have any confidence in the strategy, but she was out of options. "I was telling you the truth before. I'm a reporter for a news show with excellent ratings. Whatever you want, I can help you get it." She repeated her plea in Spanish and added, "I promise, I'm much more valuable to you alive."

Their only response was to rip off her blindfold. She shook her head as her eyes adjusted to the light. Both of the men, still wearing ski masks, were standing in front of her, one was pointing a phone at her and the other was looking at a piece of paper. She took advantage of their preoccupation and soaked up as many details as she could about her surroundings.

She was seated on a metal chair at a card table in what appeared to be a barn. The floor was scattered with hay, but for the most part, the building appeared to be clean, and there was no sign of any equipment or animals. She estimated it had taken close to an hour to get here so they weren't too far from the city, but if this property wasn't occupied, the likelihood that anyone would come along and find her was remote. Her best strategy was to escape.

One of the men slammed his fist on the table, and she jumped in her chair. He slid the paper in front of her and pointed to the camera. "Read."

She looked at the man with the phone and back down at the paper before she realized what he wanted her to do. He pulled out a knife and reached behind her to cut the restraints on her wrists. Slowly and cautiously, she brought her sore and swollen hands around in front of her. He jabbed a finger at the paper and repeated his earlier instruction. "Read."

She picked up the paper and skimmed the words. She'd imagined it would be a ransom note and it was, with a twist. The statement was short and to the point.

My name is Lindsey Ryan, and I am a reporter for Spotlight America. *This message is for Herschel Gellar. I am being held hostage and will be killed unless you release Arturo Vargas from custody and dismiss all charges against him and his brother, Sergio Vargas. You have twelve hours to comply or I will die. If you try to rescue me, I will die. I will be released as soon as Arturo is out and all charges have been dismissed.*

Lindsey read the note three times until the words swam before her eyes, but only two stuck in her memory. *Killed. Die.* Who were they kidding? No one was going to unleash a cold-blooded drug lord in exchange for a reporter, no matter how popular she was. Her captors stood to gain nothing and she would lose everything.

"This isn't going to work," she said. "They won't let him go in exchange for me. I know several high-powered lawyers. Let me contact them. You have a better chance of getting Arturo released and the charges dismissed by using the law against them. Let me help you. I will do everything in my power to secure his release."

The man standing beside her picked up his gun and pointed it at her head. He took a step back but kept the weapon leveled on her. He waved a hand at the man with the phone and then barked the command at her again. "Read."

Countless times, she'd stood before a camera and recited the facts, asked tough questions, and offered her opinions. She'd done it so often she rarely used notes anymore, preferring the spontaneity of extemporaneous speech and the realism it added to her stories. But this was different. This wasn't someone else's story for her to summarize and massage for the camera. This was her story, and deviating from the script could cost her her life. Suddenly, the mental logjam she'd experienced earlier when she'd been trying to think of things to add to her bucket list broke free, and she knew exactly what she wanted, exactly who she wanted.

Survival was imperative.

Lindsey held the paper with shaking hands and barely looked up as she read the words exactly as they were written on the page.

❖

Dale took the exit Mary pointed out. "What next?"

"Turn right at the light up ahead."

Dale looked at the road signs and then at Mary. "Are you thinking what I'm thinking?"

"Yep, and no need to speculate." She held up the phone. "They stopped moving and look where the red dot is."

"Anyone care to clue me in?" Peyton said from the backseat.

"Mary and I were out here recently," Dale said, a grim feeling setting in as she faced the fact Lindsey's kidnapping might have been a carefully orchestrated maneuver. "The farm where we found your brother is out this way, and that's where Lindsey is right now."

"The property is up for sale, but it's been on the market for a while so the likelihood of showings is pretty slim. We'd gotten a tip that Sergio was hiding out there, but we didn't find any sign of him. Maybe the intel was right on the facts and wrong on the timing."

"Okay, so we need a plan," Mary said. "I've got a couple of high-powered rifles with scopes in my bag. If they're in the barn, I might be able to get eyes on them from the attic at the house, but that means you two will need to be ready to come at them from the ground. Peyton, you up for this?"

"I'm carrying a pistol, but I don't have any extra ammo. You have anything else in that bag for me?"

Dale listened to them discuss the plan, content to let them work out the details because she cared about only three things: get in, get Lindsey, and get out.

Twenty minutes later, they pulled off one of the roads that led to the north side of the house. Mary pointed at a grove of trees. "Park over there. We'll go the rest of the way on foot."

Dale swatted at a fly circling her head as they trudged through the woods. The last time she'd been here they'd had all the power of the task force at their disposal: heat sensors, snipers, flashbangs, and over a dozen agents, armed and ready. Today they were two agents and a lawyer. They didn't know for sure how many men they were up against, and they didn't know for sure where they were on the property.

Diego's admonition to wait wasn't completely without merit. The SWAT team would have the resources they didn't, but common sense told her the longer they waited, the greater the risk. Lindsey's life hung in the balance.

She didn't know why Lindsey had been taken. It was possible Sergio's men had spotted Lindsey at Sophia's ranch that morning and concocted a way to use her journalistic skills to their advantage, but thugs didn't reward utility. They'd discard her as soon as they were done.

Maybe they should wait, but right now they had the element of surprise, and she wasn't willing to give that up in exchange for a few extra agents who had no personal stake in Lindsey's safety.

They were close enough now that she could see the house ahead and the barn on the other side. A dark blue van was parked in front of the barn, and there were no other cars in sight. Mary motioned for them to huddle behind a large pecan tree. "Here's where we part ways. You two wait here while I go into the house and see if I can get a visual. I'll send you a text when I've got eyes on the inside."

"We'll go with you," Dale said, although she was anxious to get to the barn. "If there's anyone in there, we can help you clear it."

"No," Mary said. "If I run into trouble and have to fire, whoever's in that barn will be out here the minute they hear gunshots. You need to be in place and ready."

"I should be the one to go in the house," Peyton said. "I don't have a lot of experience storming a crime scene, but I can scope things out and report in."

Mary held up an M24 rifle. "Did someone say scope? Trust me, I'm the one you want in that attic."

"We need to get moving," Dale said. She was done with talk and ready for action. Her mind was racing with crazy ideas about what Sergio and his goons might be doing to Lindsey, and all the planning in the world wasn't going to make her safe if her rescuers got caught. They needed to execute.

Mary hunched low and ran toward the house. Dale watched while she worked the combination on the lockbox, thankful it hadn't changed since they'd been here last. They waited three minutes, and then she and Peyton started moving along the edge of the house toward the barn. They were only a few feet away when Mary's text came through.

L and 2 perps in the barn. I've got a clear shot for one. The other one is right next to L.

Dale typed back. *Position?*

Dead center of the room. L's at a table.

Wait for my signal. Dale sighed as she typed the words. It could be worse. The good thing was she knew the layout of the barn and, if Mary could take out one of the men, that substantially improved their chances of getting Lindsey out alive.

She showed the texts to Peyton and they quickly hatched a plan. Peyton would bang on the shuttered window on the south side of the barn and then double back to the door. The second Peyton started making noise, Mary would take her shot and Dale would duck inside the door and take care of the other guy.

Lots of contingencies, but Dale knew in her heart they had to take the chance if they wanted to get Lindsey out alive. She motioned to Peyton and braced for the sound that would signal the start of their plan.

"I did what you asked," Lindsey said. "Now what?"

Her question was met with silence. The lack of communication was almost more disconcerting than the guns, although they'd relaxed somewhat in that regard. The man who'd filmed her statement still carried his weapon, but the man standing next to her had propped his against the wall. More than once, she considered making a break for it. She visualized vaulting out of her chair and knocking the unarmed captor over, and then making long, fast strides to his gun. Six steps, maybe five if she pushed.

As if he could read her mind, he pulled out another zip tie and said, "Stand up. Hands behind you."

This was her chance, but it was a huge risk. The other guy would likely mow her down before she was halfway there. If she thought there was any possibility they would ever let her go, she would make a different decision, but she knew deep down if she wanted a chance, she had to make one herself.

She stood slowly, with her hands gripping the edge of the table. She'd need all the momentum she could get. She was almost completely upright when she started to swing around, her fist clenched.

A loud crash followed by a louder boom rang in her ears. She looked across the room, toward the source of the noise, and the switch in her forward momentum almost made her lose her footing. The guy who'd filmed her statement was sprawled on the floor. She was struggling to process what happened when she heard a crash behind her and looked back to see the other guy had knocked over the chair in his dash for his weapon.

She took off after him and dove for his leg to slow his progress. He hit the floor, and she scrambled to keep from landing on top of him. The gun was so close. She had to get to it first. She pushed off the floor and started forward again, but iron hands gripped her from behind and held her in place. She watched in horror as the man on the floor inched his fingers toward the gun and she was powerless to stop him.

She heard someone yell, right behind her, "Don't even think about it," and the man on the ground looked at her and froze.

Lindsey recognized the voice, but wondered if the stress was causing her to hallucinate. She struggled against the grip of her captor, but the arms only held her tighter and the same voice whispered, soft and gentle, "Be still. I've got you."

She watched as a woman she didn't recognize ran over to the man on the floor and placed him in handcuffs. The second he was secure, the strong arms that held her spun her around and she was face-to-face with Dale.

CHAPTER TWENTY

*T*he roar of the explosion rocked the vehicle and rousted Lindsey from sleep. They'd been driving all night, and despite her attempts to stay awake, she'd finally given in to exhaustion and grabbed a nap while sitting upright in the back of the Humvee.

Now she was wide-awake, but disoriented about time and place and what the hell had just happened. She started to get up, but strong hands pushed her back against the seat, and a voice yelled for her to stay put.

She obeyed the order for about a minute, but then she had to investigate the piercing screams and barked orders outside. She jumped out of the vehicle and walked around to the front. Armed soldiers were running around, their activity frenzied but focused, and Lindsey quickly identified the source of their distress.

The first Humvee in the caravan was in pieces, a fiery mass of wreckage. The second one was partly crushed, and the ground outside was strewn with dead and dying soldiers, some whole, some torn in pieces, scattered around the scene.

She'd seen horrible things. Starving and disease-ravaged children, beheadings, the aftermath of torture, but this was different from anything she'd ever experienced. She'd shared meals with these men and women, listened to their dreams, their gripes, their hopes and fears, day in and day out for the last few weeks. She'd been in the fourth vehicle in the caravan. One, two, three steps removed from a fiery death at the hands of an anonymous killer.

She struggled against the sluggish realization of just how close she'd come to meeting the same fate and got to work. She had a story to tell.

"Ma'am, my name is Glen, and I'm a paramedic. May I look at your arms?"

Lindsey blinked back to the present. She wasn't on a dirt road in the Afghan countryside. She was sitting on a stretcher. She looked around. Hay on the floor. Boarded walls. She was in a barn. Black masks, gunfire, and the video—it all came flooding back. "Dale?"

"I'm right here." A hand gripped hers. Dale was crouched on the ground next to her. She was still dressed in a suit, but she looked rumpled and her face was creased with concern.

The paramedic released her other hand, and Lindsey pushed against the stretcher, but Dale held her in place. "Hang on, tiger." Dale addressed the man. "How is she?"

"She might have a mild case of shock. I'll bandage her wrists. She'll be fine, but she should get some rest. We can take her in just to be sure. Your call."

"No hospital," Lindsey said.

Dale nodded. "I'll make sure she's taken care of. Can you give us a minute?"

"Sure," he said, "I'll go get the kit."

Lindsey offered silent thanks that Dale had sent him away, but it wasn't as if his leaving gave them any privacy. The barn was teeming with agents, but she only cared about one. She put her hands on either side of Dale's face. "What about you? Are you okay?"

Dale smiled. "I am now. It's been a crazy day."

It had been a crazy day starting with her trip to Sophia Valencia's ranch that morning. Who knew she'd wind up back in the country twice in the same day? Lindsey's reporter brain kicked into overdrive. "Where are we? How did you find me so fast? Who were those men? They had me make a statement about Arturo and Sergio Vargas. It's on one of their phones. Make sure you get it."

"Don't worry, Ms. Ryan. We'll take care of it."

Lindsey looked up at the woman who'd joined them. She was the one who'd handcuffed one of her captors. The woman extended her hand. "Peyton Davis. I'm a big fan. I'm sorry to interrupt, but I need Agent Nelson for a minute."

Lindsey watched as they walked a few feet away and huddled in conversation. She couldn't hear what they were saying, but exhaustion was beginning to settle in, and she found it harder and harder to care about anything other than finding a safe place to sleep off the nightmare she'd just endured. When Dale returned to her side and asked her if she needed anything, she knew exactly what she wanted.

"Take me home."

❖

Dale unlocked the door to her apartment, held it open, and watched while Lindsey walked through and looked around. "You pretty much saw the whole thing last time you were here."

Lindsey leaned back against the kitchen counter. "I have a confession to make."

"Is that so?"

"I followed you that night. To Peyton's ranch. Alice and I kinda staked the place out."

"I know. I found out last night." Dale waited for Lindsey to put the pieces together. It didn't take long.

"So, that's why you were so angry?"

"Yes. You have no idea what you were getting in the middle of."

"I might now."

Dale nodded. "Good point." She took a deep breath. "If it's time for confessions, you should know I planted a tracking device in your suit jacket at the event today."

"So that's how you managed to get to me so quickly?"

"Yes. Plus, I had a little help from my friends."

Dale owed Peyton and Mary everything. Not only had they been her backup today, but when SRT finally arrived, Peyton had stepped up at the scene and taken control of the investigation, overruling the team commander's insistence that Lindsey leave with them to be debriefed. They'd settled on an interview in the morning, and Dale had whisked Lindsey away before anyone changed their minds.

She'd started driving to Lindsey's hotel, but Lindsey overruled that choice, calling Elaina on the drive back to let her know she was okay and that she'd see her and the rest of her team in the morning. Now they were here in her apartment and Dale was unsure what would happen next.

"Would you like me to make you something to eat?" She opened the refrigerator. "I have some eggs, and—" She stopped when Lindsey cleared her throat. "What?"

"If it's okay with you, I'd like to lie down for a little while." Lindsey glanced around the room. "Okay if I take the couch?"

"No." Dale stuttered the reply, surprised at how nervous she was at the prospect of offering something more. "I mean, you should take the bed, my bed." She held out a hand. "Come on, I'll show you."

Lindsey didn't hesitate, and her grip was tight, firm, and solid. "Only if you'll stay with me."

And there it was. The tipping point. She shouldn't be surprised. After all, Lindsey had wanted to come back here, but she'd told herself Lindsey just needed a secure place to hide away until she was ready to face questions about her ordeal.

But she'd known better. The easy way Lindsey leaned into her arms and the simmer in her eyes told her the arousal she'd felt since the moment they'd met was a two-way street. Now was the moment to back out if she wasn't ready, but ready or not, Dale didn't want to miss out on the possibility of something more.

The bedroom was only a few steps away. Dale pushed Lindsey gently back against the bed and helped her undress. With each slow, sluggish movement, she could sense Lindsey's growing exhaustion, and she knew that whatever she wanted had to take a backseat to Lindsey's well-being. She tucked her into the covers and said, "Hey, how about a little nap?"

"Perfect, yes," Lindsey murmured. Her eyes fluttered shut, and Dale stood at the side of the bed and stared. Lindsey's auburn hair was fanned out on her pillow and her face was relaxed, her expression worry-free. She started to walk away, but Lindsey reached out and grabbed her leg, her words a soft whisper. "Stay. You promised."

Dale kicked off her boots and crawled into bed, curling Lindsey against her chest. She was ready for more, but more could wait. Right now, she'd enjoy this—the overwhelmingly satisfying feeling of wanting and being wanted in return.

❖

When Lindsey woke, she was wrapped in a Dale cocoon. Dale's hands were resting on her naked stomach and her skin pulsed against the light and simple pressure. Craving more contact, she pressed back into Dale's arms. Her efforts were met with a deep moan and her clit pounded with arousal at the sound.

"You're awake." Dale's voice was husky and low, her breath warm against her neck.

"So are you."

"I didn't sleep."

Lindsey turned in Dale's arms until they were face-to-face. She ran a hand along Dale's firm, flat torso. "You're wearing clothes."

Dale smiled. "You're very observant. You should be a reporter."

Lindsey traced the buttons on Dale's shirt with her finger. "This should come off." She twisted a button loose and then looked up to meet Dale's eyes. "Okay?"

Dale's breath hitched. "Okay."

"Good." Lindsey unfastened two more buttons and slid her hands into Dale's shirt, skimming her tight abs, and teasing her by tracing slow circles across her skin.

Dale groaned. "You're making me crazy."

"In a good way?"

Dale clutched her hands and held them still. She brought them to her mouth and kissed her fingertips. "In a very good way."

"Then don't stop me." She wrestled her hands loose and reached down to undo Dale's trousers. "Help me get you out of these."

Dale responded quickly, shucking her pants and underwear and tossing them onto the floor. Lindsey lay back and admired Dale's body. She was lean and muscular without the obvious bulges of a bodybuilder. Everything about Dale signaled a quiet strength, inside and out, and she vowed to respect it. "Is this okay? Is this what you want? Because if it's not…"

Dale placed a finger across her lips. "I want you. Here, now."

Lindsey gasped as Dale rolled over and straddled her, sliding her wet center along her naked thigh. "Oh my God, that feels amazing."

Dale leaned close and licked kisses along her neck while she rocked against her leg. When Dale whispered in her ear, the soft tickle of her warm breath had Lindsey squirming with arousal. "Tell me what you want," Dale said.

Lindsey wanted hours like this, days spent touching and teasing, cresting wave after wave of pleasure. At some point she would want Dale above her, taking control, but after everything she'd been through today, she needed to be in charge. She didn't want to risk losing this moment, this momentum to her own weakness, but her inner voice urged her to trust. "I want, I need to be on top."

"Of course." Dale got it, and she could've kicked herself for not thinking of the toll this day had taken on Lindsey and that she might be vulnerable because of it, but it was hard to see her as anything but a strong, vibrant presence. She pulled Lindsey close and rolled onto her back, never losing the exhilarating contact of skin on skin. "Better?"

"Perfect."

Lindsey smiled and bent down, licking first one nipple then the other. Dale arched into her touch and cried out as Lindsey sucked and nipped at her aching breasts. Desperate to feel her, Dale reached between them and slid her fingers through Lindsey's silky wet center.

"Oh yeah," Lindsey said. "I want you inside me."

Dale inserted one finger then another, and then she eased them in and out in a steady rhythm while she stroked Lindsey's clit with her thumb. Lindsey moaned and pressed hard against Dale's hand while she flicked her tongue harder and faster against Dale's breasts. When Lindsey clenched tight against her fingers, Dale increased the pace of her strokes, knowing Lindsey needed this release now. Later, they could take their time.

Dale pulled Lindsey close as she felt the rising tide of her orgasm. "Come on, baby. I've got you."

"Come with me," Lindsey cried.

As Lindsey began to buck against her she slipped her fingers into Dale, and Dale jerked at the hard pleasure of penetration. Seconds later, they came in each other's arms.

"That was amazing," Lindsey said as she snuggled into the crook of Dale's arm.

"Absolutely." Dale studied Lindsey's face. "You okay?"

"I'm perfect, but if you keep looking at me like I'm going to break, I'm going to punch you in the nose."

Dale propped herself up her elbow. "You and what army?"

"Okay, truth be told, I don't want to do anything to mar that handsome face of yours, but trust me I'm fine. I've been through trauma before. You don't have to worry that I'm going to want to top you every time."

"Oh, I don't know, I kinda liked it."

"Kinda?"

Dale laughed and it felt good. It had been so long since she'd been intimate with anyone, she'd forgotten about the fun, cuddly afterglow. She'd always had that with Maria, but she feared she'd never have it with anyone else.

"You're thinking about her."

"What?" Dale dodged the subject even though she knew exactly who Lindsey was talking about.

"Maria. You get this faraway look. Like you're meeting her in your head." Lindsey shrugged. "Or something like that."

Dale lay back down so she was no longer facing Lindsey. "I'm sorry."

"Don't be. Unless you were wishing it was her here instead of me."

Dale shook her head. "I wasn't. I mean, I miss her. Desperately, sometimes, but I know she would want me to move on." She paused to consider her words. "I was thinking that I've never felt this way with anyone besides her."

"What way is that?"

"Exhilarated. Alive. She would be happy for me."

Lindsey put her head on Dale's shoulder and whispered in her ear. "That makes two of us."

Dale heard the screech of tires and ran to the window. The sight of the two black SUVs speeding down the street sent chills down her spine. She scanned the front lawn, but there was no one there. She prayed that because she knew what was coming, she could stop it this time.

She grabbed her gun off the dresser and ran to the front door, but it stood open and she could see the SUVs approaching fast. "Stop!" she screamed. "Come back inside!"

Her pleas were met with silence. She ducked out the door and was greeted by the ringing sound of rapid fire. She saw the body lying facedown on the lawn and ran toward her, firing her weapon until she'd emptied the clip as the SUVs roared away.

"No!" she screamed and dropped to the ground. The ripped clothes, the blood splatters told her it was too late. She threw down her gun and beat her hands on the grass. She'd been here this time and it hadn't mattered. Maria was still dead, and she'd been powerless to stop it.

She bent over Maria's body and gently rolled it toward her, but it wasn't Maria. It was Lindsey, her body torn and pierced, bloody and battered.

Dale jerked awake and sat up. Sweat poured down her neck and she struggled to catch her breath. It was dark outside, but she didn't know if it was late night or early morning. She patted the bed next to her. Lindsey. She was here, and based on the gentle sounds of her breathing, she was alive and well. Dale quietly slipped out of bed, pulled on her pants, and walked to the kitchen. She poured a cold glass of water and downed it in one drink. After a few minutes, her breathing was under control.

She looked at the clock. It was morning. She was alive and Lindsey was fine. She hadn't had one of those dreams for a while, but her rational brain told her it was just a side effect of yesterday's events and everything was okay.

"What time is it?"

Dale looked up to see Lindsey standing in the hall. She looked sleepy and rumpled and beautiful, and all she wanted to do was take her right back to bed. "It's seven. I didn't mean to wake you."

Lindsey stretched her arms and yawned. "You didn't. I'm still on East Coast time, so it's late for me."

"Hungry?"

"Actually, I'm starving. Did you say something about eggs last night?"

"I did indeed," Dale said. "Eggs are the one dish even I can't ruin."

"Make me an omelet and I'll love you forever." Lindsey froze. "I mean, well…"

Dale grinned. "What's the matter? Star reporter at a loss for words? Alert the media. Oh, wait!"

Lindsey sighed with relief. After the fantastic time they'd had the night before, she had no desire to chase Dale off by saying something she might not be ready to hear. Besides, the first time she said I love you shouldn't be because of an omelet. Time to change the subject. "You mind if I use your phone? I should check in with Elaina."

"Sure. I don't have a landline," Dale said. She pointed at the counter. "But my cell's over there."

Elaina answered on the first ring. "Are you okay? Do you need me to come get you? I can't believe you didn't come back here last night. Larry's been calling constantly."

"Tell him I'm fine."

"You can tell him. He has a surprise for you."

"Surprise?"

"I'll let him give you the details, but that Syria assignment is yours if you want it. Susan told him to give it to you."

"Syria, really?" She'd been wrangling for an assignment in Syria to investigate the growing threats from ISIS, but the network hadn't wanted to spend the money or take the risk of putting a major name in the field. "Why now?"

"Guess you haven't seen the news. I didn't think you could be more popular, but I guess saving some kids and getting kidnapped has sent your credibility through the roof."

Lindsey let Elaina drone on for a few more minutes before she interrupted to say that she'd be back at the hotel after she debriefed at the DEA field office later that morning. When she hung up she saw Dale staring at her with an odd expression.

"What's up?" Dale asked. Her voice sounded like she was trying too hard to be casual.

"Nothing. Well, actually something. It looks like I'm getting to go to Syria on assignment."

"Syria?"

"I pitched a story about ISIS a while back and the network has finally decided to back it." Lindsey saw Dale's scowl and anticipated her concern. "I won't be gone long. Maybe a month at the most."

Dale's expression didn't change. "I don't want you to go."

"I might be able to put it off for a few weeks."

"No. I don't want you to go ever." Dale's face was pleading now. "You almost died yesterday and that was here at home. Syria is exponentially more dangerous." Her voice got very quiet. "You could die."

Lindsey heard the rising panic in Dale's voice, but she wasn't willing to concede the point. "You put yourself in danger every day. Why is it different when I do it?"

Dale didn't hesitate. "Because you have a choice. You choose to put your life at risk and for what? Ratings?"

Lindsey stared, unable to believe Dale was minimizing the work she'd dedicated her life to doing. She'd never given ratings a second thought. Every single choice she'd made was about finding the truth and exposing those who wanted to hide it from people who had a right to know how their government was run, how their tax dollars were spent, and how the decisions of their leaders affected their everyday lives. The only time she'd strayed from her mission was when she'd consented to do this toothless piece of PR, but she wouldn't go back and change that decision if she could since it had ensured she'd have the freedom to keep doing the kind of stories she was known for. Not to mention she'd met Dale because of it.

She walked across the room, slid her arms around Dale's waist, and pulled her close, ignoring the way she tensed at being held. What she had to say needed to be delivered up close and personal. "Look, I get it. You're scared. Scared of what happened to Maria, to me. Scared of what happened between us. Scared of what could happen in the future. All valid. But what I do is important, not just to me, but to the public. You took an oath when you became an agent to defend the constitution. Well, the press is the looking glass through which the public makes sure that's being done."

"But, I—"

Lindsey placed a finger across Dale's lips. "Sorry, babe, I have one more thing to say and then you can have the floor. There's nothing wrong with falling in love with someone who puts herself in danger. You," she poked a finger against Dale's chest, "put yourself in danger every day and that didn't stop Maria from loving you. Maybe your sacrifice made her love you even more. Give the rest of us a little credit."

She wanted to say more, but she resisted the temptation to beg Dale to see her side of it. She knew from personal experience, strong women don't like to be pushed. If they were going to make a go of the feelings developing between them, Dale had to get there on her own.

She pulled her hands back from Dale's waist, but Dale caught them before they dropped to her side. Her grip was soft, tentative, but Lindsey was grateful for the connection, however tenuous. She held her breath and waited.

"You're brave and strong and amazing. I wish I had half the courage you do."

Lindsey heard the unspoken "but" and braced for Dale's next words.

"I just can't do it. Not again. I would smother you with my fear, and you would resent me for it. You deserve so much more."

Lindsey stared at Dale's face, wracked with pain, and all she wanted to do was comfort her, but she couldn't, wouldn't deliver the reassurances Dale needed to hear. She believed with her whole heart they could make it work despite the drive they each possessed to be authentic to who they were, but unless Dale believed it too, they would fail. Better to walk away now, before they caused each other irreparable pain.

She tugged her hands out of Dale's grasp and reached to place one on either side of Dale's face and kissed her softly before she walked away.

CHAPTER TWENTY-ONE

Dale tensed at the knock on her door. She'd been at the office for the last hour waiting on her debriefing session and wondering if Lindsey would show up. "Come in."

The door swung open and Diego was standing in her doorway. Dale wasn't sure if she was relieved or disappointed. She didn't know what she'd say to Lindsey if she did show up. She'd started to call her number no less than ten times already that morning, but each time she'd stopped before connecting the call because nothing had changed. She could concede the point that Lindsey's work was as valuable as her own, but she couldn't handle the constant worry that came with being in love with someone who took the kind of risks Lindsey did. She'd fallen in love with Maria before she'd become involved with dangerous cases so she hadn't had a choice, but now she had the opportunity to shield her heart, and it was best for both of them if she did.

"You ready?" Diego asked.

"Sure. When are you meeting with Ms. Ryan?" If she knew when, she could make sure she was out of the office to make things less awkward for both of them.

"She left a little while ago. She was here at nine."

So that was that. Lindsey had been here and left and she hadn't even said good-bye. Dale felt empty and lifeless, a complete turnaround from mere hours ago when she'd woken up with Lindsey in her arms.

She'd just have to get over it. She told Diego she'd be right there, and when he left she took a moment to compartmentalize everything she was feeling, so she could give the FBI agents investigating the kidnapping a clear picture of what had gone down.

She stood to leave and her cell phone rang. She started to shut it off, but the screen said it was Peyton. "Hey, I'm about to give my statement."

"Glad I caught you. We need to meet soon. I talked to Tanner this morning and got some scoop about the investigation. The guys at the scene were not Sergio Vargas's men."

"Whose were they then?"

"Not sure, but they both had Barrio Azteca tattoos."

"That doesn't make any sense," Dale said. "They're sworn enemies of the Zetas."

"Exactly. I have a theory, but I think we should talk in person. Can you get away this afternoon?"

"Sure, I'm only in today for this statement. At least they were nice enough to come here to do it so I didn't have to drive out to their offices."

"How's Lindsey?"

Dale should've anticipated the question since Peyton knew Lindsey had left with her yesterday, but she couldn't help but think there was something more than curiosity behind the question. "Okay, I guess. Diego says she came by and gave her statement this morning, but I didn't see her."

"Uh-huh. Well, when you do see her tell her Lily wants to meet her. She's a huge fan."

Dale resisted the urge to remind Peyton that Lindsey had been fishing for clues at Lily's mother's ranch the day before, and Lily might not be such a big fan if she knew, but she didn't feel like getting into it right now. Besides, Lindsey was probably back at her hotel, planning her trip to Syria. "I should go."

"Gotcha. Watch what you say in there. Something's off about this whole thing, and until we know more, I wouldn't trust anyone outside of our circle."

"Agreed." Dale didn't need to be told to be skeptical. Right now her ability to trust was at an all-time low.

❖

Lindsey stared at the email from Larry confirming their telephone conversation. She was being given carte blanche to make the trip to Syria and report on the growing threat of ISIS. It was a primo assignment, and she'd been wrangling for it for months. Accepting it was a no-brainer.

She pulled out her notes about the investigation she'd started on the disbanded, but still in business federal task force. Now that Dale had cut things off between them, there was no reason not to pursue those leads, but the last thing she wanted to do was stick around here and run into Dale every day. It had been hard enough this morning when she'd been at Dale's office building even though a part of her had wished for a chance meeting in the hall, one last opportunity to look into Dale's eyes and see if her no was really final or subject to bend.

No, that chapter of her life was over and it was time to move on. Far, far away where she could forget the likes of Dale Nelson, and the faster the better. With no place to live and no one to go home to, she could and should enjoy the freedom to take off at a moment's notice. The rest of her bucket list could wait. All that stuff about making different choices and finding someone to come home to had been the by-product of fear and nothing more. She responded to Larry's email before she could change her mind. *Syria is a go. I'll leave from here tonight.*

❖

Dale looked around the table. The trusted members of the original task force had been winnowed down to her, Mary, Bianca, and Peyton. The rest of the group had all been reassigned, and they were too attenuated from everything that had gone on recently to be included in this meeting. Tanner had joined them tonight at the

Circle Six as a direct result of both Bianca's lobbying and Peyton's newfound trust in her after she'd clued them in on the inside details of the men who'd taken Lindsey hostage.

"Have you seen the tape they took of Lindsey?" Dale asked Tanner.

"Even better. We located the paper they had her read from. I doubt we'll get any evidence off it, but it's being analyzed. It's strange. Whoever wrote it made a point of saying the message was for Herschel Gellar, and they ask for Arturo's release and for all charges against Arturo and Sergio to be dropped."

"What's strange about it?" Bianca asked.

"Well, the big thing is that the guys holding Lindsey and forcing her to make that statement are sworn enemies of the Zetas," Tanner said. "There is no viable scenario where these guys would risk even a paper cut to help the Vargases."

"Anything else?" Mary asked.

"Yes," Dale said. "It's not as definitive as what Tanner said, but this kind of plea is beneath the Vargases. Sergio isn't the kind of guy who bargains with law enforcement. It would be more his style to send Herschel a tape of his daughter having her head sawed off with a message that he's next." She involuntarily shuddered at her own words as an image of Lindsey at the mercy of these men materialized in her mind.

She didn't have to worry about that anymore. Lindsey was safe from whoever it was that had been behind her kidnapping. Whatever danger Lindsey faced now, wasn't her concern.

But she couldn't stop thinking about her. When Lindsey had walked out her door this morning, she hadn't truly believed it was the last time she'd see her. It was her own fault for delivering an ultimatum, but she wished she could have a do-over and, if they couldn't find a way to make it work, at least have a real good-bye.

"Hey, Dale, you with us? What do you think about that?"

"Sorry, what?" She'd missed something while she was zoned out. Right now all she wanted to do was drive back to Dallas and find Lindsey. She had to at least try to get her to change her mind without dictating the terms of their relationship.

"I was telling everyone maybe you can get your reporter friend to help out." Mary delivered the word with a wink. "She's already investigating behind our backs. Why not bring her on board? It's unconventional, but she might be able to get certain people to talk to us that wouldn't give us the time of day."

Dale started to say no way, but the rest of the group was already taking up the thread.

"Gellar would love to have a one-on-one interview with Lindsey," Peyton said. "She would have an opportunity to ask him questions no one else could."

"Wait, you think Gellar may be involved in what happened yesterday?" Dale asked, her blood pressure rising.

"He's up to something," said Tanner. "He barely communicates with me and I'm his case agent. He's very secretive about the Vargas and Gantry investigations, and he keeps all the evidence locked up. I have to check in with him personally before looking at anything."

Peyton raised her hand to take control of the conversation. "Here's the deal. Except for the people around this table, we trust no one, Gellar included, unless we all agree. Bringing Lindsey Ryan into our group would be unorthodox, but I think it might be a good idea. If we're all on board and Dale thinks she can be trusted, then I say we reach out to her and see if we can work something out. Let's have a show of hands."

Dale watched as each of her colleagues raised a hand. She didn't think there was a chance in hell Lindsey would pass up her dream assignment to work with them, but at least it gave her an excuse to go see her. She put up her hand to make it unanimous.

On the way out to her truck, Mary pulled her aside. "Do you want to grab a drink or are you in a hurry to get back to your girl?"

Dale felt the heat of a blush creep along the back of her neck, and she recalled the way Mary had emphasized the word friend when she was talking about Lindsey. "You've got it wrong."

"I don't think so. I saw the way she looked at you yesterday, and I know she went home with you last night."

Dale started to deny it, but Mary was one of her best friends and she'd never lied to her. "Whatever happened, it's over. And she's not going to be up for working with us. She just got another overseas assignment. One she's wanted for a long time."

"Is that why you have the long face?" Mary asked. "What's the matter, you've never heard of Skype? She'll be back before you know it."

"Maybe not. She's going to Syria. You know how dangerous it is over there? Eighty journalists have been taken hostage since ISIS came to power."

"Sounds like someone's been spending too much time on the Internet. She'll be fine. She seems like she's got a pretty good head on her shoulders."

"It didn't keep her out of trouble yesterday."

"Okay, okay, I get it."

"What?"

"You're scared."

Dale flinched at the words. She'd never thought of herself as being a fearful person, but in the span of a day, both Lindsey and her best friend had accused her of being scared. "No, I'm not. It just seems careless."

"Well, now you're just being a dope. You raised your hand back there and agreed she could work with us, and we don't have any idea what kind of danger we might be getting into. If you say the difference is you can keep an eye on her here, I'll kick your ass. You need a woman who was strong like Maria, not someone you have to babysit."

Dale wanted to shout. Tell Mary she was dead wrong, but she wasn't. The very qualities that could put Lindsey in danger were the ones she most admired. Mary was right. She was scared. Scared of loving, but most of all scared of losing again. Was she going to let fear continue to rule her or was she going to turn it on its head?

The minute she pulled out onto the highway, she dialed Lindsey's cell, but it went straight to voice mail. Next she called the hotel and asked for Lindsey's room. She waited impatiently, and finally the desk clerk told her that Lindsey had checked out earlier today. Another call to Lindsey's cell sent her to voice mail again. She hung up without leaving a message. Text or voice mail wasn't the right medium for what she had to say. There had to be another way to reach Lindsey without blowing up her phone with missed calls.

She scrambled to think of Elaina's last name and asked the clerk to ring her room, but no one answered. She started to give up, but then she remembered Lindsey had called Elaina from her cell that morning. She pulled over to the side of the road and scrolled through the outgoing numbers until she located a number she didn't recognize and punched the screen.

"Beall here."

"Elaina?"

"Yes, who's this?"

"Agent Nelson. I'm trying to reach Lindsey. Do you know where I can find her?"

"Have you tried her cell?"

"It's going straight to voice mail."

"I'm not sure what time her flight is. She may already be on board."

Flight? What flight? "Sorry, I didn't realize she was heading back to New York tonight." Dale started calculating how many hours it would be until she landed.

"Oh, no, she's headed to Turkey tonight. She took an assignment in Syria, and she'll be there for a while." Elaina's next words weren't as brusque. "I'm sorry. I thought she would've told you."

Dale could hear the sympathy in her voice and wondered how much she knew about what Lindsey had been doing at her house last night. She didn't like Elaina thinking she was just a one-night stand to Lindsey, even if it was true. "You know, she did tell me. I just didn't remember she was leaving tonight."

"Sure. Look, I know you've been through a lot, but if you're still interested in doing the interview, we could get someone else—"

"No, thanks." Dale clicked off the line. The only person she planned to bare her soul to was Lindsey, and she wasn't going to do it in front of any cameras. She pulled back on the road, but this time she was headed in the opposite direction. If there was any chance at all Lindsey was still here, she was going to find her and try to get it right this time.

❖

Lindsey checked into the Admiral's Club and sank into one of the large lounge chairs to review her itinerary for the next few days. She'd booked a first class flight to Turkey and she planned to sleep on the plane. Larry's assistant would email her the hotel information while she was on the flight. She'd have to stay in Turkey for a few days until arrangements could be made with the state department to let her travel into Syria.

The downtime would be a welcome reprieve from the frenetic pace of the last six months. Her only regret was that she would be spending it alone. For the first time in her life, she questioned her decision to put her work ahead of her personal life. The internal voice she'd listened to her entire life told her she was right. She'd told Dale she'd only be gone for a month, and she was ready and willing to make plans for when she returned. But their disagreement hadn't been about timing.

She couldn't start letting a lover dictate the parameters of her professional life. What kind of reporter would she be if she let someone else decide what was best for her or guide her career decisions?

Maybe that wasn't fair. After all, there were plenty of correspondents who turned down assignments to accommodate their families. She'd scoffed at their choices, but then she'd never really understood what they were choosing between. It was too early to know if choosing Dale over this trip was right for her, but if she stuck with her usual modus operandi, she'd never get close enough to find out. And that's exactly what she was doing by leaving tonight. There was no big hurry to take this trip. In fact, if she'd put it off for a week, the network would have had more time to iron out the travel arrangements. She was running and she knew it.

The question was, was she going to keep running away or was she going to run to something for once in her life?

Paging Lindsey Ryan, paging Lindsey Ryan. You have a message waiting at the customer relations counter.

Damn, she'd just gotten comfortable. It was probably from Elaina who'd thrown a fit when she found out she was leaving tonight without pressing Dale for the interview. She flagged down a waiter and asked him to retrieve the message for her. While she waited she pulled out her cell and realized the battery had died. She plugged it into the outlet near her chair, and when it fired back up, she saw several missed calls, one from Elaina and two from Dale. She started to return Dale's call, but what would she say? She knew what she wanted to say, but did she have the courage to take a chance on something other than work? How ironic that she'd accused Dale of being afraid.

"Lindsey?"

She turned in her chair, but she didn't need to look to know Dale was standing beside her. "What are you doing here?"

Dale moved so she was standing directly in front of her. She had a shy smile on her face and she looked flushed, like she'd been running. "I came to give you a proper good-bye."

"Really?" Lindsey's heart beat faster as she contemplated exactly what that meant. Dale looked as handsome as ever in her jeans and boots, but her mind flashed to last night when Dale was naked in her arms. She wanted more nights like those, long, languid bouts of pleasure punctuated by work instead of the other way around. "Good-bye like forever or good-bye like see you later?"

"Your choice, but I'm hoping for the see you later kind." Dale reached for her hands. "You shouldn't ever have to choose between doing what you love and being with someone who loves you. I'll be here waiting when you get back."

She'd said love, and Lindsey doubted it was a word Dale threw around lightly, but she had to be sure. "And if I choose not to go at all? How would that work? Even if I stay, there will be times I get into risky situations." She waited for her response, wondering if Dale was down for the long haul. It was one thing for Dale to say she'd wait, but if Lindsey stayed here, that pledge would be put to the test every day.

Dale pulled her to her feet and wrapped her tightly in her arms. "I won't say that I won't worry, but I'll do my level best not to get in your way." She leaned back and looked her in the eyes. "In fact, if you choose to stick around I may have a job where you can get in all kinds of trouble."

Lindsey smiled. "And that's why I love you."

Dale pulled her into a long, deep kiss, and Lindsey forgot about everything except the strong woman who held her tight. When they finally broke for air, Dale said, "Whenever you decide, whatever you decide, I'm here for you."

Exactly the words Lindsey needed to hear, but her mind was already made up. "Take me home."

THE END

About the Author

Carsen Taite's goal as an author is to spin tales with plot lines as interesting as the cases she encountered in her career as a criminal defense lawyer. She is the award-winning author of over a dozen novels of romantic intrigue, including the Luca Bennett Bounty Hunter series and the Lone Star Law series. Learn more at www .carsentaite.com.

Books Available from Bold Strokes Books

A Reluctant Enterprise by Gun Brooke. When two women grow up learning nothing but distrust, unworthiness, and abandonment, it's no wonder they are apprehensive and fearful when an overwhelming love just won't be denied. (978-1-62639-500-8)

Above the Law by Carsen Taite. Love is the last thing on Agent Dale Nelson's mind, but reporter Lindsey Ryan's investigation could change the way she sees everything—her career, her past, and her future. (978-1-62639-558-9)

Actual Stop by Kara A. McLeod. When Special Agent Ryan O'Connor's present collides abruptly with her past, shots are fired, and the course of her life is irrevocably altered. (978-1-62639-675-3)

Embracing the Dawn by Jeannie Levig. When ex-con Jinx Tanner and business executive E. J. Bastien awaken after a one-night stand to find their lives inextricably entangled, love has its work cut out for it. (978-1-62639-576-3)

Jane's World by Paige Braddock. Jane's PayBuddy account gets hacked and she inadvertently purchases a mail order bride from the Eastern Block. (978-1-62639-494-0)

Love's Redemption by Donna K. Ford. For ex-convict Rhea Daniels and ex-priest Morgan Scott, redemption lies in the thin line between right and wrong. (978-1-62639-673-9)

The Shewstone by Jane Fletcher. The prophetic Shewstone is in Eawynn's care, but unfortunately for her, Matt is coming to steal it. (978-1-62639-554-1)

A Touch of Temptation by Julie Blair. Recent law school graduate Kate Dawson's ordained path to the perfect life gets thrown off course when handsome butch top Chris Brent initiates her to sexual pleasure. (978-1-62639-488-9)

Beneath the Waves by Ali Vali. Kai Merlin and Vivien Palmer love the water and the secrets trapped in the depths, but if Kai gives in to her feelings, it might come at a cost to her entire realm. (978-1-62639-609-8)

Girls on Campus edited by Sandy Lowe and Stacia Seaman. College: four years when rules are made to be broken. This collection is required reading for anyone looking to earn an A in sex ed. (978-1-62639-733-0)

Heart of the Pack by Jenny Frame. Human Selena Miller falls for the domineering Caden Wolfgang, but will their love survive Selena learning the Wolfgangs are werewolves? (978-1-62639-566-4)

Miss Match by Fiona Riley. Matchmaker Samantha Monteiro makes the impossible possible for everyone but herself. Is mysterious dancer Lucinda Moss her own perfect match? (978-1-62639-574-9)

Paladins of the Storm Lord by Barbara Ann Wright. Lieutenant Cordelia Ross must choose between duty and honor when a man with godlike powers forces her soldiers to provoke an alien threat. (978-1-62639-604-3)

Taking a Gamble by P.J. Trebelhorn. Storage auction buyer Cassidy Holmes and postal worker Erica Jacobs want different things out of life, but taking a gamble on love might prove lucky for them both. (978-1-62639-542-8)

The Copper Egg by Catherine Friend. Archeologist Claire Adams wants to find the buried treasure in Peru. Her ex, Sochi Castillo, wants to steal it. The last thing either of them wants is to still be in love. (978-1-62639-613-5)

The Iron Phoenix by Rebecca Harwell. Seventeen-year-old Nadya must master her unusual powers to stop a killer, prevent civil war, and rescue the girl she loves, while storms ravage her island city. (978-1-62639-744-6)

A Reunion to Remember by TJ Thomas. Reunited after a decade, Jo Adams and Rhonda Black must navigate a significant age difference, family dynamics, and their own desires and fears to explore an opportunity for love. (978-1-62639-534-3)

Built to Last by Aurora Rey. When Professor Olivia Bennett hires contractor Joss Bauer to restore her dilapidated farmhouse, she learns her heart, as much as her house, is in need of a renovation. (978-1-62639-552-7)

Capsized by Julie Cannon. What happens when a woman turns your life completely upside down? (978-1-62639-479-7)

Girls With Guns by Ali Vali, Carsen Taite, and Michelle Grubb. Three stories by three talented crime writers—Carsen Taite, Ali Vali, and Michelle Grubb—each packing her own special brand of heat. (978-1-62639-585-5)

Heartscapes by MJ Williamz. Will Odette ever recover her memory or is Jesse condemned to remember their love alone? (978-1-62639-532-9)

Murder on the Rocks by Clara Nipper. Detective Jill Rogers lives with two things on her mind: sex and murder. While an ice storm cripples Tulsa, two things stand in Jill's way: her lover and the DA. (978-1-62639-600-5)

Necromantia by Sheri Lewis Wohl. When seeing dead people is more than a movie tagline. (978-1-62639-611-1)

Salvation by I. Beacham. Claire's long-term partner now hates her, for all the wrong reasons, and she sees no future until she meets Regan, who challenges her to face the truth and find love. (978-1-62639-548-0)

Trigger by Jessica Webb. Dr. Kate Morrison races to discover how to defuse human bombs while learning to trust her increasingly strong feelings for the lead investigator, Sergeant Andy Wyles. (978-1-62639-669-2)

24/7 by Yolanda Wallace. When the trip of a lifetime becomes a pitched battle between life and death, will anyone survive? (978-1-62639-6-197)

A Return to Arms by Sheree Greer. When a police shooting makes national headlines, activists Folami and Toya struggle to balance their relationship and political allegiances, a struggle intensified after a fiery young artist enters their lives. (978-1-62639-6-814)

After the Fire by Emily Smith. Paramedic Connor Haus is convinced her time for love has come and gone, but when firefighter Logan Curtis comes into town, she learns it may not be too late after all. (978-1-62639-6-524)

Dian's Ghost by Justine Saracen. The road to genocide is paved with good intentions. (978-1-62639-5-947)

Fortunate Sum by M. Ullrich. Financial advisor Catherine Carter lives a calculated life, but after a collision with spunky Imogene Harris (her latest client) and unsolicited predictions, Catherine finds herself facing an unexpected variable: Love. (978-1-62639-5-305)

Soul to Keep by Rebekah Weatherspoon. What *won't* a vampire do for love... (978-1-62639-6-166)

When I Knew You by KE Payne. Eight letters, three friends, two lovers, one secret. Can the past ever be forgiven? (978-1-62639-5-626)

Wild Shores by Radclyffe. Can two women on opposite sides of an oil spill find a way to save both a wildlife sanctuary and their hearts? (978-1-62639-6-456)

Love on Tap by Karis Walsh. Beer and romance are brewing for Tace Lomond when archaeologist Berit Katsaros comes into her life. (987-1-162639-564-0)

Love on the Red Rocks by Lisa Moreau. An unexpected romance at a lesbian resort forces Malley to face her greatest fears where she must choose between playing it safe or taking a chance at true happiness. (987-1-162639-660-9)

Tracker and the Spy by D. Jackson Leigh. There are lessons for all when Captain Tanisha is assigned untried pyro Kyle and a lovesick dragon horse for a mission to track the leader of a dangerous cult. (987-1-162639-448-3)

Whirlwind Romance by Kris Bryant. Will chasing the girl break Tristan's heart or give her something she's never had before? (987-1-162639-581-7)

Whiskey Sunrise by Missouri Vaun. Culture and religion collide when Lovey Porter, daughter of a local Baptist minister, falls for the handsome thrill-seeking moonshine runner, Royal Duval. (987-1-162639-519-0)

Dyre: By Moon's Light by Rachel E. Bailey. A young werewolf, Des, guards the aging leader of all the Packs: the Dyre. Stable employment—nice work, if you can get it…at least until silver bullets start to fly. (978-1-62639-6-623)

Fragile Wings by Rebecca S. Buck. In Roaring Twenties London, can Evelyn Hopkins find love with Jos Singleton or will the scars of the Great War crush her dreams? (978-1-62639-5-466)

Live and Love Again by Jan Gayle. Jessica Whitney could be Sarah Jarret's second chance at love, but their differences and Sarah's grief continue to come between their budding relationship. (978-1-62639-5-176)

Starstruck by Lesley Davis. Actress Cassidy Hayes and writer Aiden Darrow find out the hard way not all life-threatening drama is confined to the TV screen or the pages of a manuscript. (978-1-62639-5-237)